Hank Ramsan....is

The Millionaire Maverick

ISBN 1-59113-306-8

Published by
Susan James / Vast Five
Suite 218, 644 Greenville Ave.
Staunton, VA 24401 USA.

PRINTED IN THE UNITED STATES OF AMERICA

Susan James 2003
susanjames.org
Vast Five Productions

The Millionaire Maverick

By Susan James

Vast Five Publishing
Division of Vast Five Productions

Dedicated to Madonna

Contents

The Millionaire Maverick

1

Hank Ramsan, blonde, friendly and handsome. Many called him Handsome Hank or HH for short. In all of Hank's 36 years, he hadn't let his looks deter him and used them in moments to his benefit, especially now. This time he was engaging in dangerous territory which involved changing the world's money system and possible retribution.

Setting out to remedy how commerce and the world's populace had been conditioned to operate, Hank's agenda was to change it all. The powerful forces which seemed to be in control of the world's purse strings would not be happy. Hank had no idea what was before him.

Hank knew a powerful group controlled the Federal Reserve. It was owned and controlled by those who had their own best interests at heart, regardless of the affects on the various populations and societies of the world.

A new understanding of how things really worked would change it all; an event whose time had come. Hank often reasoned that he was the bearer of the gift to provide that change, no matter the cost.

Rubbing his hands through his thick blonde hair, Hank prepared for nightly sleep. Having a moment of remembering the days when he used to lie down next to the girl he cared for the most. Those days were behind him and he quickly brushed it aside, fully knowing he had lots in his life to do and someday, he would not sleep alone.

As a writer, Hank had written many books all along the theme of his own methods of design of his life. He had labeled it "User Friendly Physics," UFP for short. He was now ready to take this to an important next step; show it in evidence to the world.

Teaching the world how to become Millionaires in ease is what he wanted. He wanted the world to know how sweet the word money actually was and not the enemy sometimes it's made out to be. Lack of money seemed to kill the true meaning of the word and its spirit along with it.

Noble were his intentions, relieving humanity of disease, poverty, and lack, as they relate to money. It was however, Hank's investigative nature that always moved his passion for life forward. This was no different from any other goal he set out to accomplish and in which he always succeeded. He felt the timing was near for this goal to take form.

As was Hank's personal ritual, each night before going to sleep, he always asked for information to come to him in his dreams. Ironic even to him, he would use this information gathering system for service to others and to fulfill his drive and ambition. However, as good as his system was, he would never ask for information as it related to finding 'the right girl.'

Sometimes he would wonder why he didn't pursue another intimate relationship using this method, but as always brushed the notions quickly aside. This night as he gently fell asleep he asked to be shown how to manifest millions of dollars in ease. Hank chose this in order that the world could ease the stuck money band that seemed to keep the earth's populous in a vacuum of lack.

Hank was convinced that only a powerful few were really designing the world's rules around money and how it was to be created and used. He was out to change those rules, if not destroy them altogether.

Knowing too personally how not having enough money can affect someone's life, health and dreams, Hank now knew how to create his own life in ease and on purpose. This gave him a passion for taking it to the world in a way that all would pay attention. He knew the subject of money, more so than gold or silver, would gather much interest. Creating Millionaires out of thin air was his point and his quest.

What Hank did not know were the repercussions from the people around the world who actually control the money system. They would not be happy with someone finding the secret pill, the magic bullet, of how to create money in ease. It has always been there, Hank was about to uncover it all and tell the world, possibly to his demise.

2

A pattern for years, Hank kept a clipboard and pen by his bed to jot down moments that would come to him during the night. He always expected information to be given. What he didn't expect this night was to be given a dream of "Aladdin's Lamp" and "Ali Baba and the Cave of Thieves."

In almost unreadable script, Hank wrote down the titles of the Ancient Persian Fables as he woke during the night. He had some knowledge of Persian Fables containing ancient truth and wisdom. The stories were familiar, but this was something different.

Excitement filled him the next morning. The early part of Hank's day was to be spent in the local library. Off he goes, coffee in hand, his favorite worn torn Levi's™, his favorite soft leather boots, and his alma mater, University of Virginia sweatshirt. The same one that compliments his golden tossed hair and sparkling blue eyes. Hank was on a mission!

As if his dream was not perplexing enough even for someone like himself, who very much believes in dreams, inspirations and their symbolism, more bewilderment showed at the library.

Hank zeroed in on the children's section of the library, assuming there was a Walt Disney™ book about 'Aladdin's Lamp.' A simple story he could study for its separate parts, was the version he needed. Searching the computer, jotting down many titles, Hank in his impatience, asked the librarian if she wouldn't mind simply showing him to the section where many of the titles were located.

There they were, he and the librarian, looking on the many shelves for specific stand-alone titles of "Aladdin's Lamp" and "Ali Baba and the Cave of Thieves." Then it happened. All by itself, all of its own volition *the* book fell out onto the floor. It was one entire volume containing, many Persian fables, including the two he was seeking. The librarian and Hank just looked at one another. Hank knew in that moment, that not only his life, but that of many others was about to change.

3

Filled with continued enthusiasm and excitement, Hank rushed back to his writers loft. The writers loft, that no one who personally knew Hank understood his motives, and always badgering him as to why he seemed to live there. It was Hank's passion and will for what moved in his veins that kept him happy in his writers loft. That is until now.

Jumping into his black truck in the library parking lot, the vehicle he had dreamed of, Hank was on his way. This truck was the one he bought with a piece of paper, like he did his very first car as he was graduating from college. In college he didn't understand how the car showed up that way, he didn't care. Now he does, and he is showing others.

He had recently taken a piece of paper to his local banker. The paper showed Hank's success as a writer being rewarded, and the bank lent him the money based on the strength of that paper. Hank also used his own "User Friendly Physics" to produce that piece of paper. These same physics were about to take him to deaths door.

Previous to that point, Hank had not wanted to borrow money, and was waiting on the right circumstance to bring him the cash. That perspective changed when he read a book about 'The Disney Brothers, Walt and Roy.' The logic was, as they too did not want to build their business on borrowed money, that if they could make back each month more than the installment payment called for, then it was a good business decision to borrow the money. That was good enough for Hank.

While getting in his truck, Hank is noticed by two girls walking up the library sidewalk. He doesn't notice them noticing him. Hank is deliriously absorbed in what is before him. Nothing new, not noticing others noticing him. What he also didn't notice was someone else was watching Hank, and it had little to do with physical attraction.

Hank had reached the place in his heart that he no longer needed another person to make him happy. This was quite a great place to be based on the previous turmoil he had brought himself and others in previous relationships. Asking for happiness, on a continuous basis had brought him just that, he was grateful. Physical yearnings for someone intimate always presented themselves, however he had his own methods of relief from that.

4

Hank's writers loft was located in a second story warehouse. It was similar to the loft in the movie "Flash Dance™" occupied by the main character. This writers loft was a bit more comfortable than the one portrayed on screen, and contained a most important element in Hank's life; his famous blue leather chair and ottoman. This leather chair was that thick, deep, soft leather. Not the leather that one may question if it was vinyl or not. This was the real thing. This piece of furniture had traveled everywhere with Hank. No matter what or where he called home, that chair went with him.

This was Hank's chair of dreaming, writing, and intending, over his life. His personally designed power naps took place there. Often he thinks back fondly, to the times his girlfriend of long ago used to have her Chinese dinners on a tray from that chair. Those days of intimacy with another, in this moment seemed far away, for this now was a man with a new mission.

5

Arriving back at his writer's loft, the first order of business was to make a fresh pot of coffee. Hank was well known for his coffee habit which whenever he was invited anywhere was always was known to ask, usually before hello; "Got any coffee?" If you were an old friend of Hank's then you always had coffee. If you were a new friend of Hank's you would quickly learn to have coffee.

With coffee and his two fables of Persian wisdom, Hank threw off his boots and plopped into his favorite blue leather chair. He was eager to find what was before him.

Hours had passed, and Hank dozed off into a lazy nap. A dream ensued which startled him awake. He then realized the danger he was about to set upon. It mattered not. He was doing this, no matter what.

Hank realized he had to find the quickest and easiest way to introduce his plan to change how the world operated around the subject of money. The Internet was part of his solution. He often reasoned he could travel around the world with his fingertips, until the time came where he would need to physically travel with his concepts.

First, he needed an idea, an inspiration. Just as he was about to use some of his "User Friendly Physics" to help bring him this new idea, there was a sudden loud bang on the door. Something or someone had crashed into it.

Hank peered out his window to the parking lot, but didn't see a car and he wasn't expecting anyone. As he opened the door, a chill ran up his spine. Stuck deep into the wooden door was a huge saber with a note attached. He slams the door shut out of a moment of haunting fear, then slowly opens it to reach for the note.

6

The words on the saber filled note read:

Do not venture forward into the Walls of Wealth.
The price you pay will be the end of your Health.

After the initial fright wore off, Hank knew what he must do. Find the source of this note and the saber. It was surely a short cut to finding his answers for unlocking the ancient secrets of creating vast amounts of money in ease. A method that anyone, and if Hank had anything to do with it, it would be everyone, could use freely.

Freely because Hank knew that behind the energy of money is the same energy that makes up everything. Now was the time for the subject of money to be understood from a point of grace. Hank knew he could and would somehow unlock the key.

Feeling like he had some pieces of the puzzle to play with, Hank's investigative nature was heading into high gear. He had the two Persian fables and the arrival of the saber and note. Cautiously Hank would have to keep reminding himself that he would have to think above logic and intellect to find what he was after, especially since he didn't know what he was looking for. He simply knew what it would do. It would unlock the secrets of wealth for the entire world to share. That's what it would do.

It was decision time.

Due to the success of Hank's writing and his further investments, he had passive income that he knew he could financially afford to take off. There were no real personal ties or obligations. The timing was perfect for him to simply follow his instincts with no pressure of how he would live or pay his way to whatever he was led to next. He had taught his own UFP to himself well.

The first order of business was to trace some or any aspect of the saber and note. The note was typed, which was of little help in regards to intending on momentum of the source. Hank reasoned the saber was his quickest route to some type of discovery. He picked up his two books, pulled his duffel bag out from under the bed, and started packing for an early morning flight. To where, he didn't know.

As always, before retiring, Hank sat in his leather chair, pulled his clip-board off the ottoman, and began writing:

I intend in ease to find the source of the saber. This comes to me in the best possible way and under the best possible conditions.

Laying the clipboard aside, cutting off the light, he drifted to sleep, knowing the next day would be an eventful one. He had no idea what events were to transpire.

In the middle of the night Hank woke up and sat in bed, he knew he was to go to his computer. Into a search engine he typed: "Saber."

Not too far out into cyberspace up pops a retired U.S. undercover agent. This was Hanks next step. He chose to pay attention and simply followed what showed up. If he had thought too long about it he would have talked his way out of this being a next step on his path of discovery.

Searching more of cyberspace, Hank found that this man Saber's last known address was Houston, Texas. Hank knew where he was going now. He would be on the seven a.m. flight to Houston. Not knowing how long he'd be gone, Hank didn't want to take his own car to the airport. Calling for a taxi was his solution.

There were other things that Hank didn't know. For instance that his computer had been hacked and someone was aware of what he was doing. His phone had been tapped, and his credit cards were about to be followed along with his itinerary. Not only was his itinerary being followed, so was his taxi.

7

This was not the first time that Hank had been watched. His investigative nature had brought many tight spots that he would have to wrestle. However, this was different. This was a world power, an underlying thread through all societies and cultures that Hank was beginning to tinker with. Only this was not tinkering. This was soon to be a full fledged war between one man Hank Ramsan and what he felt inspired to do for humanity, and some powerful forces of that same humanity that weren't about to let it happen.

The search was on for the source of the saber and note, while at the same time implementing his own study of the two fables. Hank was not about to lose sight of the fact that these two stories would be a tremendous asset to his overall intentions.

The only reason Hank wanted to find the source of the saber was so he would have some idea of with whom he would eventually be dealing. This might so he thought, give him some leverage. Hank would soon find out he'd be wrong in his assumptions.

Previous investigative writing led Hank to know more detail about the money system than the average working person, both blue and white collar.

His research documented and available for public consumption shows in evidence that the Federal Reserve System which was founded in 1913 is privately owned and consists of 12 branches throughout out the United States.

In Hank's mind, The Federal Reserve is simply another business, a large corporation, which makes its own rules. Gold and silver no longer back the finances of the United States. The world's banking and financial systems are easily manipulated behind closed doors to control the world's financial streams. This often shows up in the maze of wars, drugs, and oil pipelines.

Hank's beginning investigation of how the money system really worked began his quest to find other ways for people to consider creating money. He wanted to do this without people thinking the government controlled it and took good care of it, when the opposite is the truth.

No matter how much Hank knew about how things were operating and controlled by a few powerful men, that was not his quest. He was not interested in bringing to justice any in-justice. He clearly understood the value of where he would spend his own energy and it was not to be in tearing down a group of people who would most likely see him dead before he would be successful.

Hank taught himself how to create his own wealth without using the 'have to go get and go and do, mentality,' and then have his life further controlled by the banks and financial institutions.

He remembered his reading of Richard Branson, the Founder of The Virgin™ Companies, who wrote in his book, "You are not truly free until you are free of the banks." Hank knew this as well.

There simply was an easy way to teach people all over the world to create their own wealth without having to live under the guise of a few powerful men controlling the domestic and international banking systems.

Before moving full steam into what he was learning about the mechanics of the Aladdin's Lamp, he did want to find this Saber fellow. If he could find Saber, then he felt like he may be able to stay one step ahead of those that may not want him to consummate his vision. Changing the understanding of how money shows up would be throwing up red flags somewhere. For the third time his assumptions were wrong. He had no idea the world he was about to enter, and just how many steps ahead of him, *they* were.

8

The search for a man named Saber almost came to a dead end just outside of Houston, Texas. A full day in Houston after his plane ride provided a wild goose chase courtesy of the local city records dept. There were insiders of the wealth game working for the City of Houston, and just about the time Hank felt like the search for Saber would end up cold, Alex Saber found Hank.

Saber had been following Hank for three hours waiting for him to be alone, so that he could approach him without too much notice. That moment came when Hank stopped for gas in his jeep rental.

As Hank was pumping gas, a voice behind him said, "do not turn around." Then this voice instructed Hank to pay for his gas, and to walk over to the drink machines which were at the far end of the gas station lot. The source of the voice continued further direction of Hank by telling him that he would meet him there in five minutes. Hank obeyed the instructions.

Making his way to the assigned place of beverages, Hank noticed a man sitting on top of the picnic table in front of the soft-drink shed. The man stood as Hank got closer. Hank was feeling a bit uncertain as to what this next moment would bring, but he felt safe enough in a public place to continue.

Alex Saber turned towards Hank. This man was tall, tanned, with blue black thick hair. In Hank's mind, he estimated his age at about 45, and youthful looking. His face was strong, and in this moment, not appearing intimating.

Saber got right to the point, and with no introductions said: "I know what you think you are looking for, but I can help you with what you are really needing to find."

This surprised Hank because he didn't even know what he was looking for, but he played along and asked him to continue. Saber in uninterrupted speech begins: "Powerful people have been watching you for over three years. They know what your agenda is, and they intend on not having you meet it. I can help you meet your agenda, under one condition."

Hank being silent, nods for him to continue with his terms.

"There is someone that you and I both care for. You thought this person was gone from your life for different reasons other than the truth. This person's name is *Jocy*."

Hank's heart sank as he felt a huge lump in his throat. That stinging heart break lump that won't move. Jocy was the one girl, the very woman, that Hank had wrapped all of himself around until the day she said she was leaving him. On that day, the only thing that he was wrapped around was a deep penetrating ache that lasted for almost two years. This man Alex Saber was Jocy's brother.

Alex had driven the saber into Hanks door. Knowing somewhat the investigative prowess of this writer Hank Ramsan, Saber knew it would lead them to one another. But why didn't Alex simply go to Hank instead of a cloak and dagger routine? Again, the answer had to do with Jocy.

9

Alex went on to tell Hank that Jocy was raising Imported Friesian Horses on her own farm in Massachusetts. She imported her horses from Holland, and due to the breed had many wealthy and influential friends.

Then heaviness came over Alex, as he was hesitant in what he was about to now disclose to Hank.

Alex takes a deep breath before saying; "Jocy ended her relationship with you because you were going to be quietly killed. The reason you were going to be killed had to do with your investigation about three years ago into the mineral mines in Nevada. If you remember, it was at that time that Jocy was doing some legwork for you and made some contacts there. She uncovered things that were not for anyone to know except those that were members of a closed group called *The Stiletto*."

"The Stiletto threatened to take your life if Jocy ever made mention of the information she had uncovered. In addition, to assure that this would not happen, she was to never see you again."

Alex continued. "As you will remember, it was an abrupt ending to your relationship. She said 'it was over' and then left with no further information for you to know. Being who you are, knowing in your devastation and brokenness, there was no trail to follow. She left no trace of how to find her. The Stiletto provided for all of that."

Hank is just standing there feeling a sickness in his stomach, as this Alex character continues talking.

"The Stiletto set Jocy up on her own farm in Massachusetts. They knew of her love for horses. They also knew they would be able to take advantage of one of their subsidiary businesses. The adjunct business was transporting stolen artwork that could be safely disguised through customs as the horses where transported from Holland."

"So you see Hank, it is no accident that Jocy now has very wealthy friends in her life. Many of them are unsuspecting horse lovers and breeders. A certain percentage are involved in stolen artwork and are employed by The Stiletto."

"Again, Jocy is almost a prisoner in her life and the only joy she has in it is her true love and affection for the grand spirit of the Friesian horse. Nonetheless, a prisoner due to her enduring love for you. That's her part of the deal. Your life is spared if she continues as things are. This goes without saying that if she did not cooperate and made you aware of all I have told you, she too would be conveniently eradicated."

Hank is now speechless, breathless and feeling that deep ache in his heart, and with a broken voice, asks Alex: "How is it that you have come to know all of this and why have you now told me?"

Alex begins again with a sigh. "I took early retirement from the CIA, and shortly after that was contacted by The Stiletto to work for them. At the time, I didn't know of the true implications of what they do. I personally knew some of its members, as they were friends of mine in high levels of government, so it seemed an easy and well paying transition."

"After being with them over a year, they began to take me into their subculture which involves some of the matters you may yet discover. They had no way of knowing I was Jocy's brother since in working for the CIA anything identifying me as a real person was evaporated from sight many years ago."

"I was asked to oversee the ranch in Massachusetts, just to keep an eye on things, still not knowing its true history. Then about a year ago, I traveled to Massachusetts to meet the owner, whose only name known to me was "Jessy." Jessy is the name that The Stiletto set her up with, and is what she is known by in her horse business. Some Stiletto refer to her by her real name 'Jocy.'"

"The moment we met face to face, you would have to know was something no human emotion can describe. On top of that, Jocy had thought I had died two years ago in an undercover CIA operation. My identity had to be changed again for domestic and international security reasons. And of course, there was no way I could tell her I was alive. Her life would have been at stake."

"So here is Jocy, with what she is experiencing as the loss of her two favorite men in her life, you and me, and I show up, alive."

10

Every morsel of Hank's body is now alive and on fire and he has many questions. The first one he asks of Alex is; "Why with Jocy's life at stake do you now track me down and tell me all of this? Especially since this is information that could topple lives as well as international corporations if it were to be known."

"I think The Stiletto is beginning to suspect me," offers Alex, "and that being the case, time is of the essence in order to keep all three of us alive."

It's at this moment Hank is torn between his thoughts of what Alex has told him, along with the opportunity to see Jocy again, and his quest of teaching the world to create their own wealth and never again being at the mercy of the banks. Would this come down to a choice between his quest for humanity or the love of his life, Jocy?"

Alex senses this from Hank and pulls Hank out of his dilemma, while offering him some assurance. "Hank I know what you are thinking. You feel caught between a rock and hard place. The woman of your dreams and serving humanity in some grand way."

"Hank," Alex goes on to say, "you will not meet your quest without at the same time trying to find a way to keep all three of us alive. Your mission will bring us all death. You have to include a plan to prevent that in the process."

11

"I take it you have a plan in mind?" asks Hank.

Alex without pause tells him; "I have an idea and a beginning, but Hank the bigger part will be up to you. I've been studying your concepts while I was also keeping tabs on you. I've used them successfully, but here is something further that will help you, based on your concepts."

"The Stiletto as a word, has many meanings in regard to the powers it displays of an individual or a group of individuals, sort of like a hidden antagonist. In this case, the hidden antagonist is a man who goes by the name *The Italian Dagger*. He's called 'Dagger' for short."

"The Italian Dagger is actually a very powerful Bishop in the Catholic Church Hierarchy. I can see your wheels turning now Hank. Yes, this means he is part of the world money control as held and governed by the Catholic Church disguised skillfully as religious doctrine. I know this is one of the themes you uncover as our sabotage to many things around our mass conditioning."

Hank interrupts Alex. "Alex what you are saying is that The Stiletto controls the world's money." Hank muses further; "Included among this same group of men are representatives of the hierarchy within the church, which one hand feeds the other and vice versa."

Alex quickly responds; "Precisely, and within the simple language of what you have described, are poverty, disease, war, in-humane living conditions at all levels of the earth's people. The stronghold of these two forces manipulates these conditions and at stake is humanity at large."

Alex further explains; "For what reason does this exist? To control tightly the world's purse strings by having the power of mandate over money as a worldwide asset. This affects general living and provisions of various societies, due to the sanctions placed by The Stiletto. No one will even attempt to stop them. The power of the combination of government and religion is simply to great for anyone to attempt such a feat.

Hank interrupts Alex's frustrated tirade; "Yes, it's almost as if they could withhold oxygen from the world they would do so in order to hold some type of power." Alex nods in agreement.

By this time almost three hours had passed and dusk was setting in the Texas skyline. The two men agreed that their meeting again should not be for a while, as either one of them may be followed very soon. It was time for Alex to check in with one of his Commanders within The Stiletto, he needed to cover his tracks for the past three hours.

Hank had been so jostled by all of this new information on both the emotional and intellectual levels, that he knew he would have to spend some time alone to bring himself the next step. Alex would go back undercover with The Stiletto but knew he would be aware of Hank's whereabouts since he was given the assignment to find and investigate him in the first place.

They agreed on a code to use in the event one had to reach the other. The code was simple: HH. It could be found in the classified section of The World Today Newspaper, under 'investment.' Every city in the United States carried that newspaper. However, what neither of them suspected at the time, was the fact that this huge undertaking would take one or both of them out of the United States. The World Today Newspaper would not be an available option for signaling one another of danger or otherwise.

12

Hank and Alex firmly shake hands and say their good-byes. Alex walks towards the back of the gas station and disappears as Hank is walking towards his jeep. He's not sure in this moment where to go and what to do, but decided since it's early evening he would go back to his hotel. Staying in for the evening and ordering room service was feeling good to Hank for the moment.

The Lanto Houston was always Hank's preference for home away from home accommodations. Whenever in Houston, it's where he always stayed. He felt comfortable and relaxed there and this was a time he needed to feel as comfortable as possible.

Soon he finds himself in the underground parking garage of the hotel, as if time swiftly passed on his ride back into the city. Hank's mind simply wandering over the events of the past hours.

Making his way up the elevator to his floor, Hank reaches for his hotel room door and finds it's already standing open. This did not feel at all comfortable. Slowly pushing the door open assuming that whomever had been there was now gone, Hank begins to notice all of the contents of his duffel bag were now strewed all over the room. The closet and drawers hanging open. Fortunately, Hank had taken the only thing of real value with him as he traveled around Houston that morning; his lap top computer and leather case that held it.

Considering for a moment changing rooms or hotels, Hank assumed that whomever was looking for him would find him elsewhere. He chose to stay where he was for the night but was becoming more aware of the fact that he was going to be cautious of knowing who and what to trust. In a brief moment, he even questioned if he could really trust this Alex Saber character. He decided not to begin second guessing things.

Hank once had an assignment with a tribe from the outback, and learned some tricks for setting traps around camps in order to keep unwanted humans and animals out. Setting up one of those traps around his hotel room door while he was showering is exactly what he did. He did it with the dental floss, needle, and thread kit, which were provided compliments of the hotel's bathroom basket.

13

After showering, Hank didn't even flip on the TV for noise, he called room service, ordered his favorite from the menu, fettuccini alfredo and caesar salad. It was time to get clear on his next step. Hank pulled his clipboard and pen from his leather laptop case and got comfortable to write. As of this moment due to the events of the day, he was unsure of his direction.

He begins writing and soon realizes he is to get back to what he felt he was to do in the first place. Designing how the world would accumulate money flow and not be controlled by the banks is what he needed to be doing, especially now that he knew of The Stiletto. Glancing over to the bed, he notices his Aladdin's Lamp book sticking out of the side of his laptop case. First, he thinks he's going to own a huge library fine by the time he returns, then realizes he needs to pay attention and study the aspects of the magic of the lamp.

The questions begin to flow. What did Aladdin actually do and say as he spoke to the lamp? What happened each time? What made it work? What were the mechanics? Hank began writing:

Aladdin had a wish or desire. He clearly stated it. He rubbed the lamp as he spoke his desire. The Genie appeared. As the Genie appeared time after time, the Genie would repeat: "Your wish, Master, is my command."

It seemed to be a similar pattern with the fable, "Ali Baba & The Forty Thieves." A phrase was said out loud, as was the same mechanics for Aladdin. The phrase for Ali Baba was *open sesame.*

With that one statement, the entire side of a mountain opened up the vast treasures that had been stored there.

The key elements of the granted wish seem to be in expressing very clearly what Aladdin wanted and not being vague in its description. Next was following the instructions of rubbing the lamp. The rubbing of the lamp seemed to provide a belief level from Aladdin that by doing so, following the instruction, then the Genie would appear and grant his wish.

The questions moving in Hank's mind kept coming:

What made Aladdin believe in this lamp and its instructions in the first place? What meaning was then attached to the Genie appearing and saying the words, "Your Wish Master is my command?" What did the word 'Master' have to do with it all? The same mechanics were applied to the mountainside opening as well in 'Ala Baba.' All of these questions were peppering Hank's mind.

Hank knew that Ancient Persian writings contained words carrying an energy of esoteric meaning. This often meant offering something not seen or understood for its true value on the surface, but digging deeper would be like finding gold. He was about to discover the gold.

At one point as Hank was dissecting the stories, more and more images of the mineral mines in Nevada kept coming to mind. This had been Jocy's last piece of investigative work she did for Hank before she ended their relationship. Did this have anything to do with anything? Surely it must, is his decision, giving him more clues to what he was still clueless of.

The passion and excitement began building higher and higher. Hank is on to something huge and he knows it. As he continues to write, discoveries are uncovered within the insights that seem to be flowing to him in such speed he couldn't seem to write fast enough! He almost questions where this information is coming from, but part of him knows the source. He dismisses the thought, as he does not want to interrupt the genius that is pouring through.

The flow seemed to end. All of his questions had been answered. He understands Aladdin's role, the lamps role, who and what the Genie represents, but he is a little stuck on the word *Master* but leaves it alone, knowing it will come to him at some other time.

There's a knock on the door, "room service."

Hank opens the door with a little apprehension. In walks the waiter with the pushcart of food. "Hello Mr. Ramsan," as he hands Hank the receipt for him to sign, the waiter whispers, "Alex wants you to know you can feel comfort and sleep safely this evening." The waiter again says louder, "Thank you Mr. Ramsan, have a restful evening," and turns and walks out the door.

Hank did feel a sense of relief, and was glad to know that this Alex character was apparently watching out for him. Now was the time for the next phase of his work, the actual design of the apparatus that Hank would take to the world. It had not yet come to him. Deciding to enjoy the dinner before him, Hank knew from previous experience, thoughts would then settle in with some organization.

'Fettuccine Alfredo' turned Hank into a daze for a moment. Flashes of Jocy flew into his heart and mind. She used to make it for him, it was one of her great dishes. As his mind starts to wander back to his moments with Jocy, he purposely stops. He does not want to get sentimental and emotional in the same moment with so much at stake, including her life. He would have to stay clear and on top of things. He brushed it off by saying, "this is not the time to get all sappy!"

Hank reaches over to turn on the TV for distraction and just as he is ready to flip the switch, the idea begins to pop into his mind. The design of what he would take to the world! The very item that could be freely distributed by hand, word of mouth, mail, email, the Internet, books, tapes, radio and television, newspaper! The very thing that would be an Aladdin's Lamp for each individual of the world who would be willing to use it. And, it wouldn't cost them anything to have it. All they had to do was ask someone who had one. Or they simply may see or hear someone talking about it and then ask for one! The *asking* for some reason, seemed to play in important role.

The name flew into his mind: **The Magic Wall!** It was at this point, that Hank was beside himself. He knew this was *it*. He had no question or doubt. This was *it*! All he had to do was formulate the instructions of how to implement The Magic Wall, which would make it easy for each person. Then the next part would involve the ways and means of getting The Magic Wall into the hands of the entire world as fast as he could. He knew the more people who had one, would then create more people who had one. The momentum of that would feed on itself as it is carried around the world.

Hank's direction was now clear. The reason he had come to Houston in the first place was to find some connection to Saber. That is exactly what had been accomplished. In fact easier than he thought, as Saber instead found Hank. The bonus or seemingly so, was Jocy was now back in his life on some level, although not the best of scenarios. Still she was back in his life based on the information that Alex Saber, Jocy's brother had now brought forth.

With Houston, and finding Saber now accomplished, where would he go next? Would he go back home? Going back home didn't feel right, but he needed an answer. Especially now he needed and answer because his concept was in place. Now was the time to begin the full implementation of it. Where and how would he start?

Hank did what he always did when he needed an answer. He pulled out what he had been calling his Magic Clipboard, and then 'wham' a new inspiration hit! His magic clipboard worked like the Aladdin's Lamp and was a perfect design and example for *The Magic Wall.* The excitement was almost more than Hank could stand! The flow of thoughts were pouring very fast!

These words flew from Hank's pen to paper:

I now have ease and peace at what is before me. I now ask for clear direction as to how to design, implement, and deliver The Magic Wall to the world. This comes to me in ease, peace, fun, love, and affection.

Hank set his clipboard over to the side, and pushed the food cart out into the hallway. As he was getting ready for sleep, he decided to turn on the TV for a bit to help him unwind. The first picture appearing on the screen was the Empire State Building in

New York City. In an instant, Hank knew that was his next destination.

The last time that Hank had been to New York City was to see Madonna in concert, one of the major events in his life. It was an event he created with his magic clipboard while sitting in his famous blue leather chair. It was also at this time that the Twin Towers were still standing and friends had asked to take his picture while standing in the atrium of the World Trade Center. He was reluctant at first, but then said yes.

Hank stood underneath the identifying sign that read: "The World Financial Center." This had no meaning to him until a few weeks later when he was given copies of the pictures. He knew that his standing by that sign, a symbol of the worlds money systems, would carry a much larger meaning at some point due to his quest. He had no idea at the time, what this would really mean as a sign for his future and that of the world.

Hank called down to the front desk before turning in for the night and asked that the concierge make flight arrangements for him as early as possible to get him to New York City. One of the many benefits of having money and staying in nice hotels was efficient service, and Hank took advantage of it when he could.

In the back of Hank's mind was his knowing that others would know the information about his flight to New York. However, he was not interested in watching his back. Forward was his direction, and if someone was going to follow him, whether it was Alex or someone else, then they may as well come along for the ride. He somehow felt protected.

Phone call completed to begin his next day, Hank hung up the phone, turned the out the light and fell fast asleep. The very next thing he heard was the phone ringing at six the next morning. It was the concierge informing him in a very nice manner, that Hank's reservations had been made for his flight and that a car would take him to the airport. He was to be ready in the lobby by 7:30 for the ride to the airport for the 8:45 a.m. flight.

Hank's day was a go!

He decides to eat breakfast in the hotel restaurant but had put a sign on his hotel door the evening prior for coffee to be delivered early, and a pot of it.

Just as he is climbing out of bed, the coffee arrives. This time the same waiter of last evening's fettuccini brings in the tray of coffee. Again, he leans over to whisper to Hank as he presents him with a receipt for signature. The waiter softly spoke, "Alex will be enjoying big apples as well."

Hank knew what this meant. Alex was aware of his trip to New York, and that he also would be going to The Big Apple. Hank would have company around him during his travel, and he wasn't sure if this was a good thing, but chose not to focus on that. His next step was destined for New York City; the particulars would be shown to him. Not being a doubting Thomas, Hank knew his next step would be shown. His job is remembering to pay attention and follow what shows up. So far, so good.

14

Hank pulls on his jeans, socks, and boots, and begins looking for his toothbrush. Since things had been thrown everywhere, he hadn't found it the night before, and did one of those trusty finger with toothpaste scenarios. As he's lifting up everything in search of his toothbrush, there over behind the desk, on the floor he eyes it. Bending down to reach for it, he notices there is a Gold Coin lying next to the toothbrush. This gold coin was different than any he had ever seen.

Picking it up while still crouched on the floor, he reads embedded in the gold coin was the word: **Epigram**. Turning it over, were the words: *Secret Formula.*

A surge of electricity seemed to shoot up his spine. What was an *epigram,* was his immediate thought, along with, *secret formula*? Secret formula for what? The fact that this was on a very old gold coin must also add to the mix of what he found. The question was 'did he find it?' Or was it placed there on purpose, as a breadcrumb of sorts? Something for him to pay attention to and follow? His investigative prowess was in high gear. Questions looking for answers were flowing.

Immediately Hank flips open his laptop computer and goes directly to the word processor and types in *Epigram* and sends it to the thesaurus. *Decree, dictum, edict, precept, maxim, canon, axiom, truism, verity, truth, mastery,* were the words in common with Epigram. There was that 'Mastery' word again. Just as the Genie of Aladdin's Lamp, used the word *master*. This must be a major key to what he was looking for was now on his mind.

Time to shave and get down to the restaurant. While running the razor long his jaw line something startles him and he almost cuts himself. He thinks he sees or senses someone behind him and quickly flips around but no one is there. He's anxious to get on his way and out of that room!

Hank hurriedly grabs his favorite blue denim shirt, glances in the mirror and notices his 'abs.' He hadn't made time to workout during this new mission of his, and he was noticing he was losing a bit of his six pack tone. Hank's fitness level was always important to him, as it helped him feel strong and sure of himself. It also didn't hurt where women were concerned. Again, his mind wanders to the times that Jocy would let him know when he was getting flabby. He always knew she was joking and she knew very well how to show appreciation of what his body looked liked. Hank quickly shook that thought, and knew he had to be getting downstairs for breakfast.

Breakfast was never much of a big deal for Hank but this morning he felt that the carbohydrate overload of last evening's fettuccine noodles needed some balance of a huge western omelet filled with protein, and of course more coffee. He's feeling quite good about himself as he has a great breakfast and a fun flirtatious banter with the waitress.

Glancing at his watch, he grabs his duffel bag and laptop from the restaurant seat beside him and begins his way to the front desk to check out. The concierge lets him know his ride to the airport as well as his flight are right on time.

15

Hank's car to the airport arrives just as he is glancing out the door. The concierge lets him know that this is his ride, and mentions that a friend has arranged a private car for him. Hank feeling cautious, but throwing caution to the wind and throws his duffel bag in the back seat and slides in. Immediately his eyes and the driver's meet in the rearview mirror. It was Alex Saber.

Hank was not totally surprised but a little guarded until he heard Alex speak. "Don't worry Hank, I needed to see you before you left, this was the easiest way I could do it and stay above suspicion. This car belongs to a friend of mine, and he lets me use it when I have special needs. This morning and seeing you, is a special need."

Alex begins to pull the car out of the main terrace in front of the hotel, and drives toward the airport. Hank asks quizzically. "So what's going on Alex, causing this occasion for you to meet me this way?"

Alex responds with a question. "How close are you on your part of the plan Hank? The part of the plan that accomplishes your original quest, as well as the added one of keeping the three of us alive during the process?"

Immediately Hank answers. "Well Alex, a design of what I'm going to introduce to the world is in the works. I'm now at the place of figuring out how I will implement it."

Hank continues. "I know I'm being led to New York City for part of the application, but I'm not clear on why and how it is to begin there. The particulars of the danger you mentioned we would all be in as I start this have yet to surface in any type of plan or direction."

At this point, Hank is reluctant in telling Alex about finding the gold coin and the possible role it may play in events yet to be known. He chooses not to mention it at all.

Alex reinforces the point he made at their first meeting at the gas station. "Just remember Hank. We all will meet an untimely death if you don't make that a priority in your overall agenda."

Hank is looking out the window noticing they're about 10 miles from the airport. This meeting with Alex will soon be over, and nothing new has come forth, giving any real need for Alex to be driving the car.

Hank begins to wonder what it is that Alex is not telling him. What makes him so sure of the danger being emanate. He decides to ask him.

"Alex, you mentioned that this ride was due to a special need, but you haven't said anything new. What is it you're holding back? I sense something here, so just spill it Alex. We don't have a lot of time before reaching the airport."

"It's Dagger," says Alex.

"Go on, quickly," responds Hank.

"Dagger is going to Massachusetts to Jocy's horse farm. He's never been there before. The reason he's going is because there's a very special shipment being transported along with the horses from Holland. I usually know the contents of all shipments and Dagger is never personally involved. The fact that I do not know, and that he is going to be there personally to oversee it, concerns me for the safety of Jocy."

Anxiously Hank asks; "What do you mean? If she's always been cooperating and providing a secure base for their operation, why would she now be in danger? Is her loyalty being suspected?"

"No, her loyalty seems to be right where they want it to be. Dagger recently saw a picture of Jocy, and has had brief conversations with her on the phone, all be it about business at the time. However, her picture has been playing on his mind. He asked me to lunch by his pool yesterday, knowing that I had met her and knew something of her personality. He began asking things like, 'Was she involved with anyone? Did she have a preference for the type of men she chose to spend time with?'"

Hank impatiently asks; "What did you tell him, Alex?"

"I told him I didn't know, and that our relationship was professional and all conversations were around the shipments coming and going. He asked me to arrange for him to meet her, as he needed to oversee this upcoming shipment. He went on to say that he would most certainly enjoy the company of a beautiful, intelligent, and fit woman, as a side benefit to his trip."

"Alex, tell me what the real concern is. I'm quite sure since I last saw Jocy, that she has spent time with other men, both rich and powerful. What is it you're not yet telling me?" Hank still wanting Alex to get to the point.

"Dagger, as I told you yesterday, has a large ego, he strokes this with women. If women do not return his affection, he plays very, very rough. He has been known to give both men and women facelifts that did not need them. Jocy's beauty would be no more, if she survives it. He's called 'The Italian Dagger' for good reasons."

Hank in a panic for words seeing the airport signs coming up and briskly in a loud tone says, "Alex, isn't there anything you can do about this?"

Alex quickly answers. "No Hank, not in this moment. If I'm found attempting to thwart any of Dagger's plans, either business or pleasure, red flags will go up all round Jocy and me. As of this minute, you are safe, as there is no direct connection known between you and me and Jocy. If Jocy and I die tomorrow due to me trying to infringe on Dagger's plans, you would be the only one left living. There is no-good reason for me to cause suspicion at this time. That's why you have to come up with a plan to free us all, and keep us from harms way in the process."

Just at that moment Alex pulls up to the airline entryway and as Hank opens the door to jump out, he turns and looks at Alex. Trying to be assuring, Alex utters, "Don't worry, I'll be close by eating big apples" Hank smiled and exited the cab.

16

Since Hank was traveling light, moving through airline security went smoothly, and soon he heard the boarding call for his flight to New York. He was on his way to 'next' having no idea what that was.

Not many people would be willing to depend on first thoughts, impulses, and flashes on a TV screen as a map of sorts for one's next direction. In fact, that would be the very reason not to take certain actions. However, Hank had lived the other way for too long, and latching onto the physics of the Universe and how things really worked, turned his entire life around in a short time. It took losing Jocy to take a new approach to life or be miserable for the rest of it.

Hank Ramsan discovered the physics part of life. The part where the actual dialog of how the Universe, Consciousness-Spirit-God, that invisible force talks to and answers us. He had shown it to himself repeatedly. This time although the stakes were much higher than his personal comfort, he knew simply to apply the mechanics.

Always paying attention to whom and what showed up in his space and knowing it's none by accident, Hank settles into his first class seat, and begins surveying his surroundings.

The first thing he notices is a large gold ring on the left hand of a gentleman reading the newspaper. Seated just across the aisle from him, this man's face is hidden behind the day's news. Just as Hank glances away, he senses the paper dropping to the man's lap as he is folding it.

This gentleman resembled the dark skin and characteristic of the Middle Eastern Countries, which is not rare on a flight from Houston to New York, both known as financial centers. This was a three hour flight so Hank being the friendly guy he is, knew he would have a conversation with this stranger before the end of the flight.

As always was the case for Hank, the conversation showed up for him a lot sooner than expected.

"Fruit or vegetable?" Hank hears from across the aisle in a heavy accent displaying broken English.

"Pardon me?" Hank quizzes, not sure what this gentleman had said.

"Fruit or vegetable? I noticed you ordered tomato juice, is that fruit or vegetable in this country?"

Hank muses with a smile. "Good Question, it depends on which American you ask!"

Talal explains his question. "You Americans have a difficult language to understand. So many things mean the same thing, or maybe they don't, and as you say, depending on which American you ask!" Both men laugh in agreement, and Hank extends his hand in greeting.

"I'm Hank Ramsan."

"Glad to me you," comes back. "I am Talal Halalad, please call me Tal."

"Thank You Tal, forgive my forwardness, but I am an American," grins Hank in is query, "but I was admiring your gold ring."

"Ah yes, I get many compliments upon this ring! It has been handed down to me from many Grandfathers of before. Would you like to see it?" As he is saying the words, Talal is taking the ring off of his finger and gesturing it toward Hank.

Hank accepts the ring in his open palm and the moment his eyes glance fully upon the face of the ring, his heart almost stops from what he sees engraved on its surface. The word 'Epigram.' Not only, the word Epigram but the wording somehow is wrapped in what resembles a Figure 8.

With his heart in his throat, Hank attempts to play it cool and asks Talal a question: "Tal, this is quite an unusual looking symbol and word, and you mentioned it was handed down to you by many grandfathers."

"Yes, this is true." offers Talal.

Hank begins his question. "Would it be too forward of me to ask what the word Epigram means, as well as the figure 8 symbol that intertwines within it?"

When Hank wants to know something, he always chooses the quickest route. Ask a direct question. Ask for what it is you really want to know. This was something he really wanted to know. As he was asking the question he was trying to remember if he noticed a figure 8 on the coin he found in his room. He couldn't remember.

"Mr. Ramsan," begins Talal; "The answer to the question you have asked can only be given to those who understand the implication of having it. It can be like a loaded rocket in the hands of an unknowing child, or it can be like the Magic of Aladdin's Lamp, to one who holds the wisdom to use it."

Hank now is squirming in his seat. He knows he has the wisdom, but in the moment, he's feeling like an excited child getting his very first bike. He catches his breath before saying a word. Hank is aware that although he thought his destination was New York City, that quite often it is on the way to what we think our intended destination is, that the magic of our lives shows up. This was no plainer to him than in this moment. Hank knew in an instant that this man Talal, was on Hank's path of discovery. The path to 'what' was the question.

17

A flash of how to respond to Talal's comment flies into Hank's mind. More information was what Hank wanted. Talal had managed to wet the appetite of a ferocious investigative writer with a huge quest to complete.

Hank pulls out of his left front jeans pocket, his lucky pocket, the gold coin he had found on the floor of his hotel room. The coin which displayed the same word as Tal's ring. As Hank is lifting it out of his pocket, he purposely glances at it to see if the figure 8 symbol is also embossed there. It was.

Hank motions to Talal to notice what he is about to open up in his slightly clenched hand. Talal's eyes see instantly. Tal realizes some implication that in that second that only he was privy to.

Talal's eyes meet Hank's and lock on them. Something deep has been stirred within Hank. He's not sure what's going on, but Hank knows enough about things of this nature that whatever it is, is very important.

Remaining very calm but serious in nature is Tal's demeanor. However, his new friend is extremely excited and can't wait to hear what's next. Hank is quite sure something is next.

Talal is the first one to speak. "Mr. Ramsan, know you your destination in New York City?"

Hank answers. "No Talal, I just felt I would be led there."

Talal smiles, "Good American you are, Mr. Ramsan. Might I make a suggestion?" Hank of course says, "Well yes, go right ahead."

"If I may ask Mr. Ramsan, how is your money situation?"

"My money is in great shape," muses Hank, "why do you ask?"

"Well, Mr. Ramsan, I live at the top of life and travel those circles. It is no accident that it is this way for me. I would like us to spend a few days in the company of one another. In this way, I may be able to share with you the depth of your earlier questions about the ring while offering a few answers."

"It will be better if you can travel in style so to speak, as what I will share with you needs to be seen from the top of physical life. I have two private suites at Power's One, it would be my pleasure to accommodate you in one of them. You would have full privacy and would be my guest. If this meets with your approval, we can taxi there together at the end of this flight."

Hank tries not to jump in his excitement, but does say yes, and extends his appreciation and offer to pay for his stay. Talal explains his offer; "Mr. Ramsan, Lance Powers is a good friend of mine and is one of the appointments I have while in the city. I have the good fortune that my accommodations are from the grace of Mr. Powers. Therefore, you need not concern yourself with that. However, I would like you to accompany me to my meeting with Mr. Powers. Will that meet with your agenda?"

By this time Hank is beside himself, and blurts out a boyish, "Well heck yeah!" Talal smiles. Then as Hank seems to wander off in a fun daydream of what all is transpiring before his eyes,

Talal breaks his pondering with a question. "Mr. Ramsan, how did you come by having the gold coin in your possession?"

It's at this time that Hank begins to give a little background of his plan for changing how the world populations can create unique and new understandings of the subject of money. How along with that, various financial equivalents can be given new powerful meanings and direction.

Hank continues describing for Talal how the two Persian fables flowed to him, and how he'd been dissecting them for information. He reminded Talal of his comment on the Aladdin's lamp, as he discussed earlier with Hank, the properties of the ring.

This showed them both that this was a coincidence created by the very physics that Hank had learned to apply.

At the time, Hank saw no reason to bring up the other part of the story unfolding with Jocy and Alex Saber. There was no concrete reason to believe if any part this had to do with Talal Halalad.

Talal listens intently to Hank's summary of how things transpired leading to the coin. However, Talal also notices some holes in the story as Hank tries to tell it leaving out the developments with Alex Saber.

Tal being very wise and knowing asks Hank point blank. "Hank, you are leaving out some major dynamics of your story and the coin. It is only through such dynamics that a coin of this nature would show up in your life. You have to know you can trust me Mr. Ramsan, and in that I can help you with the momentum of fulfilling your quest."

Hank immediately thinks; 'Here is it again, someone seemingly offering to play an important role in his self-imposed project. This same person also offering him momentum, just as Alex Saber did. Also saying, as Alex did, that he Talal, had information to help him find what he needed. It was all a quandary to Hank, when not even he knew what he needed.

On the other hand, two men are telling him they have information to fill in the blank spaces and that he can 'trust' them. At minimum, he knows to pay attention to what is showing up.

Hank notices the three-hour fight is soon ending, and he decides to give the full content of his journey to Talal, and tells him; "Talal, you are correct. There are pieces of this that most likely are important for you to know. However, we are landing soon and there isn't the time for the history of it.

Talal agrees and thanks Hank for offering to be up-front with more of his story of the gold coin. They agree after settling in at Powers One to meet in Talal's suite for dinner so they would have no distractions or interruptions.

Talal reaches into his soft brown leather suede blazer side pocket and hands Hank two of his business cards with these instructions; "Hank, this is both my cell number and my room number at Powers One. I can be reached by cell 24 hours a day."

Hank notices only one set of numbers on the entire card, neither Talal's name nor business is listed. In the center of the card, are three numbers **426**. Hank has to ask. "Tal, I can understand how

426 could be your suite number at Powers One, but do you have any other prefixes to go with 426 as your cell number?"

Talal smiles affectionately saying: "Mr. Ramsan, the office that over sees the assignment of cell numbers has a board chairman, who also happens to be one of my very good friends. I had asked him for a special dispensation of numbers, and he knowing who I am, granted my request."

Hank couldn't help but blurt out, "Well then you know I must ask, who are you, Mr. Talal Halalad?"

Talal takes a third card from his blazer pocket, one of the same cards with the 426 in the center. On the back of the card he writes something and offers it to Hank, saying; "Hank, the numbers on the front of the card correspond to who I Am. These numbers match the numbers on a telephone-dialing pad. I have written those letters on the back of the card.

Hank takes the card and quickly flips it over. He almost loses his breath. The letters he sees are: **I AM**. Hank looks over at Talal, again their eyes lock. Talal calmly offers, "I'll help you in further understanding as we meet later this evening." Hank shakes his head in bewilderment and agreement.

18

After the necessary movement from their seats to the walkway of the plane, Hank assumes the next stop is the baggage area for Talal to collect further luggage. However, Talal as well as Hank, travels light and they instead walk briskly to the taxi area outside the lower lobby.

Quickly Hank begins waving his arm up for a cab. Talal laughs and stops him by saying; "Dear Mr. Ramsan, do you not remember me saying I travel at the top of physical life? We have a private car waiting for us."

Just as he said the words, along side the curb drives up a beautiful white with gold trim, stretch limousine. On the license plates Hank notices the word 'Tacks E' and looks over at Talal grinning while saying; "Ok I get it. The plate says *Tacks E* but what I thought was *taxi*. I do suppose you're going to tell me the significance of the word on your license plate?"

"Well of course my good Mr. Ramsan," chuckles back Talal. "*Tack* is another name for *aim*, and the letter *E* stands for energy. *Aim Energy*." Hank smirks at Tal's answer. Both men knew without speaking exactly what the term 'Aim Energy' is about.

Hank is soon to find out how much more these two men from different parts of the world have in common.

The two men enter the limo, and Hank glances up to the driver and the rear view mirror. His and the driver's eyes meet. Hank's heart is all of a sudden in his throat. It's Alex Saber.

In this brief moment, Hank doesn't know whether to mention this to Talal or not, since they had yet to discuss the other details going on with Hank. Just as he's having those thoughts, Talal leans over to Hank and whispers, "No need for concern, Mr. Ramsan. Alex Saber is on our side."

"So, you know Alex?" blurts Hank.

"Yes," answers Talal, "oh, and in case you are wondering, I know of the situation he discussed with you regarding Jocy, the horse farm, Dagger, and the art work."

"To cut to the chase Hank, as you Americans say, there is a background going on of which you know not of, but have been on the path of finding."

Tal continues with Hank's full attention. "The gold coin plays a major discovery in what you are intending consciously to do, and it meets a higher plan. This moment is not an accident for you, but you could have changed the course of it happening at most any moment. It is your overall intent that has kept you on course, which is being of service to your fellow man in what you are understanding as the financial arena of life."

The questions are piling up quickly in Hank's mind as to how Alex and Talal know one another. What is all of this really about, and what does it have to do with Jocy and the artwork? How does all of this fit into what Hank is thinking is his plan to take to the world?

Talal interrupts Hanks thoughts and assures him by saying; "Hank I know you have many questions as to how all of this fits together. You will have all of your answers in due time. First however, we must prepare you with new information so that you may use it as a tool to move forward. We will be sharing some of this information with you over the next three days."

Hank thanks Talal for giving him straightforward information to calm his impatience, and then asks, "What of the arrival of Dagger at Jocy's farm? Is there concern over the timing of that, and is it not imperative that something be done to protect Jocy, Alex and myself?"

"The knowledge you will be given over the next three days will prepare you for what may be ahead." Talal continues. "Dagger's trip to meet Jocy in Massachusetts is being delayed because the shipment of the horses is being conveniently rescheduled due to a paperwork mishap. Some friends of ours in Holland are arranging this delay. We have time to put things in order."

"We are now arriving at Mr. Powers' building. Let us get settled and refreshed and we will begin our meeting this evening at seven, assuming that's a fit for you."

Hank agrees, as it's now three in the afternoon in New York, as that would give him some time to walk the city a bit.

19

The *Tacks E* pulls up to the outside curb of Powers One, and the valet quickly moves toward the car to open the back doors as Talal and Hank exit. The valet leans into Talal and whispers, "Mr. Powers requests the pleasure of your company as soon as you arrive, assuming you can arrange."

"Yes, please, lead us to our host, it would be our pleasure," as Tal looks over at Hank and winks.

Hank is still a playful boy at heart, which keeps his open mind always saying yes and keeps his life full of excitement and newness. Hearing that he was going to be in the same room as Lance Powers for a private meeting was a little more than he could stand in this minute. He vowed he would muddle through somehow as he his responding in gesture to Talal's approving the visit with Lance Powers.

Entering the front lobby, they walk into the atrium of Powers One and over to the right is a huge registration desk made of marble. To the left is a long escalator. Hank is assuming they will use the escalator and begins to walk that way. Talal quickly motions to Hank informing him of other directions. "Hank, we will be taking Mr. Powers private elevator to his suite, come this way." Hank blurts out laughing, "Yes, I knew that!"

Powers' offices displayed his love for architecture. Various books and articles depicting the Powers Empire and acquisitions was at one time study material for Hank. He was fascinated with what these structures went through under the guidance of a man like Powers. Many of these buildings were exquisitely portrayed along the corridor in acrylic pieces of artwork displayed as they exited the elevator. These colorful pictures and paintings lined the wall and entryway of Lance Powers' main office.

Powers' assistant thanked the valet for escorting them, and Hank turned to offer him a tip. The valet responded, "Oh, thank you Mr. Ramsan but I am quite nicely compensated for the pleasure of escorting you here, please spend your money in the city!"

The assistant takes both hands and opens inward two huge mahogany doors leading into what Hank was feeling as huge wealthy air pouring over him. Powers is standing in front of his mammoth desk as if waiting in earnest for the arrival of Talal Halalad.

Both men greet each another warmly with a double handshake and an embrace, and then Talal turns to introduce Lance Powers to Hank Ramsan.

"Ah yes, Mr. Hank Ramsan, Talal mentioned you briefly in a call from the airport, you and your proposed project. I do hope I may be of some benefit."

Hank is trying to remain composed in this moment, but all he can think is, 'Lance Powers, one of the wealthiest men on the earth is offering to help me? What planet am I on?' He does however pull himself out of his stupor and politely gestures the honor and pleasure it is to meet him, while yielding to Talal next, to help him not look so green!

Talal, as Hank has shortly learned, moves quickly to ease Hank and he says to Mr. Powers. "Lance, it would be appropriate due to shortage of time and to ease Hank's query, if you would show him what the two of you have in common."

Hank can't imagine what's to happen next or what in the world Powers has in common with him other than they both have blonde hair, blue eyes, and are tall good looking men. Powers smiles and acknowledges Talal's request as he reaches into his left-hand suit trousers pocket to show Hank what he was carrying.

Hank's heart is again in his throat. Powers displays in his hand, the same coin, that Hank had in his possession. The one with the word: *Epigram* surrounded by a *Figure 8* symbol.

All three men are silent. Hank doesn't know what to say. He's not clear regarding the implication of the coin, and now added to that, Lance Powers has one of the same coins, matching the insignia on Talal's gold ring.

Talal gestures to Powers with a nod. "Go ahead Lance, briefly explain to Hank."

Powers begins: "Hank, you are here to do what I was destined to do at one time but I got sidetracked. I've had this coin for over 20 years while I have built my empire. I have used the secrets of the coin to help me in my wealth acquisitions. Talal came into my life at the same time the coin showed up. He explained to me what had happened; things I was not aware of relating to what I was destined to do, but ignored along the way."

"After he explained it all to me, he then asked would I now be prepared to move back in line with destiny and assist humanity in some way. Of course, I said yes. Since then, I have followed various forms of unique guidance and have been applying my wealth both publicly and privately toward certain intentions. There was some indication about three years ago that someone, 'you' may be able to take up with what I was supposed to do but did not. I could then assist in many ways in helping the potential path of you, humanity, and myself. Again of course I said yes."

"Various things have happened along your life recently that looked as if this meeting would finally take place. That moment is here, and here we are, you and I."

Hank is both dumbfounded and awestruck. He of course believes it, but can't believe it. Nevertheless, he believes it. Back and forth, his mind is working overtime. Finally, Talal feels the emotion of it all coming from Hank and gently says, "Hank, think with your heart, in this moment, and you will calm yourself."

Hank takes a deep breath, closes his eyes and thinks from his heart.

Suddenly he feels an outpouring of love and emotion. It is intelligent love and emotion, but sent with warm fire running through his body. He then extends his hand to Lance, and thanks him for the honor of taking up the baton from where he, Lance Powers had left it.

20

Eager to feel the energy of the New York City streets, at the close of the meeting, Hank takes the elevator back down to the lobby area, and hurries out the front door. As he is standing on the sidewalk in front of Powers One, looking left, then right, trying to decide which way to go, someone walks up behind him. There's a sharp punch to the center of his back and a heavy, tall sounding voice tells him not to turn round. Hank quickly senses it's a gun, and the male voice says; "Into this car now, do not make any gestures, just get in."

Having no choice, he gets shoved into the back seat of a large black limo. The windows are darkened glass all around, and there's a partition between he and the driver. Hank cannot see the driver, or where they are going as the car speeds off into traffic.

Turning to look at the man who pushed him into the car, a big man with dark features, sunglasses and well dressed, the big guy says with force in his voice to Hank, "face forward, do not speak."

Immediately the thought of missing his seven o'clock appointment with Talal, and what would happen regarding what he was to do with Lance Powers, ran through Hank's mind. His thoughts were interrupted, as he is able to hear the car entering an underground-parking garage.

It seemed they'd only gone a few miles when they entered the underground area. He was hearing the echo of other voices, and not other cars, as one may assume you would hear in an underground parking garage. This gave Hank the impression that this was a private building of some type, with its own underground access.

The car stops, and someone on the outside opens the door behind the driver's seat, which is the side in which Hank is sitting. That someone turns out to be a very huge man. No gun was used. He just picked Hank up by his jacket and yanked him out of the car shoving him in the direction of an elevator that was standing open.

There are now four larger than life men in dark suits surrounding Hank in the elevator. Looking down, he notices they all were wearing the same boot designs with some type of insignia. As he was trying to zero in on the boots, one of the huge bodies nudged him hard and said; "face forward, do not speak."

The elevator comes to an abrupt stop, unlike the smooth ride of the elevator in Powers One, and opens up into a dark corridor. One of the big guys pushes Hank out in front, and says, "walk."

All five of them file toward a large door, which just as they are ten feet from it, opens automatically, swinging inward to a large office suite.

There are a table and chair centered in front of the room that seems to not be part of the decor, but there for a purpose. Hank is guided over to the table, and then in a deep electronic tone over a speaker system a voice is heard. "Welcome Mr. Ramsan," comes first from the voice, then, "please empty the contents of all of your pockets onto the table."

Hank decides to be bold. "Why am I here?"

No sooner had those words rolled off his tongue, he gets a blast in the back of the head with a huge hand. Letting him know to empty his pockets or he would be assisted in doing so and he wouldn't appreciate the assistance.

Emptying his pockets, he's aware of the special coin in his left pants pocket, and purposely does not bring it out onto the table.

Finishing the task, one of the large men walks over, looks at what was placed on the table, and shakes his head as if he were saying "no."

The voice over the intercom, which was clearly electronically distorted to disguise any traces of recognition asks, "Mr. Ramsan, is that the full content of your belongings in your pockets?"

"Yes, it is," replies Hank.

Suddenly, three of the four men grab Hank so that he can't move. The fourth man then reaches into all of Hanks pockets. As the left pocket of his jeans is being searched, Hank begins unsuccessfully to try and break apart from the hold. Then out of his left pocket, in the hand of one of the men, appears the special gold coin.

The fourth man holds the coin up to an eye in the ceiling, a camera eye, and the voice again comes forth, "Mr. Ramsan, we mean you no harm. This coin is what we wanted from you, now listen carefully."

Hank is silent. The fourth man takes out of his own pocket a coin resembling Hank's gold coin. The voice tells him he is to now carry this coin, and to behave as though it is the same coin in the event he is asked by anyone. "And if you do not, Mr. Ramsan, then your friend Jocy will meet with a long painful, agonizing death at the hands of men you hope you would never meet in your worst nightmare."

The voice instructs the men to take Ramsan back to where they picked him up. Three of the four men begin their way towards the large doors that brought them all into the room. Big guy number four nudges Hank to hurry as he places things back into his pockets.

Hank looks down at the table as he lifts the contents to put back into his pockets. His eyes are carried further down to the floor where beside him is a huge pair of those black boots that he noticed in the elevator. They belong to the fourth man. He's moving slowly to see if he can make out the insignia, just as he does, he's pulled back to get him moving. However, this time Hank was able to make out the symbol on the boot. It was a very sharp long knife with a defined handle. As this is running through his mind, in a flash, he feels chills run up his back. The knife is the insignia of the group called, *The Stiletto.*

After being forced back into the car and driven back to Powers One, Hank tries to listen intently for any signs of where he may be. He hears different sounds of the street, but can't pick up on anything significantly different from street noise.

It's 7:30 p.m., as Hank glances at his watch after being safely delivered back to the front of Powers One. He's late for his dinner meeting with Talal. How will he explain it, knowing that his coin was taken, which seemed to be an important aspect of why he was in Talal's company in the first place? How would he explain himself while also being aware of the threat on Jocy, if he did tell anyone about the last hour or so?

21

Hank is perplexed about as much as anyone would be under the circumstances. Thousands of thoughts are running through his mind as he knocks on Talal's door.

Talal opens the door and notices the sweaty warmth of Hank's handshake, and unlike Hank, he doesn't greet Talal eye to eye.

Not being one to mince words or play guessing games Tal immediately addresses Hank. "Hank, I know where you have been the last hour or so, and I surmise that your gold coin no longer is with you." Hank felt relief and surprise at the same time.

"Let me guess, you have been threatened in some way regarding your safety and possibly Jocy's, if you were to talk of the incident, is that correct?"

Shaking his head acknowledging 'yes' is about all Hank has to offer in this moment.

"All right Hank, it's time we get down to business. We must have the coin back. It is disaster for many, if it remains in the wrong hands. It's like an Aladdin's lamp, and will work for constructive or destructive intentions."

Hank interrupts, "How did you know where I had been?"

"Hank, you are yet to realize, how important you are in the scheme of things. Many are, and have been watching you for some time. Let me just say that I have my own special force watching over you, and they are fully aware of your movement.

You were thankfully not in emanate danger, as it's not the style of The Stiletto. You were simply a means to their end of getting the coin, and they now have it."

"However, they are yet to realize that there is a power to the coin, that can only be invoked with a special set of words, and the understanding of *The Epigram* and *The Figure 8*. We know they do not yet have that information, nor do they know it is required to unleash its power."

"If they had known this piece of information, then they would've assumed that you knew the combination of the symbol and words to unleash its power. The coin operates similarly to that of rubbing the Aladdin's Lamp and the Genie appearing. They certainly would have attempted to extract that information from you."

"However, they are an intelligent group and at some point, they will find out that they need more information to invoke the power of the coin. Most likely, they may come after you again. Even if you told them you did not know, they wouldn't believe you and would do whatever it would take to try and extract the information."

"Having said all of that Hank, it's still important that we continue with our set agenda, and you will have the information of the coin."

Hank interrupts. "Why would you give me this information, knowing they will do all they can to get it from me, may kill me anyway and then they could have the power of the coin? It seems you would want this information protected in some manner."

"Because Mr. Ramsan," answers Tal, "it is *you* that is to have the information to do what you have originally set out to do. In the event the coin again would come across your path, even under dire conditions, it would be better for you to have the knowledge and die for it, versus not having it and dying for it."

"Somehow," Hank interjects, "that doesn't make me feel any better, but I think I understand."

Over the next several hours, Talal explains in depth the meaning and use of the gold coin, the word *Epigram*, and the *Figure 8* symbol. Hank is mesmerized at what he is hearing.

Finally, Hank tries to put it all in his own words and he stands up to recite it back to Talal.

"This is what I understand: When I have this coin in my possession, treating it in the way you described, then as I teach the world about The Magic Wall, the use of the coin adds momentum to the power of The Magic Wall for all who choose to understand and apply its use."

Talal is enthused by Hanks clear remarks; "Yes, that is quite a perfect summation. So, do you see why you have to have the coin back? It plays a vital role in the implementation of your financial plan for all that choose to use it.

And do you further see why The Stiletto, who controls the worlds background of wealth including minerals, gems, all forms of currency, and all financial instruments, does not want this to happen? Do you see why The Stiletto does not want you to teach what you know, nor have the tools to do it with?"

Hank shakes his head in understanding and half bewilderment.

22

Hank brings up the next natural question. "What do we do now?"

No sooner had he presented that question, did he ask another one. "Did anyone try and take Powers' gold coin from him?"

"Your second question is the easier of the two." Talal answers. "No one knows that Lance Powers has this special gold coin. Before you ask why no one knows about his, but they do know about yours, it's because of your investigative nature that has brought this to you. Lance Powers is very good at keeping things close to his vest. It was when you and Jocy began looking at the mineral mines out west, you then became someone to watch."

"Apparently you have been watched for some time, and somehow they were made aware of the gold coin in your recent possession. Most likely your room was under surveillance and they saw you pick it up off the floor."

Talal pauses as he notices Hank beginning to understand a little more of how circumstances are unfolding.

Hank concedes, "That would explain why the waiter kept whispering to me then."

"Yes," Talal inserts, "he is a friend of ours, and knows the decorum of matters such as these."

Hank blurts out; "Ok, how did the coin end up on the floor in my hotel room, apparently for me to discover?"

"Hank, if you remember, that coin showed up after your room was ransacked. At the time, the people looking through your room didn't know what they were looking for. They since have found out. They found out because your room was under surveillance. The coin was placed there by a similar power to that contained within the coin."

"Ok I'll bite. Who or what had the power to place the coin there for me to then find it?" Hank now insisting; "Talal, how did the coin get there?"

Talal looks at him, sternly but with an affectionate smile. "I placed it there, Mr. Ramsan."

The questions were now erupting from Hank. Talal put up his hand in a gesture of 'stop.' "Hank, this is where you must exercise your wisdom. You will only receive certain levels of information, as you are able to understand it. For me to tell you in this moment is not the way of wisdom. Will you accept that for this moment?"

Hank in his care and respect for this Talal fellow, whom has become a friend of his, answered; "Yes Talal, I understand."

"As to what the next step is," continued Talal, "that is now being arranged. In the meantime, we need to continue as planned and meet Lance in his suite for an early breakfast. Since it's almost midnight, I suggest we retire and reconvene here at 6:45 in the morning."

"Yes, that's good for me Talal, I'll not wander off this time!"

Both men chuckled, but knew the seriousness of the statement. Hank turns to go out the door, with Tal reminding him; "Hank, you are safe in your room." Hank nodded 'thanks,' and closed the door behind him.

23

A nice hot shower and bed were the only things on Hank's mind as he opened the door to his massive suite. Just as he walked into the dark foyer of his room, he noticed a red light blinking on and off. At first, he was alarmed, but quickly calmed as he discovered it was his phone blinking, letting him know a message was waiting.

Picking up the phone while punching in the codes to check the voicemail assigned to him, Hank's heart drops as he listens. It was Jocy's voice. He was first breathless at hearing her voice, almost ignoring her words. Nevertheless, her words brought him back to reality.

"Hank, this is Jocy, no time for warm hellos. The Stiletto knows they need more information to have the power of the coin do its bidding for them. They assume you have this information. They want it."

"My call to you is a friendly invitation for you to give them what they want under no physical threat or other wise. They are giving you three days to contact them. When you are ready to give them the information, you are to go to China Town to the shop of Lin Chow. He will take you to The Stiletto."

Jocy's message continues echoing in Hank's mind. "If you are followed, Lin Chow's family will be killed. Lin Chow is not part of The Stiletto and his family is being held in captivity. He however, must perform certain tasks for The Stiletto successfully, before his family can be released. You are the last task he is to perform, and his family is then set free."

The message and Jocy's voice ended as abruptly as they had begun.

Hank's mind is swirling as he prepares to shower. The hot water will help him unwind and think clearly for a few moments. Those thoughts are interrupted as he notices a large piece of white paper has been slipped under his door. *Please come to my room now, the door is open.* The note was from Talal.

Almost relieved to see the note, Hank briskly walks next door and helps himself in without knocking.

Talal greets him with, "Hank, I know of your message from Jocy but I didn't want to knock on your door in the event your room was being bugged. I do not honestly know how that might happen, as Lance takes proficient care of these things."

Then just as Talal finishes, Hank's thoughts immediately flash to the coin in his pocket that The Stiletto had given him. He pulls it out and shows it to Talal.

Tal being an electronics expert looks at the coin and tells Hank that this does not appear to be a sound mechanism, but that it does look like it's capable of putting out a signal of radar.

In his gazing of the coin, Talal explains further to Hank; "We are safe that they have not heard my instructions to you about the coin. We already knew, they knew your location. Nothing alarming here.

However, we do need to consider the 3-day ultimatum you were given, and Mr. Chow's situation within it."

Noting the time is almost one in the morning, Talal suggests Hank get some sleep, as they have their breakfast meeting with Lance. The two men say goodnight as Hank turns again to go to his room.

24

The shower that kept escaping Hank is now running down his weary body. Weary from all of the information, the heightened danger, and the emotional play of hearing Jocy's voice. Hank feels himself begin to relax within the hot water steaming over his head, and soon he knows he will be fast asleep.

No sooner does Hank's head hit the pillow that he hears the phone ring. The voice on the other end saying; "Good Morning, Mr. Ramsan, this is your six a.m. wake up call."

Hank can hardly believe his ears as he feels like he just went to bed. Thoughts of last night come rumbling to his mind, and he remembers his breakfast date with Talal and Lance Powers. No time to think about how intense things are appearing.

Rumbling through his duffel bag, he notices he's down to one clean shirt. Finding time to have them laundered as well as pick up few new ones was a priority. A new pair or two of jeans wouldn't hurt!

Just as Hank is heading to the bathroom to shave, there's a knock on the door. The man appearing in the peephole is the same waiter that brought his coffee when he was staying at the Lanto Houston.

A full pot of coffee passes in front of him on the waiter's tray. Hank just looks at him with a grin and a question mark.

"Mr. Ramsan, your coffee service is provided by Mr. Powers. Please enjoy your morning. Might you need anything?"

Hank starts to say 'no,' and then remembers his shirts. "Well, as a matter of fact, I could use some clean shirts. Can you take care of that for me?"

"Why yes, my pleasure Mr. Ramsan. They will be waiting for you within three hours. Simply call the front desk and the porter can bring them up to you."

The waiter takes Hank's laundry bag full of clothes as Hank thanks him with a quick quip; "Great! The one easy thing I've been able to do!"

The waiter leaves, and Hank realizes he has 15 minutes to finish getting ready in order to meet Talal by 6:45. He hurries to finish combing his hair, noticing he's due for a trim. Grabbing his shirt from the bathroom door, quickly tucking it in, Hank looks around wondering if he's to take anything with him.

His laptop is the only thing of real value and he had checked that in the hotel safe the night before, per Talal's suggestion. The gold coin that The Stiletto had given him caught his eye and he wasn't sure whether to carry it or not. He had taken it out of his jeans the night before to be laundered. Since it was a homing device, he decided not to bring it. Out the door he goes.

Just as he's about to knock on Talal's door, Tal opens it, welcoming Hank inside. Talal is putting on the same leather suede blazer he wore on the plane, and Hank takes the opportunity to mention he's in need of some extra clothes.

"Fine, yes, most certainly Mr. Ramsan! Let's give your requirements to Lance at breakfast and he can have some new clothes provided for you to choose from." Hank likes that idea a lot, as shopping for clothes is not one of his favorite pastimes.

Gesturing that he's ready, Talal led the way toward Powers' private elevator. Asking Hank if he slept well, Hank blurts impatiently; "Slept great, it simply felt like a 10 minute nap, before the wake-up call came in!"

"Yes, I understand completely. But what you will find Hank as you become more comfortable with the instructions I gave you last evening, you will require less and less sleep, but still feel quite invigorated in your day."

The elevator door opens, Hank and Talal step on with Tal continuing the conversation.

"Let me brief you quickly to save time as we soon meet with Lance. As soon as you left last night, I informed Lance of what transpired with the phone call from Jocy and the 3-day ultimatum combined with the plight of Mr. Chow and his family. Lance has begun to put some things in motion, and he will fill us in over breakfast."

Hank was silent knowing his day was to be quite full, with who knows what with, at this time. In his own mind, Hank was trying to keep some levity, otherwise, the seriousness of it all would allow fear to take over. He had too well trained himself against giving fear much room or attention.

The elevator opens into Lance Powers' office suite, and as the two men walk in, Lance waves them a good morning. He hangs up from a phone call. Powers then reports; "We have things in motion, let us have a good breakfast while I fill you in." Lance escorts them into the veranda, which overlooks New York's business district.

25

The sky is a beautiful blue as the brightly-lit sun is reflected off the veranda by a special tinted window. This special window allows both the scenery and the light to be enjoyed without discomfort due to heat or brightness.

Powers poses a question to Talal. "Talal, do you want me to give my coin to Hank, so that he may complete his mission?"

Talal immediately responds. "No, no Lance. I appreciate your offer and I understand why you are suggesting it, but we cannot take the chance of The Stiletto having two of the coins, and no one knows you have one of them. We must get this coin back, in order for Hank to accomplish what has been set out long ago."

Lance in full understanding gets things underway. "Ok, I thought that would be your response, but I wanted to be clear as we begin. So let's begin! Have a seat gentlemen."

Lance begins briefing Hank and Talal.

"Here is what we have found in the short time between last night and this morning. Lin Chow is indeed an innocent party in this arrangement. Therefore, we must protect him and his family. Being at the top of the financial markets, we, and by 'we,' I mean those in my organization whom I trust with my life, are well aware of The Stiletto. On occasion, we have had dealings with them that were seemingly from our viewpoint above board. Whatever The Stiletto had to do to bring the deals to the table, of course we were not privy to, nor needed to know."

"They want the power of the coin number one. The reason they want it, is to make sure no one can tamper with the financial markets of which they help to create, monitor and guide in their favor. This is due to their heavy influence and control in high places of all different types of funds and financial instruments."

"Secondly, they are beginning to feel creative in having the type of power they understand the coin to have. Those two reasons are enough to make sure that Hank brings them what they need on both counts."

"They are very efficient at applying strategic pressure when needed, and only begin applying physical harm and other means of torment, when they are not satisfied within a reasonable amount of time. The type of strategic power they use is similar to what you are aware of with Jocy and now Lin Chow. They will use the lives of innocent people and of those they care about, to exert influence in order to extract what they want."

"This works most of the time, and The Stiletto is able to keep the blood off their hands as far as any authority is concerned. It simply keeps it a cleaner, more efficient operation for them; a business decision, you might say."

"We will need every bit of the three days in order to have things in place to protect Hank from any harm, while also attempting to determine the whereabouts of the coin. Someone has it, or knows where it is."

Hank inserts a question, as Lance takes a sip of coffee.

"Ok fine, but what if they are able to get to me in some way? Although I would not volunteer the information, I'm quite sure they have drugs or other means to get me to spill the beans. What will happen then? I'm not asking so much for my safety, but based on my understanding of the power of the coin, it's not what humanity at large would want. It could be the very downfall of much work over many, many years."

Talal sits forward, puts his cup down, and looks at Hank. "Hank, this kind of power was not set forth without a mechanism to protect itself from that happening. The coin and *The Epigram* along with the symbol *Figure 8* is designed only for good."

"It is designed only for raising vibrations and frequencies of light within individuals, which brings them an easier life, filled with the bounty of all that the God-filled Universe contains. It has that much power for good."

"If ever the coin is used for lower light vibrational work, meaning, control over others for the sake of power; then the force of the coin travels back to the ones who set forth the dense lower light. In other words, it's like a gun that misfired and shoots the gun holder in the face. Therefore, the boomerang effect would destroy all who were associated at any level in its use for control and manipulation."

Talal continuing in order to cover any skepticism in Hank's mind offers forth more. "That sounds like an ok arrangement on the surface, which would lead to this question: 'Why not just let them do themselves in; use the power and then be destroyed by the same power.' "

"However, a part of that mechanism also includes the coin destroying itself after it has searched out all associated with its use in lower energy light situations. It will self-destruct, unless someone of a higher light vibration is present to cancel the self-destruct mechanism."

"We have to have the coin Hank, in order to complete the task you were sent to accomplish. If we allow it to self-destruct then this opportunity will not come around for many more centuries. Humanity needs this now, not centuries down the road."

Hank naturally wanted to know why couldn't Powers' coin be implemented in some way for this.

Talal answers him this way; "If The Stiletto uses your coin for lower light work, and we have Lance's coin for higher light work, then we have a negation of energy. Null and void. They cancel each other out, even if the boomerang mechanisms were not in place. Lance's coin plays a different role in all of this. At the proper time, if needed, you will be shown its role."

"Hank," Powers continues, "It looks like you will be meeting with Lin Chow in three days. There's not much of a way around that. We have to do it this way, so that Lin Chow can have his family back. We can monitor this closer than fleas on dogs. The Stiletto will keep its word to Lin Chow, and will release his family once you are delivered to them. They do have some honor in what they call their 'word.' We need you with The Stiletto in order to take the next steps to retrieving the coin."

"It's at this point that I turn this over to one of my Captains, so to speak. I cannot be found out to be an active player in the coin.

All The Stiletto knows to date, is that Talal and I are business friends, and that I take good care of him when he comes to town."

26

Noting the time, and feeling like both Talal and Hank have been adequately briefed, Powers reaches over to his phone and hits a number. Into the receiver Lance says; "We are ready for you now."

All three men stand as they hear the doors from the side wall open; Hank's mouth also drops open.

A very tall, strikingly beautiful, blonde woman with skin and other attributes that would surely make men weep, walks slowly into the room.

Hank is mesmerized. Talal speaks first as he walks over to the new entry into the room. "Maddy, always a generous treat to see such an expression of God's beauty."

Maddy thanks Talal, extends her hand to meet his, and in Talal's gentle style, kisses her hand, as he then accompanies her over to where Hank and Lance are standing.

Powers makes the proper introduction. "Hank, this is Maddy Monroe." Hank looks at Lance as if to say; 'You're joking right?'

Powers continues. "Maddy, this is Hank Ramsan. Hank is the one I've told you about, and the one who must have the coin back in his possession."

Maddy is noticing Hank noticing her. She smiles and picks up his hand from his side, because in his being taken over by her beauty Hank forgot his Southern manners! Maddy attempts to comfort him with a few words. "Hank, we will be successful in this, please feel secure."

Lance pulls up a chair for Maddy and all four are seated for coffee. He furthers his details and introduction of Maddy. "Maddy is in full charge of everything that takes place from this point forward."

"As you noticed Hank, Maddy and Talal know one another. The good part is that The Stiletto does not know Maddy, and as you know, The Italian Dagger, as do many within The Stiletto, have both a preference and a weakness for beautiful women."

"Hank, do not let Maddy's beauty fool you. She is highly trained and skilled in areas you do not even know exist. We have top security clearance for special operations from time to time. This is partly where my use of the coin has been beneficial, and that's all you can be privy to for now."

"We will arrange for you to meet with Lin Chow, but will give you no other details. This way you will not know anything or anyone that may be around you. It is best this way in order that you be of greater assistance. Just prepare yourself for the fact that you will be taken to The Stiletto and we will fill in the rest." Powers rises from his chair after finishing his briefing.

Glancing at his watch, Powers notices it's almost 10:30 and tells his three friends of his meeting with the Mayor at 11, and that he must leave them now. Everyone stands, as Lance heads back into his main office; looking back at Hank and saying; "On God's wings you go."

Maddy, turning to Talal and Hank, "The next time you hear from me, will be when all has been aligned for Hank to go to China Town."

The three say their good-byes as Hank and Talal begin their way toward the elevator. Talal suggests since they forgot to mention Hank needing some new clothes that they take a break from the intensity, and find him some new jeans. Hank is ready for such a break, even it means shopping!

27

Talal asks Powers' assistant, David, if he would arrange for a car to take them to the 5th Avenue shopping district. David agrees, picks up the phone to call their driver, as Hank and Talal exit to the elevator.

Hank appeared to be more quiet than usual on the ride down to the lobby. Noticing this, Talal breaks the silence. "Hank what's on your mind?"

"Two things really, Talal. First, things seem to be getting complex and dangerous and secondly, Maddy."

"Ah, yes, Maddy. She will stir your soul most certainly." Hank inserts laughing, "Well, yes, but more than my soul for sure is stirred! How did you meet her Talal?"

"Hank, that story would take a while to tell. Perhaps over lunch I can fill in some spaces for you. But for now, simply know that you are resting in trusting arms." Hank liked that idea in more ways than one.

The elevator door opens to the lobby, and the escort is waiting to take Hank and Talal back to the car. The escort, surprises Hank and he asks Talal, "Talal, with everything as it is, how did you know this escort is someone we can trust with our day? Do you already know him?"

"No Hank, I had not met this escort before. However, he offered forth code words, which let me know who he was and that we were under protection. Now is the time possibly for you to be aware of those code words."

"The escort said these words to us as we exiting the elevator. 'Gentlemen, I am at your service for your shopping trip and we will arrive in some special shops within about eight minutes.' The code words were: *I Am* and the word *eight*, as in figure eight."

Hank exclaims, "as in The Epigram!"

Talal further explains. "Yes, exactly Hank. And whether or not it takes us eight minutes to reach our shopping destination is beside the point. The delivery of the coded message to let us know we were in good hands was the intent of the statement from this valet."

The escort walks Hank and Talal to the car and as he opens the back seat doors tells them that there has been a slight change in plans and that David will be driving them today. David turns around from the driver's seat and greets them. "Gentlemen, it seemed under the circumstances that it would be best that I accompany you on your shopping trip."

It took no more than three minutes in traffic to arrive in the shopping district. The car pulls over to a curb, and David walks around and opens the back seat door for Hank and Talal to step out. David asks them to follow as he leads the way into an art gallery by the name of 'Visions.'

Hank glances at Talal, apparently confused and says, "So I guess we are going to find me some new Levi's™ in an art gallery?"

Talal puts his index finger up to his lips as if to say, 'Quiet, and you will see.'

They enter a large hallway with many specialty shops that seemingly are hidden from the general New York City shopper. Talal pauses in his stride. "Hank, remember I mentioned to you early on, that I travel in high circles of influence? Well this is where folks like that shop." David proceeds in guiding them to a boutique called 'The Pinnacle.'

Immediately, an attractive woman appearing to be close to Hank's age, approaches welcoming them to the store. Her nametag reads, 'Jenny.' "Gentlemen, I have been briefed that Mr. Ramsan is here for a new set of casual clothes preferably along the lines of his favorite jeans!" All four including David laugh in agreement.

"Mr. Ramsan," Jenny continues, "if you will step back here with me, I may have some clothing that will suit your fancy."

"Well, I don't know how fancy jeans are, but lead the way!" chimes Hank.

The door opens to a large dressing room where there are six pairs of jeans and matching shirts. Matching in a way that Hank would match them; meaning, they didn't really match much, but they looked good on him, and that's all he cared about.

Hank noticed there was a belt provided, and he didn't wear belts with his jeans. He called Jenny back and mentioned he was not in need of the belt.

"Oh, Mr. Ramsan," answers Jenny, "I am quite sure in the eight days ahead, you might find a belt quite fitting." Hank almost begins to once again say, 'No thank-you,' but immediately is reminded of what he just heard Jenny say: *I Am* and *eight days*. He knew, although not why in this moment, that he was to begin wearing the belt provided.

Finishing trying on the various jeans and shirts, Hank comes out of the dressing room dressed in one of the outfits. It looks familiar to his normal attire; blue denim shirt, and jeans, except for one thing, he has added a belt.

"Ah, Hank . . . you look so, well 'the same,'" as Talal, chides Hank.

"Oh, but you are incorrect my Dear Talal! Have you not the keen sight of my new belt?"

Talal smiles and lifts his own shirt from over the top of his pants, and there shows, he too is wearing a replica of the same belt.

"You are always full of surprises Talal, and another story about the belt is being added to all of the other things you have to tell me about."

"Hank, we are actually pretty even in our understanding of the belt. I was just given the belt by Jenny a few moments ago, and along with the belt she said: 'I am quite sure that eight notches will give you plenty of room.'"

Hank understood exactly this time and asks Tal, "Talal any chance our friend David can guide us to some coffee?"

David is standing close by and interrupts by saying, "Why yes, Mr. Ramsan, New York City has some of the finest coffee in the world. I'll take you to a place you will enjoy both the atmosphere and the coffee."

All three men turn to leave the store carrying Hank's new clothes and Hank stops abruptly saying; "Wait, I have not paid for these yet!"

"Mr. Ramsan," answers Jenny, "your clothing has been taken care of compliments of Mr. Powers."

Hank now gloating; "Wow, this being taken care of thing could be quite addicting!"

Then Talal without a blink of an eye follows up with, "Hank, and it is this type of care and living that you will be offering in opportunity to others."

Chills ran up Hank's spine. Part of him knew this as well, but in all of the new circumstances that had shown up, he'd taken his mind off the focus for a day or two. He was trying to place the confusion and intense circumstances somewhere in his mind so that he could function from a balanced place.

28

David had parked the car in front of the building, another perk of traveling in higher circles. Talal is first to climb in the back seat, and as he is doing so, his cell phone rings. It occurred to Hank that this was the first time he had heard it ring since he'd met him.

Talal with the cell phone still up to his ear asked David where they were going for coffee. David answers: "Coffee Empire on Fifth," and whomever was on the other end of Talal's phone call heard David's response. Apparently, the caller said to Talal, 'they would meet the three of them there.' Hank was surmising this from what he was hearing from Tal's end of the conversation.

"Sounds like we're having company for coffee," inquires Hank. Closing up his cell phone, Talal answers, "Yes Hank, and things are beginning to move along very quickly for your meeting with Lin Chow. Someone's coming to brief us."

For a moment, Hank considered maybe it was Alex Saber that would be coming along for the briefing and he asked Talal just that. "Talal, is Alex the one coming?"

"No, Hank, Alex has gone to Massachusetts to begin things on that end, he left hours ago."

The sleek white limo in which they were riding pulls up outside of the Coffee Empire and Talal and Hank jump out. David tells them he will wait in the car, as Mr. Powers needs to speak with him by phone. David proceeded to call his employer, Lance Powers, while Hank and Talal went for coffee and their meeting.

Just as they are seated and beginning to place an order with the waiter, a familiar face comes up to the table and asks if she may join them. It's Jenny from The Pinnacle. Jenny quickly places an order with the waiter. Talal looks over at Hank and reassures him that yes, Jenny is 'with' them.

Jenny asserts herself into the conversation. "Gentlemen, we haven't much time so please excuse my candor. Here is the plan: We all will enjoy our coffee in a leisurely manner and Hank will pretend he has asked me here as a possible companion while he is in New York City. I will say yes, and I will accompany Hank to China Town to meet Lin Chow."

Hank interrupts Jenny. "Great, but no one is supposed to follow me or accompany me to China Town, as this will endanger Lin Chow and his family."

"This is true Hank," Jenny continues, "but I didn't tell you how I was to accompany you. This is where that belt you didn't want enters the picture. The fibers within the belt put off a special type of radiation. It's a radiation that I am trained to pick up on quickly. I prefer to follow it with special instruments but if those instruments are not available, I can hone in on it intuitively."

"In the event, your belt is removed for any reason, which is possible for The Stiletto's security, the same fiber has already embedded itself in your jeans. You are wearing hot pants, in other words!"

"If your pants are removed, again for security, the radiation has already gone through to your skin and cellular structure. In other words, we will not lose you."

"We will know how you are and where you are at all times. The only way the radiation would fail us, is if they took the skin off of your bones, then at that point, finding you wouldn't really matter, then would it?" Jenny flashes a smirk Hank's way.

"Oh great, you are a comedian aren't you Jenny?" Hank plays back.

"I just wanted you to feel a comfort Hank, that we will know where you are at all times and can sense your level of danger by what you put out through the radiation."

"Ok, I have a big question." Hank leans over as if to whisper. "I know all of this with Lin Chow is important along with getting the coin back, but what about the timing of this and my ultimate intention of offering a way for humanity to spring themselves forth into financial heaven? Is there a time frame to when I am to present this so that it is it's most effective?"

Jenny begins explaining in depth so that Hank has full understanding. "Hank, linear time does not play a significant role here, however, all the wheels are in motion for this to happen now. People are now showing up at the right places at the right time, and with the right questions. They would be more open to what you have to bring to them now versus even one year from now. So to quote a cliché, we need to 'strike while the iron is hot.'"

"This development with The Stiletto having the coin, will work to our advantage once we retrieve it. The reason is that we will know our opposition and have them where we want them. This is helpful in order to thwart their further efforts as you begin your ultimate mission."

"Speaking of linear time Hank, we are so prepared for this, that we have bumped up the meeting with Lin Chow to tomorrow. This will catch The Stiletto a little off guard, as they will assume you needed all three days to figure something out. It would be best if you and Talal had dinner in Talal's suite this evening, as we know everyone is safe there."

Talal voices his agreement. "Yes, good idea Jenny, and that way too, I can fill Hank in on Maddy."

"Oh, Hank has met Maddy?" Jenny grinning again with a smirk.

"Why yes, Jenny," as Hank playfully banters back, "you jealous so early on in our relationship?"

Talal then enters the fray. "Hank, you might want to tread lightly with Jenny, as Maddy trained her. She could break you in two with a stare."

"Well if it's my heart she will break, then I will certainly keep my distance!" They all laugh as they begin to stand with Hank offering to pay the check. Talal and Jenny glance at one another and Hank says; "Oh wait, let me guess, coffee compliments of Mr. Powers!"
Jenny and Talal nod their heads in a 'yes'.

29

It's 1:30 in the afternoon, as the three of them stand outside of the Coffee Empire. Hank glances at his watch, noting the time, asks about lunch.

Talal suggests that if Jenny is free, that she shows Hank to a nice place for lunch as Talal had an appointment in lower Manhattan in thirty minutes. Hank looks at Jenny; "Well you did mention we were to look like companions while I was in the city!" Jenny, not to miss a golden opportunity says, "Well it's hard work, but somebody has to do it!"

Talal senses an agreement between them for lunch and offers his good-bye as he slides into David's waiting car. "See you for dinner in my suite around six, Hank?"

Hank agrees, "Yes, that'll be perfect Talal, that'll give Jenny a chance to really get to know me!" They all chuckle under their breath as the white limo pulls away with Talal and David.

"I'm all yours, Jenny, where's a good place for lunch?"

"Well, French Cuisine does not seem to fit you for some reason Hank, am I right?"

Hank smirks as if to say, 'do I look like a guy who eats French food other than french fries?'

"Well you know the saying Hank, when in New York, you do what New Yorker's do, and that means New York Deli's. There's a great one just a block over from here, do you think you can walk that far without whining?"

Hank laughs as he much appreciates a great sense of humor, especially in women, and especially in attractive women.

Crossing over the street in the middle of traffic, Hank grabs Jenny's hand to be helpful in their plight not to be hit by cars flying by. They both sense an easy comfort between them.

Now in front of the deli, Hank notices the name on the billboard out front. 'Deli Empire.' He laughs while asking Jenny, "What's the deal with first the Coffee Empire, and now the Deli Empire?"

"Gee, Hank I thought you were a little brighter than that. Let me give you a hint. Powers One, Powers Two, through Powers Nine, doth and empire make?"

"Oh, I get it! Powers owns these, which is also why it was so easy for him to take care of the tab when I saw no one around telling the waiter about whom to bill the check to."

"For a southern blonde boy, you do ok!" Jenny nudging Hank in his side with her elbow; "And yes, you are correct. We felt it safer to also keep us all under some level of protection. We are very well protected within any of the Lance Powers' facilities."

Greeted by the headwaiter, Hank asks if they have a booth available. The waiter shows them back to the corner of the room while Jenny explains the location of the booth to Hank. "Hank this is a special booth, in that cameras and other sensitive equipment are around this table."

With a wink, Hank says: "So, no hanky panky for you and me, huh?"

"Yes, that's right Mr. Big Pants." However," Jenny continues, "this booth has come in very handy when we needed information from the underworld, as they were unaware of the attributes of this table."

After placing their order, Hank begins to get inquisitive. "So Jenny, tell me, what's an attractive girl like you doing in a business such as this, and by the way what business is this you are in, anyway?"

"Well Hank, you will learn more of 'this business I Am in' as Talal talks to you further of Maddy, and how they became acquainted. This particular type of business is of a higher nature, as you are already aware of on some levels due to your own study. Your interests in how higher vibrations affect the world at large will now be put into full practice."

Hank comments on his recent experience with The Stiletto. "It seems dangerous from what I've seen so far."

Jenny agrees by saying, "Well yes, in appearance it would seem that way. However, those of us working at this level of business have special tools at our disposal. These tools remove the perceived danger, so that we can do what we need to do. You Hank, bring two aspects to the table."

"You have your human personality characteristics. In addition, you bring the study of the higher aspects as you have applied them to your own physical life. That's why you are part of this unfolding. Not everyone is willing to study higher material, and if they do, they fall short of the evidence of it showing in their lives. The evidence does not show because they have chosen not to apply the wisdom."

"What you will be doing with your mission, as well as other things of which Talal will introduce to you, is that you will make the transition so much easier to implement than before. In other words, it will be easier for those in mainstream to take advantage of the wisdom, proving its use in their lives without the self created frustration of not applying what is before them. It will simply feel easy and natural. That is what you are doing Hank. The best part is that you are affecting the stuck money band across the earth that has held so many captive. This is what The Stiletto does not want to happen."

As Jenny is finishing her last sentence, her cell phone rings. She hangs up and looks at Hank. "Hank, it's time for you to get back to Powers One. You are to meet at five with Talal in his suite instead of six, so let's hurry on. Oh, and before you ask, and before I say it, 'yes,' this is being taken care of compliments of Mr. Powers. David is waiting out front to take you back and my walk is only a block, so I'll leave you now."

Hank asks his companion, "Jenny, will I see you again?"

"Most likely yes, Hank, and remember, I'm with you in your belt, your jeans and under your skin!" says Jenny as she hurries off.

30

By now, it's getting close to four p.m. as Hank exits the car in front of Powers One. Deciding to shower and fit a nap in before meeting with Talal at five, is on his agenda. Hank suspects he'll be given lots of new information and he wanted to be refreshed to take it all in.

Flipping on the TV in his room, Hank hears the news of a Holland freightliner being held up by some international authorities en route to the East Coast. Sitting on the edge of the bed watching, he wonders if Alex Saber had anything to do with this delay. 'Possibly,' Hank muses to himself, 'Talal would fill him in during dinner, if in fact this was the case.' In the meantime, Hank checks his watch while preparing to shower.

Showered and refreshed, the TV off, Hank sets his cell phone to wake him up at 4:50 p.m., and then he immediately dozes off to sleep.

The cell phone had other plans. At 4:30 it rings, and it's Talal asking that Hank come as soon as he can. Hank thinks to himself, 'getting rest is impossible with this crowd!' His feet hit the floor quickly as he begins dressing and combing his hair. Checking out how good he looks is part of his routine as he smiles back from the mirror. Out the door he goes.

Arriving at Talal's open door at 4:45, Tal without a hello, asks him if he saw the news about the Holland freighter. Hank responds "yes," and related his thought that he was sure that Tal had further information.

"Yes, as a matter of fact, I have lots of information." Tal not wasting a moment in the briefing. "A sticky wicket here Hank. We, meaning Alex, put things in order to hold up the freightliner from Holland, that's the good news. It gives us time for what we are intending to do. The bad news is that this ship is where Lin Chow's family is being held."

"The timing on this has to be perfect. Hairline perfect. I'll get to that part in a bit. But first as promised, and what will be of some value to you, is the story of how I met Maddy."

"Let's have some coffee and room service is scheduled to deliver our dinner at six. Does this sound all right to you Hank?"

"Well of course Talal, and with coffee in my hands, I'm a happy attentive guy, so please continue. I'm ready for a good story."

"Get comfortable Hank, this is better and bigger than any story you've heard prior to this day."

Talal begins: "Are you familiar with Mt. Saffron?" Hank shakes his head, 'no.'

"Mt. Saffron, is a sanctuary of sorts held in seclusion. Seclusion in the meaning that it exists in another realm, not able to be seen or felt by human means, but exists all the same. I'm not at liberty to tell you where this sanctuary is, only that I have been taken there."

Hank interrupts. "Talal, if you are human and have been taken there, how do you know it exists, since you said it is in another realm?"

"Well Hank, that's a natural question, but although I am human, I have an energy radiance available to me that allows me to see into the other realm. But let me finish, as you will have a peppering of questions and I'll never be able to finish the story!"

Hank apologizes and says he'll hold his questions.

"Thank you Hank, and what you may find, is that all of your questions will be answered as I tell you the story."

Tal continues where he left off. "The fact that this other realm exists, one of the many reasons it exists, is to be of service to earth and humanity. To be sure that it does not shoot itself in the foot, in other words, due to misuse of its potential."

"There are individuals of that realm that travel back and forth into earth's three-dimensional density. Maddy is one of them. All of the so-called individuals of that realm are strikingly beautiful, including the men. They carry a certain perfection within them that also displays itself physically."

"I know you're really not too surprised at this, as you have studied material along these lines. You just may not have actually known you would be some fabric within it at some place in time. However, that is exactly the case now."

"The world's financial structure is very powerful. Over the past decade, it has been known to us, that now was the time for the pendulum swing, in whom actually held the financial power."

"As long as lower, more dense forms of individuals controlled the world's money system, then it would stifle other physical beings. This would show up in regard to their creative gifts of which they came to offer. It would seem hard for them to pursue their gifts and live happy abundant lives along the way. All people of earth have a sovereign right to prosperity. They just don't know it, nor do they know how to tap into it. This is where you come in Hank. You will show them how to tap into it."

31

Talal continues with his story as Hank's blue eyes are wide open and attentive. "Part of your place in this Hank, is to introduce a simple, easy way for those who have been living under imbalance in regards to money, to the opposite of that, which is wealth. Wealth created in ease."

"Once the shift begins to take place, then untold gold and minerals will be released from the ethers for mankind and for all the good it will do."

"If it were released before the shift, then the same people and organizations that currently control the world's wealth would do their best to take charge of the material being released. We see the beginning of this happening with The Stiletto wanting the gold coin and its understanding of the mechanics. Again, Hank, this is why you have shown up."

A knock on the door interrupts Talal's story, as "room service" is heard coming from the other side of it. Talal walks over to the door, and looks out the peephole. He turns to Hank, as he is opening the door and says, "it's Alex."

Alex pushes the dinner cart in, "Good evening gentlemen, I trust you will enjoy your dinner, as breakfast comes a bit early!"

"My Dear Good Alex, your appearance here means something, since I was under the impression you were far away. I'm sure you bring us a bit of something other than the personal delivery of our dinner!"

"Quite right Talal. As you know the situation with the Lin Chow family and the Holland freightliner. Well we've had to alter our course a bit."

Alex continues with further instructions. "Hank is to take a car to China Town tomorrow. David will drive him, but drop him off about a block from Lin Chow's establishment. This will catch The Stiletto a bit off guard, as they would have expected him on the third day and not the second. They already have to reorganize on their end due to the ship being held up. The Stiletto has customers waiting and impatiently so, I might add, on the shipment. This means, there is room for error and mistakes on their part, but there must not be on ours."

"Hank, you won't know the next steps, but you will intuitively know what action to take. Has Talal told you of Maddy?"

Talal answers. "I was just getting to the good part, when you knocked, Alex."

"Alright then Gentlemen, I'll leave you to your dinner and evening of discussion. Oh and Hank, David will be in front of the building at seven in the morning. Please remember to wear your belt."

Alex has his hand on the door ready to leave, as Hank replies; "Got it, Alex," Hank confirming, "I'll be there with my belt on."

"Great, then I'll see you soon enough I am sure!" Alex reaches for the door handle to leave, and turns to Talal, "Have you told him about Jocy?"

"No not yet, but I will," responds Tal.

"Ok later." Alex closes the door behind him.

Hank wants to know now. "Ok Talal, give, what about Jocy?"

"Hank, as a form of insurance that you would appear at Lin Chow's and give information on the coin, guess who in addition to Lin Chow's family is now being held on the freightliner?"

Hank for once is silent.

"The Stiletto flew Jocy by helicopter to the freightliner. Apparently, they had a sense that something else was at work in the shipment being held up. They know now that you were involved, so it made Jocy an even bigger pawn than before for receiving what they want."

"The Stiletto assumes that you will show up at Lin Chow's, and that Lin Chow will deliver you to the designated place. However, they want to further assure themselves that you 'will' give them the mechanics of the coin. If not, then for sure, Jocy will perish. Most likely, they will let Lin Chow's family go. He would have lived up to the bargain, and again they do have some honor in their business."

"Our framework of time will be from the moment Lin Chow delivers you, until the freightliner shows up. You will have a bargaining tool, in that you will insist on seeing that Jocy is ok. That will bring the two of you within the same space. The freightliner will arrive with the stolen art and the Lin Chow family on board. They will be witnesses to the very kidnapping of themselves. Whether or not they will testify against The Stiletto is another story. However, this may never reach a court of law, and will need to be taken care of in other unseen ways."

By now, Hank is getting uncomfortable. "What do you mean, 'unseen ways,' Talal?"

"It has to do with Maddy and the realm of which I spoke. There simply is power available to her, which can transcend any physical activity. What we don't want, is for any imbalance to occur, and that is why the timing must be perfect."

Continuing their discussion, Talal gives more information to Hank, which he would not find in books. This level of detail is helping him to understand the larger role in what is happening, and his place within it. As their dinner is about to end, Hank reminds Talal that he has yet to tell him how he met Maddy.

In respect of time, Talal gives Hank the short version.

"Hank, I met Maddy the same way that you met me. A simple way to explain it is this: All of us have higher selves with higher goals, and 'they,' work together to put the right people at the right place, at the right time for the overall service to mankind."

"You are in that loop. The thing that makes you or anyone a part of that loop, is both the willingness to study the 'more,' and then by applying the wisdom found within it, the rest takes care of itself."

32

Noticing it's close to 11 o'clock, Talal suggests they call it a night. He feels that Hank is adequately prepared for what is about to begin. Thus far, only information and conversations have transpired concerning various events. The time is fast approaching where all the various data must be applied. The beginning of the preparation is with the meeting of Lin Chow the next day; Hank will then be on his own as events begin to unfold.

Now very good friends, goodbye handshakes are followed by Hank embracing Talal. He's thankful for this man showing up in his life and providing part of Hank's 'next,' including leading him back to Jocy.

"Where will you be while all of this is going on Talal?"

"Oh, you might just be surprised where I'll be showing up Hank. Just know that we are all around you. Feel safe as you move forward and make the choices that will come up very quickly."

Hank still wanting some reassurance from his friend, "I will be seeing you again, won't I, Tal?"

"Oh yes, Hank, we have much to do together! Now go on your way, and sleep well."

"Oh Talal, before I forget, should I check out of the room or pack anything when I leave in the morning?"

"No Hank, for now please consider that suite as your home, and your laptop is still under secure protection in the hotel safe."

Hank's hand is on the doorknob to leave. "Thanks Talal."

"On God's Wings, Hank," is Talal's response, as Hank closes the door to go back to his adjacent room.

There's a lot going on in the heart and mind of Handsome Hank as he prepares his clothes for an early rise in the morning. So much has happened in such a very short time. Information has been entrusted to him, that few people would know about, much less accept, or try to understand.

However, Hank Ramsan has been a good student of life. Part of him knows that this is a big deal he's privileged to know. Still, there is the other part that is connected to Jocy. He wonders, assuming this would all somehow work out, meaning he and Jocy live through it, would they have a second chance at sharing one another's lives?

Hank's insecurities begin to show when he gives much thought to he and Jocy. He quickly dismisses those thoughts, knowing he has to be on top of himself in every way for he and Jocy to even be a remote possibility. They do have to do whatever is to be done and not be killed in the process.

The reasons Hank is involved in part, of what some would deem risky behavior, are for intentions much larger than his own physical desires. A constant reminder of this helps to keep him balanced and moving forward.

Setting items from his pockets on the large mahogany desk, including his new belt, Hank picks up one of the resort magazines, which is supplied by Powers One. Flipping through the pages as he sets on the corner of the bed, he stops on the section of Las Vegas.

Las Vegas is where Lance Powers has more Powers' architecture, one photograph specifically catches Hank's eye. The building is named *The Magic Presence*, *The Tower of Wealth and Power.* It's a fitting Las Vegas name. This is a building of such stature and magic that just looking at the picture in the magazine would let one know that this building was indeed magical.

Hank reads more about the location of The Magic Presence; then all at once he sees it. It was like he was meant to see this. It was as if a bolt of lightening burst into his mind. The Magic Power Tower is located on top of one of the earth's hidden gold mines and it's one of the secret places Talal mentioned during their discussions. Jocy was also investigating this mine prior to ending their relationship.

Quickly realizing that The Magic Power Tower, had begun initial construction three months after Jocy had discovered some unique information, Hank's mind is swirling. Jocy's discovery, had she gone further, may have led to the full discovery of the mine. Hank was not quite sure what to make of what he was beginning to think. The only thing he could come up with that made any kind of sense, was that Powers built his huge massive powerful structure on top of the mine to protect it from being found by groups such as The Stiletto.

Hank's mind was now a whirlwind of streaming questions:

How much had Jocy found out about the mine at that time, and how much of what she knew, did The Stiletto think or know that she knew? Did they think that Jocy had uncovered some information about the mines that they had not yet accessed?

Was this somehow part of why she was taken abruptly away from his life? Or maybe they have no idea what she found out. But that she was getting to close to The Stiletto's own interest of the Las Vegas area and its many gold and silver mines. Maybe they don't know what she knows. His mind was racing with questions. He wanted and needed answers.

33

By this time, Hank is wide-awake. He has to speak with Talal, and he calls his room. "Talal, this is Hank, sorry if I have disturbed you."

"No of course not Hank, what is it?"

"I've just been flipping through the resort area magazine and have been reading about Powers' new business out there . . . and;"

Talal stops him, in mid-conversation. "Hank, best not do this over the phone, come on over."

Hank walks through Talal's open door, and as soon as he walks in he sees Alex Saber. Alex turns to Hank. "So Hank, I gather your mind is quite full in this moment!"

"Well yes, Alex, any chance either of you would care to fill me in on some details?"

Talal begins. "Well instead of answering your questions Hank, I'll just tell you what you saw as it relates to the magazine and Jocy. I assume that is where your questioning was headed, correct?"

"Yes Talal, I'm all ears." Hank pulls up a chair.

"I mentioned to you earlier this evening about the hidden sanctuaries and the gold that is available to humanity once the shift takes place. One of these gold mines is in Nevada and was in danger of being discovered. The reason it was in danger of being discovered had to do with one event. Expansion into the higher vibrations that both you and Jocy had achieved both consciously and unconsciously."

"It's automatic Hank, that as humanity, meaning individuals as well, rise in light vibration, or radiation, that they will then attract higher known experiences to them."

"It is this exactly, that led Jocy to the mine of which up until then, no one of pure physical characteristics had been given knowledge. That was one of the two events that came into play. The other was, that anyone that begins investigating mines in any part of Nevada is known quickly by The Stiletto. They assign a special group of individuals to watch every step of whoever is looking for such information. Jocy fell under their self-imposed jurisdiction, so to speak. Those of the other realm I spoke of earlier, were also aware of Jocy's investigation, and the fact that she was under the surveillance of The Stiletto."

"It was at this point, we chose to throw Jocy off the trail. This was for her protection as well as that of humanity. It would contradict the entire cosmos for a group such as The Stiletto to find any of the hidden sanctuaries including, but not exclusive of the gold mines."

Tal continues as Hank is glued to his chair.

"What we did, was place a valuable piece of information in front of Jocy about another mine. The Stiletto was under the impression that they were the only ones who knew about this particular mine in Nevada. When she started uncovering things about what they claimed as 'their property' even though it was not legally obtained, they decided to show themselves."

"Things happened fast from that point. They also knew of you, since you and Jocy were communicating back and forth. Therefore, they knew her emotional attachment to you and were going to use that to stop her. They also knew that both of you had many powerful and influential contacts that could really put a vice on their operations. There was a chance that too much would be discovered and revealed to the public. All of this would have alerted the authorities resulting in many secrets of The Stiletto being in jeopardy."

"The Stiletto and their sub-culture controls and designs the financial wealth of the world according to their agenda. This includes all of the various financial instruments and mining operations. They were not about to let anyone curtail or even dent their operation."

"Their next step was the one you are most familiar. Jocy abruptly ended her relationship with you and gave you no explanation."

"Our next step was to make sure this sacred mine was protected. This is where Lance Powers and his gold coin with the epigram came into operation. It was the power of that coin, which built a very Magical Tower. This tower protects the mine and it's setting right smack dab on top of it."

"Not only that, but it is surrounded by a vibration that can never be noticed by human means or instruments. So, you see Lance Powers has played a very important and crucial role in something of much importance not only to humanity at large, but the entire balance of the cosmos."

"The power of the epigram coin allowed all of the red tape normally that goes along with things such as this to melt away. That was a primary reason construction began within three months. Normally for a venture such as this would take a minimum of three years and that would be if the wind was at ones back."

"Now do you see Hank, that it is imperative that you deliver your Magic Wall to the world, so that the gold can be realized from the ethers and used to propel the creative good?"

"Once humanity knows and experiences they have this power in their very hands and apply it, then groups like The Stiletto will melt away. The very existence of a group such as The Stiletto depends on the powerlessness of the stuck money band."

"You, Hank, are cutting that ribbon to freedom with your Magic Wall. However, having said that, you need the power of the coin to assist you in this, as it carries a vibration to help enhance your plan. It carries a blessing and power of the Gods so to speak, and we must have it back. We *will* have it back so that you can do what you really came to do in this incarnation."

By now, Hank is mesmerized and speechless. He knows the depth of what Talal has entrusted him with, and he has no questions.

Talal grinning, "What no questions, Mr. Ramsan?"

"No Talal, but I do have a deep understanding, and now we begin to implement it. Goodnight gentlemen. I have a cosmos to save!" Hank left, with simply a nod goodnight.

34

Thoughts of Jocy were clearly on Hank's mind as he turned and walked back to his room. Until this time, she didn't appear to be in emanate danger, but now that seemed to be changing. They both were being used as a pawn for The Stiletto, with both their lives, as well as others, at stake.

Humanity was not on his mind now, it was Jocy; he and Jocy. Half occupied with calling the front desk for a wake up, and pulling his jeans off to climb into bed, Hank's mind wanders back to their first moment. Their first kiss, the first time he knew that for him, it was Jocy.

He wasn't sure what it was, what it felt like, he simply hadn't felt anything that ever looked like this before. All he knew was how he felt, in that moment.

They kissed. He was speechless. There were no words in Webster's entire dictionary to fit this that he felt. It was like all of Hank's dreams had come true in one moment. He was speechless while breathless, and grateful.

That one kiss, Hank felt from the bottom of both of their souls. He could not breathe for a moment, and felt as though this person with whom his lips and mouth had become one, was breathing for him.

In one brief moment, all of Hank's reasons for being born, all that he had done and ever would do, was being answered by all of the Angels of the Galaxy. It was as if they wrapped their arms around him and said; "This is home, this is where you belong. You can rest here."

For Hank, it was like he was the inside of a smile contained in the sweetest mouth there could ever be. Jocy's kiss was sweeter than the sweetest kiss he had ever known. For a moment, he thought he had died and landed in the land of golden chocolate, free to come and go between worlds as he chose. Free with the ability to do and be anything he could ever desire. It was Heaven. That's what it was.

Following those sweet memories, Hank fell fast asleep.

35

"Good Morning, Mr. Ramsan, this is your six a.m. wake-up call," was half heard in Hank's ear as he was fumbling for the phone on the night stand.

He hangs up, and lies back down for a moment to get his bearings. Then he remembers his last thoughts before going to sleep. He and Jocy. A quickening of sorts went through his bloodstream, and he sat up alert. He knew what this day was.

It was a new beginning, maybe for him, maybe for humanity, maybe for Lin Chow, and maybe, yes God, maybe for he and Jocy.

This was one of those days, that if you were to ask Hank what he was doing in such a rush, his answer would be; 'Gotta see a man about a horse.'

That was his way of moving on, and answering no questions. 'Just move and get out of the way, I have things that must be done!'

Breaking his thought was a knock on the door; it was room service, so he thought. Looking out the peephole he sees that it's Talal. He pulls the door open and in walks his friend with a silver tray of coffee, bagels, and cream cheese. Hank's favorite way to begin his morning.

"Good morning Hank! I just wanted to make sure you run off to school with a full tummy!" Hank laughed while thanking him for the breakfast, especially the coffee.

Talal responded with; "Well Hank, Supermen as you know, must be supercharged!"

Hank had a feeling that there was more to that statement, and he wanted to ask, but knew there wasn't time. It was now 6:30 and he needed to be in front to meet David and the car by seven.

Talal said his goodbyes so that Hank could continue dressing and be on his way without rushing.

With 10 minutes to seven on the room clock, Hank grabs his second cup of coffee, sticks a bagel in his mouth, reaches for the door handle, and stops. Turning to look back at the room, he wonders how long it would be before he sees this 'home' again. Out he goes, a fast clip to the elevator.

Exiting the elevator, he sees David and Lance standing in the lobby and they both turn toward him. Powers walks over, greets Hank with his right hand extended, and grabs Hank's shoulder with his left hand.

"Hank, you can do this, and you have power with you and around you of which you are not yet fully aware. It will be great to hear your stories when I see you again."

Hank thanks him, and David signals that they must be on their way.

David opens the front door instead of the back door of the car. Hank kiddingly asks, "What you are not a valet anymore?"

David replies with a smile, "It must appear that a friend has dropped you off. This way The Stiletto will not know the nature of the friend, and it will keep them on their toes. If they trace this car, it will lead them to a dead end. Keeping some mystery around even this simple ride, is very important."

Hank agrees, "Ok, thanks David. Can I pick the radio station?" David just looks at him with a smirk.

During the 20-minute ride through traffic, Hank asks David some personal questions about his life. 'Was he married? Did he enjoy working for Powers and just what was his job, as the only thing he saw him do, was move people around in cars.'

David summed things up for Hank in answer to all of his questions.

"Yes Hank, I am married to the pinnacle of any human woman. We are compliments to each other and laugh and have fun constantly."

"My job with Mr. Powers? I am his best friend, and he mine. We have a very special relationship. I am one of his closest, if not closest confidantes. I do not 'need' to work. I do what you see me doing as well as many other things, you do not see. Being a taxi driver, is one of the fun things I do. It gives the appearance that I am just a chauffeur, which allows my ears and eyes to see things, that may not normally be seen if people knew my relationship with Lance."

"As you might guess, this is very beneficial to Lance the person as well as his business."

Gladly responding as Hank loves this conversation with David, "Yes David, I can see the benefit. It's also quite interesting to get to know a little bit of Lance Powers the man, versus the celebrity."

David continues, "The celebrity comes with success at the level of someone like Powers. It's a very human thing and need to want to look up to others for grabbing a piece of ourselves; Lance provides that for many, as you will Hank."

"What do you mean," asks Hank, "as *I will*?"

David explains his comment: "Hank, you are going to change things for millions of people. Human nature wants to know what is behind this change, and who the person or people are. All roads will point to you."

Just as Hank is about to blurt out a comment, David stops the car.

"We're here, this is where I leave you." David pointing, "Can you see that red neon sign, with 'Lin Chow', about a block away? That is where you're to go. From there you'll be in Lin Chows' hands and you'll know what to do with each choice that shows up."

"How do you know that David?" Hank feeling a little shaky.

"Because you would not have been put in, nor put yourself in this position, if you were not ready. You are ready Hank."

David extends his hand to say goodbye and good luck. After they shake hands, Hank exits the car and begins is way down the block.

36

Although his stride is brisk as he heads toward Lin Chow's, Hank's stomach is beginning to feel uneasy. He knows what to do. He just keeps thinking and saying; "Peace. This is going to be fine. I am going to be fine. I am okay." Within about 100 feet of the store front he stops, takes a deep breath, and repeats, "I Am Safe, and this is only all good."

Hank gingerly grabs the doorknob to the store pushing it open. The cowbell above the door clangs letting the storeowner know that someone has entered his shop. Hank looks over to the counter and a small man in stature, apparently Chinese, looks up to see who has entered.

First, the man stares, then both the expression of sadness and hope seem to fill his face in the same moment. The storeowner comes out from behind the counter and greets Hank. "Mr. Ramsan, I am Lin Chow."

Extending his hand, Hank asks, "how did you know who I was?"

Lin Chow pulls a picture from his back pocket. It was a picture of Hank. He goes on to explain. "I was given this picture and told that you would show up soon, but tomorrow was the day. I was given further instructions that I was to take you to a designated place. Then and only then, would my family be released. I am quite happy to see you as you might imagine, Mr. Ramsan. Please come and I'll fix you some tea."

"Any chance you have coffee?" The usual Hank response.

Lin Chow turning again to Hank, " I have instant coffee and hot water, will that do?"

In Hank's usual politeness, since they had just met, "Yes, that will be just fine, thank you."

Hank begins asking Lin Chow some questions which stops Lin Chow from going to the back of the store.

"Lin Chow, maybe you are limited in what you can tell me, but how did you become involved with The Stiletto and being assigned delivery of me to them?"

Lin Chow wanting to be as helpful as he can begins to explain to Hank: "The Stiletto owns, and at minimum is active in a large part of China Town. The Chinese Mafia is under the organization of The Stiletto, they have their own branch, so to speak. They own my shop."

"I have a successful business here Mr. Ramsan, but I do have to pay a percentage to The Stiletto. If I don't, they put me out of business, and I have no where else to go. I need this business to produce income as well as send money back to relatives, not fortunate to be in the USA."

"When The Stiletto needs some special project done, they often choose those of us here, because they know we fear them greatly. When they wanted you to come to them, they used my family as the tool. As you can see, it worked. Here you are, and I am most grateful that you came, Mr. Ramsan."

"Lin Chow, do you know anything else, as to why they want me?"

"No, I do not ask questions, and they wouldn't tell me anyway. My role, in order to get my family back, was when you showed up, to bring you to them."

Hank begins to press a bit. "What makes you so sure they will return your family, after you deliver me?"

"It is their way, Mr. Ramsan. They keep their word in things of this nature. That is all I know."

Hank impatiently wants to know what's next. "What next, now that I am here, Lin Chow?"

"Well, Mr. Ramsan," Lin Chow replies, "since you are a day early, I will need to make a call for instructions. I'll do that in just a few moments. First, allow me get your hot water. I do not know what this means for you, as they want you for something, but I thank you for returning my family to me, Mr. Ramsan."

"Well, I won't go as far as to say it's my pleasure Lin Chow, but you are welcome."

"I understand, Mr. Ramsan."

As Lin Chow exits behind the curtain to get the hot water, Hank looks around the shop. He notices behind the counter pictures of Lin Chow's wife and two daughters. He's somehow thankful that he is able to bring them back together, and tries not to think past that for the moment.

"Here you go Mr. Ramsan, all the necessary ingredients to make some not so great instant coffee!"

Graciously Hank accepts his coffee; "Thank you Lin Chow, I'll enjoy it just the same."

"Ok, good, I'll make that phone call now." Once again, Lin Chow exits behind the curtain, which closes off the back of the store.

37

Approximately 10 minutes had passed when Lin Chow comes out from behind the curtain. "Mr. Ramsan, I have my instructions, may I recite them to you?"

"Yes, of course, Lin Chow," responds Hank, "please begin."

Lin Chow begins reading from his notes: "We are to leave here as soon as possible and take a taxi to Pier 17. Pier 17 is about three miles from here. The exact taxi of course will be provided for us, and should arrive here within the hour."

"At the end of Pier 17 will be a small motor boat with one driver who will be your brief escort. You are to take that motor boat out to a yacht that is moored in the harbor."

"According to my instructions we will be able to see it from the pier. The name of the yacht is 'The Fancy Madame.' That yacht will then take you out to sea. At the proper time, the helicopter that is stationed on top of the yacht will take you further on your way. The helicopter will fly you to a freightliner which is in a holding pattern."

"The same helicopter that delivers you to the freightliner will also bring my family back safely to me. That is all that I was given, Mr. Ramsan."

After sitting patiently, Hank says to Lin Chow, "Ok Lin Chow, then I am ready."

"Would you like something to eat, Mr. Ramsan, while I prepare to close the shop down for a few hours?"

"Yes, that would be great Lin Chow. Food may help settle this queasy stomach a bit." Hank was always glad to respond to a free food offer, no matter the circumstance.

"I have some fresh Hunan chicken simmering, would that do for you?" inquires Lin Chow.

Not one to mince words over food Hank gladly accepts; "That's my favorite, Chinese food! Do you mind that I call it Chinese food Lin Chow?"

"Well you know Mr. Ramsan," responds Lin Chow, "I love American cheeseburgers, and to me that is my favorite American food. That is what I ask for as well, when I refer to my favorite American food!"

"I'll be back in a moment with lunch, but we must eat fast, so this will be fast food Chinese food!" Lin Chow again exits to the back.

Quickly returning with a tray of wonderfully aromatic Hunan Chicken and hot tea, Lin Chow sets it on a table at the end of the shops counter and pulls over two chairs. "Enjoy your meal Mr. Ramsan. I'll join you as soon as I close out the cash register and lock up the back of the store."

Hank lifts the silver domed lid off of the plate of hot food, and spoons it onto his plate. He knows rice is under the other dome. However, Hank never eats rice with his Hunan Chicken. As he is lifting it onto his plate, his thoughts briefly go to Jocy, as this too was her favorite. She had introduced him to this seasoned dish of chicken and broccoli soon after they first met. He quickly dismisses where his mind was going, he knew he needed to stay alert.

After taking a few bites, Hank notices a fortune cookie setting next to the tray on a gold saucer. Thinking to himself that he could use some good fortune about now, he decides to open it instead of waiting until he's finished eating, which is the normal custom.

Breaking apart the cookie and reading the small piece of paper brings Hank a shift in his chair. In handwritten gold letters was this message; "We are with you, Signed Maddy."

This note takes Hank by surprise and he looks around to see if anyone else was in the store. There was no one. Just as he's glancing around, Lin Chow pulls his chair up to join Hank.

"Lin Chow, this is quite good. By the way, where did the fortune cookie come from?"

"What fortune cookie Mr. Ramsan? I did not bring you a fortune cookie."

"Well, this one.." As soon as Hank went to show Lin chow both the saucer and the remains of the cookie, the saucer had disappeared.

"Oh, what I meant to say, was are you going to give me the customary fortune cookie?" Hank catching himself in mid-thought.

Lin Chow innocently answers, "Well of course Mr. Ramsan, this is Chinese food!" They both break apart a laugh, which helps with some of the anxiousness.

Although Hank didn't understand what had happened, he somehow felt better about what was ahead of him. He knew that although he had little information as to what was transpiring, perhaps others could see further ahead. That thought did help him to feel better.

As Lin Chow is spooning rice onto his own plate, Hank being his inquisitive self begins asking some questions. "Lin Chow how long as The Stiletto had your family?"

Swallowing some tea before speaking Lin Chow replies; "Just about three days, but it has felt like three frightening months."

Lin Chow begins telling the story of what happened: "I left to do an errand one afternoon, and when I returned, the shop was locked. It was open for business when I left, my wife and daughters inside running the store."

"When I returned and unlocked the door I cautiously walked in, not knowing what to expect. Looking around and calling for my wife, I suddenly noticed a large note hanging from the cash register. The note had a phone number and a message to call that number if I ever wanted to see my family again."

Hank interrupts. "What phone number is that, Lin Chow?"

Wanting to oblige, Lin Chow answers; "I can easily give you the number Mr. Ramsan, but it will be of no help to you. It is a familiar number in China Town. From that number, they then either give instructions or tap us into another line. The instructions were given from this number, and I was to press an automated system for my message."

Hank still pressing. "And what did the message say?"

"The message said exactly what you already know," answers Lin Chow, as he repeats the message to Hank.

'Lin Chow, we are holding your family in exchange for delivery of one Mr. Hank Ramsan. Mr. Ramsan will show up at your store within three days. When he arrives, you are to immediately call this number for the next set of instructions. You will find Mr. Hank Ramsan's picture under your cash register drawer, so that you will know him when he arrives.'

"That was the end of the message. I knew all I could do was wait and pray that you would show up, and you did." Lin Chow finishes his story of the events leading Hank to his store and noticing the time says to Hank; "Mr. Ramsan, if you are about done, we probably should get ready for the taxi's arrival."

"Sure, Lin Chow, thank you very much for lunch. This was helpful for whatever is before me."

Hank of course, meant the message from Maddy, but Lin Chow understood it to be about the food.

"You are welcome Mr. Ramsan. I'll just put these things away, and we can walk out the door upon the arrival of the cab."

Lin Chow begins to clear the table and Hank helps by moving the chairs back to where they were.

Walking out from the back and drying his hands, Lin Chow mentions to Hank the location of the restroom, in case he needs it before they leave.

Hank goes to the side wall of the store and walks back to a small one-stall restroom. Standing over the sink washing his hands, he looks in the mirror and says: "Ok, here we go!" Grabbing the door handle, he moves swiftly back out to the main part of the store.

Just as he appears from the restroom, Lin Chow tells him the taxi is waiting outside, and it's time to go.

"Of course, Lin Chow, I'm ready!" Hank responds trying to sound enthusiastic.

Walking out the door, Lin Chow turns to lock the door behind him. Hank opens the back door of the cab and gestures Lin Chow in and then follows. He closes the door, and then glances to the driver who was American in appearance. The visor was open above his head, and the symbol of The Stiletto was boldly displayed. There was no mistake, they were in the 'right' taxi.

The driver made a short clear statement: "No conversation, please gentlemen. I am to take you to Pier 17. Those are my instructions, enjoy the ride."

With that comment from the driver, the partition goes up between the front and back seat. Although it was a darkly tinted partition, Hank was sure it was bullet proof.

Hank and Lin Chow look at one another. Next stop, Pier 17.

38

The taxi pulls into the pier area, driving by pier 11 through 16 and slows as it approaches Pier 17. The cab stops, the driver doesn't say a word. Hank and Lin Chow look at one another. Lin Chow tells Hank that he is to walk with him to the end of the pier and watch him get on the escort boat. The escort boat will take him out to the yacht, 'The Fancy Madame.'

Hank turns to Lin Chow, "what are you to do after you see me off, Lin Chow?"

"I am to take the same taxi back to my shop and wait." answers Lin Chow.

Helping Lin Chow, while opening the door, Hank says, "ok, then let's go!"

Cautiously walking down the long pier, they notice fishermen with large coolers full of fish, but the men behind the coolers don't look much like fishermen. They have on those familiar Stiletto boots and not fishing footgear.

Hank keeps his thoughts to himself, assuming they are being watched for anything that Hank may do to cause havoc at the last minute. However, Hank had no such plans. He was going to see this first part through as best he could, for the sake of Lin Chow and his family.

Reaching the end of Pier 17, Hank and Lin Chow begin glancing down the loading ramp, where there is a surprise. A nice surprise for Lin Chow. His family was there! He would not have to wait or wonder in fear.

Sharing Lin Chow's enthusiasm as his family begins their way up the ladder, Hank asks him why he thinks they were released before Hank was taken to the freightliner.

Answering Hank as quickly as he can, Lin Chow offers his guess: "Mr. Ramsan, The Stiletto keeps their word. And although yes, we have to live under their rule, they are honorable to an extent. This keeps the Chinese from revolution within China Town. The Stiletto would win any revolution, of course, but they prefer no bloodshed or anything that upsets the ongoing daily success of the business. They choose to keep large amounts of money flowing without having to rebuild or clean up an organizational mess caused by bloodshed. Interruptions of this nature would be expensive in many ways."

"They do play rough, but they have honor within it. I have honored my part of the requirement, and now they have honored their end with no additional strings. My having to wait until you were on the ship would be a string attached. I have delivered you. They have honored their end. Deal is closed. Thank you Mr. Ramsan. I know not your fate, but you have saved mine."

Hank gestures to Lin Chow that he is welcome, however Lin Chow's attention is diverted to his family. They are now on the pier level and running to meet Lin Chow. Hank moves out of the way for the reunion and then someone grabs his arm.

"Mr. Ramsan, it's time for you to get on the boat waiting below, please descend the ladder, I will follow you."

This fellow was very polite, but also very big and fit. Hank began the climb down the ladder and as he turned to steady his footing, he noticed the escort in the boat. The escort's back was turned away from Hank while securing the rope. Hank steps down into the small boat and immediately the escort turns around. The boat escort then proceeds to acknowledge the presence of the two men, Hank, and the big fit guy.

Suddenly, Hank catches himself before he almost says something that would have jeopardized everything. The escort turning around, catching Hank off guard as he was greeting them was none other than Alex Saber.

Alex didn't say a word as he started the boat's engine. The big guy untied the last rope holding them to the dock. The boat begins pulling away from the pier, leaving Mr. Big Guy behind.

Hank didn't say a word, he didn't know if the boat in which he and Alex were riding was being bugged in some way. He would wait to see what would come from Alex.

Causing fright to fill Hank's entire body, Alex turns around pointing a gun at him. Immediately Alex said in a low tone; "Hank, this is for appearance. We are being watched from the yacht and shore, but they cannot hear us. My instructions were to keep a gun on you until I have you to the yacht. So please keep that frightened looked on your face." Alex holds back a slight grin, while watching Hank recover from the initial shock. He had no problem looking a bit scared.

Alex speaks quickly. "I have to be brief in my words with you, as they would not expect us to have a lovely conversation. I'll motion you over here with the gun, and you move over to where I can see you and steer the boat at the same time. I will give you information that will be helpful."

Alex begins motioning the gun for Hank to move over to the front of the boat. Speaking just above the noise of the motor, Alex begins to brief Hank.

"The reason it's me that's here Hank, is because you are valuable cargo, and I'm a very trusted person within The Stiletto. This is a normal task for me under the circumstances, since I tend to be at the front of the things. We don't have much time before we're at the yacht. Once you are there I will leave you to your own resources."

"There is nothing for you to do once aboard the yacht except to pay attention. You know they have Jocy; they know you know, that they have Jocy. Therefore, it would do you no good to try and invent some maneuver at this point. But any intentions you may have up your sleeve when you get to the freightliner, may be useful."

"One thing to always observe, and maybe you didn't see it when the guy brought you down to meet me, but they all wear earphones. Even your taxi driver had them on. They are connected into The Stiletto's main headquarters. I don't always have them on, because they let me make some decisions on my own."

Alex continues briefing Hank as quickly as he can. "Those big guys are mainly just that. Big guys to move physical bodies around with no interference. They are not paid, nor on board with The Stiletto to 'think;' they are there to push if something needs to be pushed, as in bodily harm. They follow directions and that is all. There will be five of this level of men on the yacht. No decision-makers around at this time. Just big guys that can push you down hard, if you don't do as you are told."

"I get paid to think, not push, and they pay me well. Therefore, I'm in a good position to know what is really going on at all times. This has been very beneficial for the, well let's say, the higher good, that I am in a strategic position with The Stiletto."

Alex seeing they are soon to the yacht speeds up his delivery of information to Hank.

"The yacht will travel about an hour out to sea. This is to keep up appearances, as this will be far enough out that it is too far for the regular coast guard patrol to be aware of any foul play. The Stiletto is careful to stay on the right side of the law, however superficial."

"When you reach a certain marker in the sea, you will then board the helicopter that is already on board this yacht. The helicopter will take you to the freightliner, which is about 30 minutes by air."

Hank interrupts. "What do you know about Jocy and the ship?"

"I don't know a lot about the freightliner Hank," replies Alex, " nor Jocy's where-abouts on it. The freightliner is run by the Holland end of The Stiletto, they get their instructions directly from The Stiletto's headquarters."

"Since I oversee Jocy's ranch, artwork, and horse operation, I knew enough information as to which freightliner to hold in limbo. I needed to be able to do this until Maddy and others could get things in a ready position. It was easy because that's part of my responsibility with The Stiletto. But the actual running of the ship and its primary service belongs between The Stiletto and the Holland organization operating under its long arm."

"The yacht is ahead Hank so I will not be speaking much more."

Hank quickly asks, "What happens next with you, Alex?"

"Well Hank, I will know where the freightliner is at all times, "Alex reassuring Hank, "because it has the artwork and the horses on board. However, I'm privy to very little information as it directly relates to you, Jocy, and the reason they have her. They are keeping this coin thing within the higher levels of the organization. I'm not trusted with that since I am just an employee, and this is a very large transaction personally involving the higher ranks of The Stiletto. Once you are on the Holland freightliner, you are on your own."

"Oh, and one other thing Hank. Will that Magic Wall of yours really work?"

"Yes, Alex, no question," responds a confident Hank, "The Magic Wall is the one thing I am sure of along with my place within it."

Glad to hear Hank's answer, Alex replies; "Good, then see that you stay alive and in one piece to do what you came to do."

"Your lips to God's ears, Alex," whispers Hank in a low tone as they approach the yacht.

Alex held back a grin.

Just as they bumped up against the yacht, ropes were eased down to tie them close. Then an aluminum ladder extended down to Hank for him to climb, leaving Alex behind.

Hank begins up the ladder and no further words or motions were exchanged between Hank and Alex as they parted ways.

39

'The Fancy Madame' was beautiful. It was a black, shiny velvety black, and the emblem along side of the name was a symbol that Hank had grown familiar with, 'The Stiletto' *knife*. The only other yacht of this size that Hank had been on, belonged to one of the publishing tycoons that hired him for some freelance work.

The moments of drifting back in memory were cut short as his hand reaches for the last rung on the ladder. One of those five big guys helps to pull Hank the rest of the way. With both feet now on deck, the big guy that helped him on board introduces himself.

"Mr. Ramsan, my name is Marty. I'll be your supervisor of sorts for your stay on board. I am limited in information that I'm at liberty to tell you, so your questions may be best held to your imagination."

"Please follow me to one of the private dining rooms on board, where you will be served a light refreshment and available food choices before dinner."

Hank follows Marty while trying to be observant of every room and person that he's able to take in along the way to the dining room. So far, he is being treated as a guest, but he knows he is really a prisoner.

Being keenly aware is one thing, but Hank knows it's in the best interest of all involved to just do as he is told. He plans on playing it safe until something would have him change that. Hank knows Jocy is on board the freightliner, so he wants to make sure he is able to get there and not jeopardize her life, out of some lack of control on his part. Staying low key would be the only acceptable behavior at this point.

Marty interrupts Hank's thoughts as he shows him into a magnificent stateroom with a huge oval shaped conference table with black leather chairs surrounding it.

"Mr. Ramsan, you will notice to the left, a buffet table with a variety of food and beverage. Please help yourself and then be seated as soon as you are comfortable. A message will be forthcoming. I will leave you to your refreshments, Mr. Ramsan."

After giving Hank his instructions, Marty leaves the stateroom closing the door behind him. Hank hears a click in the door lock, letting him know he is now a fancy prisoner for sure.

Dangerous territory or not, Hank starts looking for coffee. Sure enough, fresh brewed french roast, one of his favorites is calling him. He pours himself a cup, and as he's beginning to savor it, the food items catch his attention.

Wanting to keep alert, Hank chooses to build himself a sandwich of the gourmet looking turkey slices and swiss cheese. "Ah, but have they really done their homework?" He mumbles to himself and then, "Yes!" His favorite mayonnaise and in packages of plenty! "Good undercover work by The Stiletto's big boys." Hank was having fun in his own mind keeping calm, while talking to himself.

Trying to stay in a humorous mood, because he knows this will keep him open to inspiration, Hank begins whistling. It's something that he always does. If he gets tense or begins to think about the possibility of dying soon, he will close off any good ideas that could prevent him from just that.

Hank moves his coffee cup over to the table and turns to get the plate holding his sandwich. He's looking forward to this sandwich. It's his favorite. As he bites into the sandwich, he silently is hoping this is not his last meal. Otherwise, he would have chosen prime rib with the works. It would have taken him longer to eat it!

Just as Hank is comfortably settling into enjoying the tastes filling his mouth, he hears: "Good Afternoon, Mr. Ramsan, it's good to see you again."

This was the same distorted voice that he had heard when he was first pulled from the street and taken to The Stiletto's headquarters. This same voice had his gold coin removed from his pockets by one of the big guys.

Hank continues eating, but offers; "You'll have to pardon my manners but my mouth is full."

"I trust you are enjoying the provisions so far, Mr. Ramsan?"

"Yes, I am thank you very much." Hank wants to blurt forth questions, but chooses only to respond when spoken to; he knows he's safer that way.

"As you are aware Mr. Ramsan, we are heading out to sea to meet the freightliner. We will be having our most intensive discussion once we are there."

Hank knows what intensive may mean, but does not respond. Again keeping his thoughts to himself as he continues eating.

"Mr. Ramsan, Marty will be escorting you shortly to your private suite. I'll inform you now that this suite is sound proof, and we have no surveillance equipment within that room. You will have 100% privacy while you are there, which will be approximately three hours. Then at that time, we meet up with the freightliner. We have also provided you within your suite, ample refreshments and yes, coffee, Mr. Ramsan, so that you may enjoy your stay."

Hank is wondering why he is being told this, but again does not ask and just listens.

'The Box' continues addressing Hank from some type off a speaker or intercom. "We ask that as soon as you are taken to your suite that you remove all of your clothes. Marty will stand there watching you undress, so that all clothing is handed over to him. You will find on your bed, a warm-up suit, undergarments, and other essentials. We also ask that you shower while Marty is in the room."

By now, Hank can't hold back any longer and asks; "Why does Marty have to see to it that I shower?"

The mechanical voice offers, "because Mr. Ramsan, we want to be sure our security system is not breached in any way, this assures us of that. Please comply, otherwise, Marty will have to help you with your shower. We assume you'd prefer not to shower with Marty."

"Oh, you have a sense of humor, Mr. Box. I will do as you say, and take a shower." Hank concedes this one.

The Box gave further details. "Good, thank you for your cooperation under less than perfect circumstances for yourself, Mr. Ramsan. The next time you hear from me will be as we approach the freightliner. It is our hope that you will be very talkative and open regarding a matter of most importance to us."

Hank is again silent.

Just as Hank is about to finish his last bite, he hears the door unlock, and it's his shower partner, Marty. "Mr. Ramsan, are you ready to move onto your suite now?"

"Sure, lets do it Marty."

"You may leave your dish on the table, Mr. Ramsan. It will be cleared away."

Hank sets things down, as he was quite used to cleaning up after himself, but when on yachts, you do what the yachtsman say.

Marty escorts Hank out the door and suggests he go left down the corridor. Hank notices the hallways feel wide for a yacht and quite roomy. The green color of the carpet throughout was quite rich feeling. This is as it should be for a group in control of the world's money system.

"Here we are Mr. Ramsan, your suite." Marty stops behind Hank, and points to the door. Hank had walked past it, since he was walking in front of Marty.

Opening the door, Marty shows Hank in and then follows. The door closes behind Marty as he nods over to the bed where the warm-up suit sets waiting. He points with his body language as if to say, 'There you are, take off your clothes and get in the shower.'

"I guess you have to watch me Marty?" Hank wants to be sure.

"Yes, Mr. Ramsan," politely replies Marty, "but I have seen many men without clothes, do not be embarrassed."

Hank trying to make light of the moment replies; "Well Marty, I'm not embarrassed, I have a pretty decent body don't you think?"

Marty tries not to laugh, but he is beginning to feel some brotherly affection for this blonde handsome man, of whom he is in charge. "Hard to say, Mr. Ramsan, they all look the same to me."

Sharing a laugh, Hank thinks maybe he has a little bit of a new friend in Marty, but he's not counting on it just yet."

Hank removes his underwear quickly and grabs the towel that's lying on the bed next to his warm-up suit. "Is that good enough for you Marty?"

"Yes Mr. Ramsan, you have handed me all of your clothing except your belt. It seems to have dropped to floor. I'll need that."

Hank had hoped good ole' Marty wouldn't have noticed the belt he tried to slide beside the bed. However, the big guy is observant. Hank hands Marty the belt. "Ok, is that it, Marty?"

"Well one more thing Mr. Ramsan, the shower?" You didn't think I would forget the shower, did you now Mr. Ramsan?" Marty playing a bit with his new friend.

"Well damn, Marty, nothing gets by you, now does it? Are you going to wash my back?"

"No, Mr. Ramsan, I'll leave as soon as I know you are soaping up."

The bathroom has a very large standing shower and Hank moves toward it. The shower can be seen from the main part of the room, where Marty is standing supervising. Hank gets in, turns on the water, and begins to soap up. He hears the door close, and knows he is now alone.

40

Cutting off the water from his shower, Hank reaches for the towel, while stepping onto the thick bathroom rug. As he begins to wrap the towel around his body, he hears the door close. He calls out to Marty thinking that he's returned for some reason. Hank leaves the bathroom and begins to look toward the main suite door.

His eyes glanced forward. *She* is standing near the door. His eyes lock on hers. Hank's face grew warm, the corners of his mouth turned up into a glowing, beaming smile. It was Jocy. Dear God, he didn't know how; all he knew, *it was Jocy.*

She looked straight at him in disbelief, as neither of them had any prior knowledge of this moment. Jocy looked at Hank and could not take her eyes off of him. He was still as handsome, blonde, and tanned, as she always knew him to be. The best looking blonde chest in the Universe adorned this man. They both are speechless, as they are caught in a moment of an affectionate stare.

Before Hank knew it, the subtle danger no longer existed. In a brief instant, Hank's eyes went to Jocy's mouth. That mouth, her soft lips, that lipstick. She was wearing the same plum color. That mouth, which once had been all over his body. That tongue, he still knew and felt. In a sweet instant, he is reminded of the very first time that tongue was in his mouth. It made him gasp for breath then, and made him breathless now, as he dared to remember.

Both standing in a daze, locked in memory, no words yet spoken. Every nerve ending in Hank's body is screaming out for her.

Every sense of self-control and discipline had left the planet. His only thoughts were: 'God I do want her.'

Stuck in this moment, this incredible moment of pure desire, of wanting something more than he needed it, was all that was going on in Hank Ramsan's mind. Wanting this person, this individual whom he had loved, whom he still loves, and with whom he had made love. Passion was invented for Hank when he was with Jocy.

Now, here she is, within 10 feet of him. His conflict was to reach for her tearing away at her clothes no matter the cost for either of them, or to reach for her just to hold her. After all this time, of not being able to just hold her, it's now consuming him.

Millions of seconds are burning a hole right through him. Hank had no thought, no thinking going on at all; then she came closer. He was still just standing there gazing at her in utter amazement as to what was going on within himself. She knew.

She knew very well what was boiling under his skin; it was under hers also. She started toward him, he couldn't move. She knew, because she felt the heat just the same.

They still had not spoken; they both knew that words would ruin it. Then into each other's arms they flew.

They couldn't talk, but they laughed. This was a wonderlust, funny, exhilarating moment. Just to be close to one another again, in the same room, just to enjoy one another. However, the joyful moments were being taken up with a sense of urgency. Hank had to bring himself back to what was ahead of them.

He somehow regained some sense of where he was, whom he was with, and why that moment was even created. However, before he completely came back to the reality of where they were, she placed her lips softly on his.

Then he couldn't breathe; her kisses always took his breath away. Being lost in Jocy's mouth not wanting to find his way out. He didn't want to take his mouth from hers. Maybe if he stayed there, the world would go away.

Suddenly, the towel that was clinched around his waist fell to the floor! "Whoops!" came from Hank while his mouth was still on Jocy's, and they both broke out in laughter. Their loving laughter which helped to ease both the passion and unease of the moment.

Jocy reminds him; "Well, I've seen that before!"

Hank responds, "yes but don't you think it's so much healthier than the last time you saw it?" This again brings smiles, and remembering how good they were together.

Hank, instead of grabbing the towel reaches over and picks up the pair of warm-up suit pants. Jocy compliments him by saying, "Well you did always have a great butt!" He grins as he puts the pants on.

Motioning with his hand patting on the bed, he asks her to sit down beside him. "Jocy," Hank begins, "you know I could get lost in this moment with you, and most likely that was the plan of The Stiletto, but we don't have much time. What I guess is that they put us together, so that they could then threaten us with each other's lives at stake. Having us spend some alone time together would make it more emotionally pressing."

"Yes, you're right Hank, and yes, too, it is emotionally pressing just being with you after all of this time, I've missed you very much." Hank holds her and expresses the same, and then Jocy stands up.

"Ok, Hank, it's time to get serious about us getting through this alive. Why are you here, do you know?"

"I'm here Jocy because of a very powerful gold coin that works like an Aladdin's Lamp when used in a certain way. They took the coin from me, but did not know that there were instructions in implementing the coin in order for its power to be shown. When they discovered that they couldn't release its power, they came after me. I'm assuming they have you involved, in order to entice me into showing them how to distract the power from the gold coin."

Jocy places her hand on Hank's knee while asking, "I assume you know of my involvement with The Stiletto, the artwork and horse farm operation?"

"Yes I know," answers Hank, "and I know you did that to keep me alive." For a moment, they get lost in each other's eyes.

Jocy breaks away from the longing stare, and says: "Well, it would appear that they think they have us both right where they want us, in order to get what they want. That's how The Stiletto operates. But I have an ace up my sleeve that they don't know anything about."

"What's that Jocy," queries Hank, "can you tell me?"

Jocy begins, "have you heard the distorted voice yet?"

"Oh, you mean, Mr. Box? Yes, I've had the pleasure, twice. Once when they took the coin, and then on board here today."

Jocy continues with her surprise, "I know who Mr. Box is."

Hank looks at her. "How did you find that out, Jocy?"

"Have you heard the name, Dagger?"

Hank now impatient on top of curious. "Yes, go on.'

"He was scheduled to come to the horse farm, but due to the freightliner being held up, that got postponed. Apparently he made some kind of arrangements to meet me on the freightliner last night."

"I knew what he wanted, and I was prepared."

"How did you find out?" Hank wanting her to hurry before Marty showed up.

Speaking in a fast whisper, Jocy continues. "I received a message in a bottle. No joke. I received a telephone call about thirty seconds within the delivery of a bottle. It was a woman's voice on the other end and she said, 'Open the bottle carefully, there is a message inside.' Then she hung up."

Hank instinctively thinks maybe it was Maddy.

"I opened the bottle and the message read, 'Dagger is arranging a little meeting for the two you on board the ship. The enclosed tranquilizers might come in handy. They are horse tranquilizers. In the event you are searched, it would not be out of the norm for you to have them in your possession.'"

"So, with that, I mixed up a powder that would be tasteless and harmless and kept it with me. I didn't know what to expect or when. Then around four yesterday afternoon, I got a message from Alex that a helicopter would be arriving to take me to some boat to be Dagger's escort for the evening."

"Dagger shows up and long story short as he began to make his move, I poured some champagne and I spiked his with the white powdered horse tranquilizer. He became giddy, lightheaded, and very free. He started to talk about different aspects of The Stiletto. Dagger was like an excited child telling me his show and tell for school. He loves The Stiletto and the power it gives him."

"I gingerly began to ask him some questions, as we were playing a little affectionate on the sofa. To my surprise, he answered them all having no inhibitions. He kept asking for more and larger glasses of champagne. I kept pouring and each time I put a little more of the powder in his glass until he was closer to falling asleep."

"Then the moment came when I asked him. 'Are you the boss of The Stiletto organization?' Dagger's response was, 'Oh no! The boss of The Stiletto is more powerful than the heads of 10 countries.'"

"Dagger then asked me if I wanted to know who it was. I told him, 'only if he wanted to tell me.'"

"And then like a little boy, he says, 'Ok I'll tell you but you must promise not to tell anyone, it's a big secret!'"

"And then he just blurts out the name!"

"Who is it Jocy?" Hank is dying to know by now.

"You won't believe this Hank, it's ..."

Just as she is about to tell him, there's a loud knock on the door.

41

"Mr. Ramsan, it's Marty, may I enter?"

Hank calmly responds, "yes, Marty we have our clothes on."

Marty enters the room and acknowledging them both saying, "you are requested in the main dining suite, if you would follow me."

Both Hank and Jocy knew it would be best not to exchange further words as Marty was wearing his earphones. For a brief moment, Hank thought that if they were going to follow Marty, maybe they could jump him. That idea quickly cooled because as soon as they went out into the hallway, there was another big guy waiting. 'So much for that idea,' Hank thought to himself.

They entered the dining suite where Hank was first brought for his second conversation with Mr. Box. Marty shows Hank where he is to be seated, and then walks Jocy over to her designated seat across the table from Hank.

Marty proceeds to set a coffee serving down in front of them both. Jocy holds back a smile, because she knows Hank is happy with his coffee in front of him, despite any present danger.

Hank breaks the silence. "So Marty, we going to be hearing from Mr. Box?" Marty politely replies, "yes, Mr. Ramsan, I suspect so."

Then over the hidden intercom the voice comes: "Hank and Jocy, I trust you had a nice reunion?"

Neither of them answers.

The Box continues speaking. "Well then, lets just put our cards on the table. Mr. Ramsan, we want the instructions of how to activate the coin. If you do not give it to us, then we will end Jocy's life and you will be a witness to each moment of her pain."

Without skipping a beat, Jocy begins speaking. "Mr. Box, since we are putting our cards on the table, I have one to play. I know who you are. And so that we don't play any guessing games as to whether you are sure I know or not, I will tell you that Dagger told me exactly who you are, while under the influence of spiked champagne. You really should not have a ladies man in your high-ranking positions Mr. Box, it makes you vulnerable."

"I will go on to tell you that if I am not returned to my home by three p.m. tomorrow, your identity goes to all of the world's newspapers. I've left instructions that in the event of me calling and begging for my own life that I will be under duress to do so, and it is not to be honored."

Jocy keeps her pace. "This is a world issue, Mr. Box. If you even attempt to harm Hank or me, I have a special code embedded within me that will trigger my death, keeping me from torture. I will end my own life, and the newspapers will be notified by three o'clock."

Hank is sitting there, not believing what he's hearing but realizing how close to the edge Jocy is playing this card. It appears to be working, as during her entire citation, there was erry silence, you could have heard a pin drop.

Hank notices that Marty is getting a message from his earphones.

Marty speaks. "These are the instructions I have been given: I am to return both of you safe and sound to the ranch by three p.m. tomorrow. That is all the information that I have. There is no reason to detain you further, under the circumstances. We shall ready for departure within the hour."

This sounded fine and dandy on the surface, except for one major thing. Hank needed the coin back. On top of that, he cannot imagine that The Stiletto will just drop this matter. One word from Jocy could bring the entire Stiletto empire down. This was far from over on both sides, and Hank knew it.

Returning Hank and Jocy to her ranch would buy The Stiletto some time. They would surely attempt to design some other way to get the information regarding the coin's power and remove the threat of Jocy toppling The Stiletto.

Score one for the good guys.

42

Hank needs some time to talk to Jocy alone, so he goes for the soft spot in the heart of the big guy, Marty. "Marty, is there any reason that you can't take us back to my cabin? I mean, it's been a while since we've seen each other. How 'bout it Marty?"

Marty looks at them both, "Well all right Mr. Ramsan. I was not given any instructions to separate the two of you for the duration of this trip, so I will oblige your request. Follow me and I'll escort you to your room."

The four of them began their way toward the cabin; Marty, Jocy, Hank and the other big guy bringing up the rear. Marty opens the door, shows them in, and tells them he'll be back in under an hour. The door closes locking Hank and Jocy inside.

Hank turns to Jocy kissing her on the cheek. "That was a pretty bold move, playing that card, Jocy."

Jocy takes his hand, "Well Hank, we had no choice. I had the only thing available that could save us from harm and buy us some time. This was one of those times when that good ole feminine touch works well with guys like Dagger."

"Well, I wouldn't want to be in Dagger's boots about now." Hank smirks to himself, but loud enough for Jocy to hear and shaking her head in agreement.

"I have an idea." Hank begins to talk swiftly. "We haven't much time. I could most likely try and break free on the way to your ranch, but at this point, I wouldn't even know where to go. It might just keep things a little smoother if I played it safe and had them take me along with you."

"Jocy, I have to get that coin back! Wait, I know what I'll do. There's got to be a pen and paper in here somewhere."

Hank goes over to the desk, he knows this suite is a fully operational upper-class suite and sure enough just as he suspected, in the desk are pen and paper.

"What are you doing?" Jocy watches Hank rumble through the desk.

"Hang on Jocy and you'll see. This little thing I am doing is part of what The Stiletto does not want me to show the world. Watch this!"

Hank writes something on the paper, and then takes one of the framed pictures down from the wall, so that the nail is protruding. He then takes the piece of paper containing the words he had written on it, and sticks it up on the wall, fastened by the nail.

Jocy, walks over to the note now hanging on the wall, and reads it out loud. "I have the gold coin in my possession. The location of it comes to me in ease and peace."

"Ok, Hank, give. What's with the note on the wall thing?"

Hank answers as quickly and clearly as he can, provided the shortness of time. "Jocy, this is the simpler version of what The Stiletto does not want the world to know. The world and its people can generate their own wealth, money, and resources simply by placing it written on a wall. It works like the Aladdin's Lamp, and it's called The Magic Wall."

"Ok, I'll buy that for now," says Jocy, with an inquisitive eye, "but what does the gold coin have to do with it? Why would you need a gold coin, if you can put something up on a Magic Wall and then you have money and wealth? What's the point of the coin?"

Filling her in with some details as he takes her hand and guides her to sit with him on the bed, Hank begins: "Jocy, there is power in the coin that would help bring an understanding to the masses of people with some momentum. The Magic Wall alone will work, but the coin would add rocket fuel to its progress, both in the knowledge given and experience of many around the world."

"So you see Jocy, if people knew they could produce their own money, wealth, resources and other material manifestations, why then, would they need the banks approval and scrutiny over exchange of goods and services around the world?"

With her usual trust in Hank, Jocy tells him, "I think I understand your concept in theory, but you'll have to help me understand its depth and further implications."

As Jocy is telling Hank of her need for more information, she's walking over to the bathroom.

From the bathroom Hank hears, "Hank, you might want to see this!"

Hank thinking she is being playful walks into bathroom. Jocy is just standing there with a puzzled look on her face letting Hank know, this is something else other than Jocy being playful. He looks at her and says, "what Jocy, what is it?"

"Over on the mirror Hank, look on the mirror!" Jocy nodding as if pointing with her head.

Hank turns to look on the mirror, and written in large script writing are these words: 'The coin is in London, find Sir Max.'

Seemingly, as soon as Hank read the words, they disappeared from the mirror.

"Hank, where did that message on the mirror come from, and how did it just disappear?" Jocy now very curious as to all that is happening in front of her eyes.

"Jocy, remember the message you read in the bottle about Dagger?"

"Yes," she replies.

"Ok, what color was the writing?"

Again, Jocy's reply, "Gold."

"And what color was the writing on the mirror?"

She's locked into Hank's questions, "Gold."

Hank with another question, "Then, do you see the message is from the same source?"

Jocy not quite sure of what she is beginning to think, answers, "keep going Hank, what source is that?"

"For now Jocy, lets keep this simple, this source has a name; *Maddy*."

To further explain, Hank begins to back up a bit by offering a comparison. "Jocy, do you see a connection here between what I wrote on the wall, and what showed up on the mirror?"

Jocy's face goes almost white in disbelief, but belief catching up fast as these words fumbled out of her mouth; "It worked like the story of Aladdin's Lamp."

43

Knowing they didn't have much time before Marty would come to collect them from the room, Hank asks Jocy of any connections she may have in London, which may help him find Sir Max.

As of the message on the mirror, Hank does not know if Sir Max is a good guy or bad guy. Is he the one with the coin, or is he the one that can lead him to the coin?

Jocy already wise to what she is picking up from Hank, asks him, "Hank, why didn't the mirror note give you that information?"

Hank pauses for a moment and laughs under his breath as he tells her, "Jocy those answers were not shown because I did not ask clearly enough."

"It's one of the tricks to getting what we want from The Magic Wall, and really, life itself. So since I was not clear, I received more general information, this may cost me some time. But, as I move forward, I'll simply ask again. In the meantime, I've got to get to London as soon as I can, and it looks like I may be heading there from your ranch."

Jocy has an idea or two that may help Hank get to London. "Well if we are at the ranch by three, then it'll give me some time to make a few phone calls to see if we can expedite your London trip. Are we under any time constraints?"

"Well Jocy, we have to assume that The Stiletto is going to try and come up with something to get me to tell them about the coin, while at the same time removing you as a threat to telling the world who they are. So yes, I'd say the sooner the better, and hopefully this will keep us at least one step ahead of them."

Jocy follows up with her next idea. "I've got a friend who's an art dealer in Manhattan. He's back and forth to London constantly, and has his own plane. He's offered it to me anytime I have need of it. I'm sure he'll be glad to help. You could be in London within 24 hours."

Jocy and Hank continue to discuss the logistics of things and then Hank remembers something of importance. "Jocy, there's a good chance that all of your calls are bugged and your contacts in the art world are well known to The Stiletto. I have a better idea. I'll call Lance Powers, he can get me to London."

"You know Lance Powers?" Jocy asks with a raised eyebrow.

Hank grins, saying, "yes Jocy, I seem to be moving in higher circles these days!"

Jocy having no real idea of the double meaning of his answer, remarks, "Well if you've got Lance Powers helping you then you have it made I'd say!"

"Yes, but I can't just call him." Hank thinking out loud to himself, "I know what I'll do! Alex. Alex can get it done for me. Will he be at the ranch Jocy?"

"Most likely yes Hank, because I would assume that the freightliner will be back on its course soon. And that ship has my horses and some intended artwork on it as well. Alex has to be around to oversee that shipment."

Just as Hank is about to ask another question, there's a knock on the door. "Mr. Ramsan, it's Marty, time to go."

Speaking loudly enough for Marty to hear him through the door, Hank answers back, "Ok Marty, just two minutes."

Hank moves closer to Jocy and takes her face in his hands, tells her he loves her and kisses her forehead. Then he moves his way to her lips, and lightly places his lips on hers. She remembers his kiss, it's the same, and she has missed it. They stand in that kiss and the warmth of it, until they hear the door unlock.

44

Marty enters the suite and tells Hank and Jocy, that as they may have suspected, they would not be going to the freightliner. This is due to the turn of events, regarding Jocy's information from Dagger and the identity behind The Stiletto. Marty informs them that they will be taken to the ranch by helicopter.

Marty continues, "The authorities are still discussing release of the freightliner. It is expected to be soon off the coast of Maine in its usual docking location, assuming the paperwork is in order."

Jocy has never known of the exact location of the ships docking. That information had always been kept from her. It was her job to keep art dealers, horse breeders and owners happy, while at the same time conducting business with them throughout both the Art and Equine world.

"Please follow me," instructs Marty as he turns to go out the door.

Suddenly Hank remembers he has that note up on the wall, and does not want to leave it there. Out of not knowing what else to do, he impulsively jumps on the bed and grabs the note off the wall.

Marty hears the commotion and turns to see what Hank is doing. Hank by now has the picture frame in his hands. "Sorry Marty, I had taken this down off the wall to show Jocy something, and I forgot to put it back."

"Fine Mr. Ramsan. If you are ready now please."

After Marty's direction, Jocy looks over at Hank and whispers, "good punt!"

The four of them walked out to the deck, and above the yacht, they hear the helicopter blades swirling.

Instructions again from Marty, "Mr. Ramsan, please escort Jocy and yourself to the above platform for your helicopter ride."

Hank turns to Marty as he steps up on the ladder to the next deck. "Marty, will I see you again? Probably not huh?"

"Well, Mr. Ramsan, I am sure that eight hours of me is enough."

As soon as Hank heard Marty say, *I Am* and the word *eight*, chills flew up his spine. He didn't know if they had been on board for eight hours or not, he knew that didn't matter. The message did. Marty was a good guy, a very good guy. Hank and Jocy were in good hands all along. Hank didn't know it then, but he knew it now.

Although Hank's boyishness wanted to tell Jocy about this, he knew she wouldn't fully understand. They wouldn't have time for further lengthy explanations. However, Hank felt they would have a very long time to tell each other plenty of stories assuming they live through this one!

On board the helicopter, it's the pilot and one other big guy. No one speaks, and Hank reaches over and takes Jocy's hand. He had always loved just holding her hand.

45

Hank glances over at Jocy as they begin their way above the water and says, "so, what's for dinner hun?"

Jocy gives him that look that he remembered just like it was yesterday. That look that says: "Well it depends on what *you* are fixing, hun!"

He loves her so much. He's just melting inside with each second that they are together. Smiling blonde boys are very attractive, and Jocy is taking in all of his smile.

"Ok, what's up with you, Hank? We're playing with dangerous people and you look like you just found the golden chocolate ice cream and haven't told anyone yet."

"Jocy, it's you, it's just you."

Jocy knew what that meant. He had told her many times before. Hank didn't need to explain further. She knew, and leaned over and gently kissed him. Kissing an already smiling blonde boy has a real sweetness to it.

The noise of the helicopter is too loud for them to talk without shouting. They both sit close enough to feel that feeling of sitting next to someone who means the world to you.

The helicopter ride over the sea, back to Jocy's ranch in Massachusetts would take about an hour and a half. This would be a good time for Hank to practice some of the things that Talal had told him over their time together in New York. He knew use of this information would be vital to him getting both the coin back and staying alive in the process.

Closing his eyes so that he wouldn't be distracted by the ride, Hank began to ask himself some questions. He already understood before he had met Talal, that asking clear questions to one's self can bring certain levels of success. This would work for any endeavor. Hank needed it to work for this one in addition to staying alive.

This was one of the shortcuts he used while business associates chased and banged into projects. Then as they tired of that, they would have to dig themselves out from where they were stuck. Skilled at avoiding the turmoil often involved in business ventures, Hank usually came out on top.

Hank's first question to himself involved the coin. He needed to be very clear on its properties. Understanding its use and power were a priority, because as soon as he had his own hands on it, he would have to use it immediately to further his safety in keeping it.

The first question showing up in his mind was: *What does the coin look like? What are its physical characteristics?* This answer flowed to him: *It's pure gold, with the phrase and words 'I Am' on one side and an Epigram on the other side. The Epigram was a symbol in the form of a Figure 8.*

Until Talal's explanation of the coin, Hank's comprehension of its place and value was little more than superficial. Having an understanding of the phrase *I Am* and the symbol of the *Figure 8*, would allow a power to be born through its application.

It would be with this new appreciation of the power of the coin that Hank would be able to convey the use of The Magic Wall to the masses with some momentum behind it. This momentum and knowledge would expand due to the use of The Epigram.

As Hank is sitting there musing in his own world, Jocy nudges him. "We're here."

Hank can't believe over an hour had passed as he was daydreaming the moments away, but sure enough he looks down, and sees about twenty beautiful black horses grazing in a field.

"Jocy are those all yours?" Hank asks, breaking his thought pattern.

Jocy gives him some background of what he sees below. "Well, Hank that's not all of them that you see there. I have about 100 imported Friesians, four of them are mine, and of course are the best ones! The others belong to the elite of horse people, and they bring them to me for upkeep and training. Then after they are trained for their greatness, we return them to the owners."

"There are some Friesian owners that have them as a pure investment, and those horses never leave the ranch. We are under contract to care, board, and train for future resale."

By now Jocy is shouting over the propeller noise, and tells him she'll fill him in on more of the ranch after they land.

46

The helicopter began its descent to the landing area located at the edge of the bay, which borders the ranch. The Helio pad is off to a distance from the main ranch house.

Hank nudges Jocy, "someone is standing down there, Jocy, can you see who it is?"

"Yes," Jocy responds, "it's Alex."

The helicopter begins pulling up its power as its runners prepare to touch the ground. Just as they land, Alex rushes over to help Jocy and Hank step down to the platform.

With the chopper's blades still roaring and wind blowing everywhere, all three hold their heads down as the helicopter begins to lift back off the helicopter pad. The three of them standing together for the first time in a mini reunion, but one they could not openly express. The instructions to deliver them safely back to the ranch had been completed.

The loud noise of the helicopter is now off in the distance. Alex turns to them saying, "glad you both made it here safely, and we have only just begun what needs to be done."

"Ok, fill us in Alex." Hank answers quickly, as Alex hurries to recite all of the information he wants them to know.

"I can only give you the highlights for now. We have about 100 feet to walk, before our voices will be picked up by The Stiletto's new surveillance equipment. So beware, all of our conversations are overheard as well recorded once within the boundary of the ranch. Also, know that there are hidden cameras everywhere."

Alex continues, "First the good news. As you might have suspected, Dagger has met with an unfortunate accident, and is no longer with us. As in, he's dead. I am his replacement."

"The down side, is that I am to find a way to remove Jocy as a threat to The Stiletto and I have to do it within a certain amount of time. If I don't take care of her, then they will do away with me."

"But let's not be concerned about that part for now. What's your plan Hank?"

"I need to get to London as soon as possible, the coin is there. Can you get Powers to help out?" Hank asks Alex in a clear but hurried voice.

"Yes, of course." Alex continues, "listen, we are about in the boundary of the house. Lets keep our discussion as real as possible and getting you to New York can be part of that. It's natural that you would want to leave, and I've not been given any instructions to keep you here. But just understand, you are being watched."

"The Stiletto has two big problems with the two of you. It will be primary that they solve them quickly." Alex finishes abruptly.

With Alex's last comment, the three of them walk within the boundary of the house, very aware that their conversations will be overheard.

Hank begins by telling Alex that he has to get back to the city, and asks if it's against The Stiletto policy to deliver him back.

Alex responds as the loyal Stiletto employee, "Mr. Ramsan, I see no problem with getting you back to the city, but I will have to check in for proper authorization."

No sooner than Alex had said the words, he stopped. He was getting a message in his earphone. Alex reports the message he was just given. "Mr. Ramsan, I've been given instructions to arrange your way back to the city. Perhaps you'd like to freshen up from the days activities, while I organize your transportation."

"Yes, that would be fine, Alex."

Alex continues playing his part, "I also must tell you Mr. Ramsan, as we get back to the ranch, I will have to keep you and Jocy separated for the duration of your stay. Those are my instructions, Mr. Ramsan."

Hank and Jocy look at one another, knowing it may be awhile before they see each other again, while both hoping that they live to see that day.

They all step up on the patio, which is at the back of the house. Alex instructs Hank to follow him, then quickly tells Jocy that he will be with her in a few moments. Alex makes sure to add in Hank's presence, that there is information regarding the shipment and he will fill her in after he gets Mr. Ramsan settled.

Jocy stands watching the two most important men in her life walk down the enclosed patio foyer. Hank turns to get one last glance at the one he has missed for a long, long time.

Hank turning his head back to ask Alex a question, "Alex, how many horses are here on the ranch?"

"Mr. Ramsan, I'm not at liberty to discuss any particulars with you. I'm simply to arrange your transportation back to the city."

"Ok, got it. How much time before we leave?" Hank showing signs of impatience now.

"I should be able to have you a ride within the hour," surmises Alex. "There are some fresh clothes in the closet of your room, which you may find suitable, Mr. Ramsan. I'm sure you will find something appropriate for your short time here. A duffel bag is also provided for you to carry your current clothing back to the city."

Alex guides Hank fully into the bedroom suite and without a goodbye, closes the door, and locks Hank inside the room.

It would be natural for Hank to grab a pen and paper to help him get clear on some things so that he'd be open for any inspiration, but he doesn't want to show The Stiletto any of his methods. For now, Hank keeps his thoughts totally to himself. His primary intention is regarding this 'Sir Max.' Did Sir Max actually have the coin, and was he a good guy or bad guy?

Hank glances at his watch, and decides he doesn't have to be in a hurry to change clothes. He almost talks himself out of a shower, since he had one on the yacht earlier in the day. Nevertheless, since he didn't know what the next 24 hours would bring, he decided hot water would be in order.

Standing at the window and looking out over the beautiful property of which Jocy has been a prisoner, Hank notices Alex in the circular driveway talking with a large big fellow. Assuming this is to be his ride back into town, Hank then sees Alex hand the big guy a gun.

A little surprised, but remembering that Alex too is a prisoner of sorts and that he must appear loyal to The Stiletto. His giving this valet a gun was part of the appearance. He calmed himself with that, at least for now.

Choosing to begin the shower and get ready for the ride to town, Hank walks toward the bathoom. On is way he flips on the TV, continuing to the bathroom and the encased shower stall to turn on the water.

'Freightliner held up at the dock,' was heard coming from the television.

Hank walked back in to see if there was more information from the news. He thought to himself, 'maybe this is what Alex was going to discuss with Jocy,' but he knew he couldn't concern himself with that now. He had a pond to cross. London was his next step.

47

Hank begins pulling off his shirt as he walks back into the bathroom for the shower. He stands back up after pulling off his jeans, and he sees it. Right in front of him, written in the steam of the shower stall, 'Sir Max has the coin. He is Stiletto.'

Immediately Hank's thoughts went to five minutes ago, when he asked in his own mind about the coin and which side Sir Max was on. Now right in front him, the answer shows up. He was just as much intrigued in how his answer showed up as he was the actual answer regarding Sir Max.

Hank is beginning to understand at a new level the power and new conditions that The Magic Wall will bring to the world. He has to make this happen, no matter what.

The shower is a short one, as Hank becomes preoccupied with getting to London as quickly as he can. Just as he is toweling off, he hears a knock on the door.

"Mr. Ramsan, your ride to the city is now ready. Please come out to the driveway as soon as you can." Then the door unlocks. It was Alex giving him his instructions from the hallway.

Hank's first impulse was to hurry dressing and since the door was now unlocked without anyone there, he would go and find Jocy for a last minute goodbye. However, just as he has that idea, he walks into the main part of the bedroom, and there is a big guy standing in the middle of it. The big guy has his instructions. "Mr. Ramsan, I am your escort down to the driveway."

"Well, of course you are!" Hank realizing he should have known better.

While tucking in his shirt, Hank says, "Ok big guy, lets go."

Both Hank and the big guy walk down the hallway and back out the patio doors leading to the driveway. The driver opens the back door of the limo, and without a word, Hank gets in.

As the driver, another big guy, gets into the driver's seat and closes the door, he tells Hank that they are driving to a small airplane hanger about 5 miles away. It's from there, that Hank will be flown into the city, and another car is waiting to take him back to his current home at Powers One.

Hank begins to say something, and the driver throws up his right hand. "Those are my only instructions, Mr. Ramsan, I'll thank you to enjoy the short ride to the airport."

Under Hank's breath he says, "Well, I should have known that!" He's getting the real jest of the efficiency of The Stiletto. Musing to himself, that all the big guys are 'Stepford Wives™.'

48

Meanwhile, back at the ranch . . .

Alex and Jocy are back into their roles. She the broker of original, authentic artwork, stolen in many cases, and purebred Friesians. Both the artwork and horses were toys as well as investment properties of the rich and famous. Alex was back in his role as the new supervisor of the ranch and other Stiletto dealings of which Dagger was previously in charge.

Alex begins catching Jocy up on what is happening with the freightliner. "Jocy, the coast guard is again holding up the ship. You and I know what this means. It means that if it's not released soon we are going to have some very unhappy clients. And these are people we do not want unhappy."

Jocy agrees. "Yes, Alex and the type of customers we have could make things uncomfortable for The Stiletto, especially since they work very hard at keeping things calm. They go to great lengths to be sure that no attention is drawn to them, even for the slightest reason."

"Ok Jocy, you know which customers are involved in this shipment, can you appease them in some way, before anything gets out of hand?"

"Well Alex, technically, this shipment is catering to only one customer. He has deposits on artwork as well as the horses. He's already assigned and designated them to others for investment purposes. It's those other investors that we are to deliver the products directly to and service."

"Who is this apparently very wealthy customer, Jocy?" Alex pretending that he didn't know.

"Lance Powers," came back from Jocy's lips.

Without skipping a beat, not to let on at all that he may have known about this prior to his asking the question, Alex asks her; "Can you keep him calm Jocy? Most certainly he has heard about the two hold ups of the freightliner."

"Well, I don't know," Jocy hesitating, "I've never talked with him personally, only his representative."

Alex now sounding concerned, "Well, you'd better begin to see what you can do, before any of this escalates."

"Ok, I'll call his office today." Jocy tries to reassure herself.

Alex begins to leave by saying; "Good Jocy, I've got much to take care of on my end. You know how to reach me."

Jocy sees him to the door, "thanks Alex, I'll keep you posted."

Alex leaves and Jocy begins making fresh coffee. As she is doing so, her thoughts naturally go to Hank. She notices this has not happened for a long time, where Hank just pops into her mind. It was something she missed. She paused for a moment and under her breath said; "Come back to me, safe, and smiling, Hank Ramsan."

In the middle of her drifting off, the phone rang. "Jocy, here," as she answers.

"Jocy, this is Maddeline Lamp of SK Investments. I am inquiring of a possible delivery date of the investment property I'm purchasing through Mr. Lance Powers."

Jocy, always professional begins to stumble a bit, as she knows this is an important investment partner of Powers, and she does not have a good answer for her.

"Ms. Lamp, thank you for your call. We are arranging those dates and schedules presently. May I have your number where I can reach you once all is confirmed?"

Maddeline answers clearly and with no emotion, "Jocy, sorry to not be able to oblige on this, as we keep our lines of communication always protected. I will call you within two days for the update. Will you have more information within that time?"

"Yes, Ms. Lamp, that should be sufficient time to have all in order for your delivery. Thank you for your call, and I'll speak with you in few days." Jocy thinking and hoping to herself as she answers.

"That's fine, and that is two days, Jocy, I will call you within two days." Again, the clear Maddeline Lamp responds.

Feeling uneasy, Jocy hangs up the phone. This apparently is a very powerful woman, this Maddeline Lamp person. Jocy's anxiety starts to rise as she has no idea when the goods will be delivered. She figures now is the time to call Lance Powers. Hopefully, he could keep his clients like Maddeline Lamp off her back until things were sorted out and shipments delivered to her own ranch first.

Jocy pours herself a fresh cup of coffee, sits down at her large mahogany desk, thumbs through her address book, looking for Powers' representative. She pulls the card from her file, takes a deep breath, and begins punching numbers on the phone pad.

Although Jocy knows she has a big piece of information revealing The Stiletto's identity, she also knows it's important for appearance sake that she keeps things running efficiently as she always has. She knows that keeping things running per the usual Stiletto expectations would give Hank more time to do what he is doing. Doing her best to play the game was all she could do at this point. There was much at stake in this particular game, and she knew it.

49

Jocy dials and the phone rings twice on the other end and is answered swiftly: "David Tate."

"Hello David, this is Jocy Preston, I'm calling to see if I could speak with Mr. Powers personally about his shipment?"

David half-chuckling, "oh, do you mean the one that is now being held up for the second time?"

"Yes David, I need some help in keeping Mr. Powers investors calm while this unravels itself."

"I understand Jocy, and yes many of Mr. Powers friends and investors can be, well, shall we say quite demanding and insistent?"

Jocy feeling more at ease, says, "that would be a very diplomatic way to state it David, and thanks for your understanding."

"Sure, let me put you on hold for a moment, and I'll see if Mr. Powers can take your call."

Jocy's listens to Bach while on hold, which helps in her further calming. As she is waiting, she's not quite sure what to say to Lance Powers. She's never spoken to him before, and now was not feeling like a great time to discuss a huge investment that appears to be stalled out in the water somewhere.

"Jocy?" David back on the line breaking her from her quandary.

"Yes, David, I'm here."

David suggests something that Jocy had not anticipated.

"Jocy, Mr. Powers would find it a pleasure to discuss this matter of most importance with you, but he prefers to do so in person. Can you arrange to meet him in the city for dinner this evening or possibly an early lunch tomorrow? His agenda is quite full after tomorrow."

Jocy immediately goes into a slight panic. She doesn't know how to answer. Up until this time, The Stiletto has made it quite clear that all of her meetings are to be done over the phone, or on the ranch. Only on rare occasions has The Stiletto allowed her to travel outside the ranch, and then under heavy escort.

In her fumbling, she starts to put David off by telling him that she would have to rearrange her schedule to do so. She asks if she can give him a call back to confirm. This, she thought, would give her time to talk to Alex and see what The Stiletto wanted her to do. She knew they would not want her to make this particular decision on her own.

Just as Jocy is having anxious thoughts, she sees a light on her other line, the line directly into The Stiletto. She is never to call that line, only to answer if it rings.

David, I apologize. Can you hold a few seconds? I have a call coming in that I have to take, but I don't want to lose you."

David in his accommodating demeanor replies, "sure Jocy, I'll just push some paper around for a few minutes, take your time."

"Thanks David, back in a moment." Jocy presses the light that is flashing on her phone pad. "Jocy here."

She recognizes the voice. It's Mr. Box. "Jocy, go ahead and make the arrangements for lunch with Powers. Keep him calm, until we can work the shipment situation out. Have Alex take you into the city. We will brief him. That is all." Then there was a click. The Box hung up.

Jocy hits the key to get back to David's line.

"David?"

"Yes, Jocy, I'm still here."

Jocy in a sigh of relief tells David of her phone call. "That call happened to be about my agenda for today and tomorrow, it turns out, I can come into the city tomorrow for lunch with Mr. Powers."

"That's great Jocy, and possibly I'll get to meet you in person as well! As I look at Mr. Powers' agenda, tomorrow would actually work best. Can you find your way to Powers One by 11:30 in the morning and we can go from there?"

"Sure David, I'll just get it done! I'll plan on seeing you also if it works out. And David, thank you for helping to take some of the sting out of this for me."

"My Pleasure, Jocy, see you tomorrow morning."

Jocy hangs up with a sigh of relief. There was a little pressure building up over this one. Normally she doesn't have this kind of anxiety as her efficiency, as well at that of The Stiletto, keeps things running very smoothly.

This was the first time that there had been a glitch in a delivery, and for it to happen with one of the most powerful and wealthiest men in the world simply created some tension she was not accustomed to feeling.

As she's sitting back in her chair getting ready to call Alex, in he walks through her office door.

"I understand you have had an interesting morning!" Alex half smiling.

"Yes Alex, do you already know the details? And if so can you fill me in? Also, why is the Stiletto so willing for me to go into the city to meet Powers in person, when they are so protective of me ever leaving here for business or pleasure?"

Alex eyes the coffee table as he answers, "yes Jocy, I'm aware of the call and I have plenty of information, got any coffee?"

"Sure Alex help yourself."

Alex walks over to the coffee maker, pours himself a cup, and asks Jocy if she needs a refill.

"Yes thanks Alex, I love to be waited on!"

Alex starts to talk about his favorite coffees.

Jocy interrupts him, "uh Alex, are you playing me with me here? My veins are all constricted between the shipment and the meeting with Powers, can you fill me in now? Then you can tell me of your love and care for all the coffees of the world!"

Alex laughing, "sure Jocy."

"Jocy, The Stiletto needs some time to work things out in regard to this shipment. Anything that can be done to help keep someone like Lance Powers calm during this time, is only of benefit to The Stiletto in the long run."

"If Powers is unhappy, then it will affect his referrals and lineage of investors of which he has sent us many. Mr. Powers is unaware of the true nature of our products and how we do what we do. We want to keep it that way. It's much better to have someone like Lance Powers with us, instead of against us, so to speak."

"Aside from all of that Jocy, Mr. Powers is currently unattached in regard to female company, and as you know in your experience with Dagger, sometimes that is an asset. This may be one of those times."

"The Stiletto sees your lunch with Mr. Powers as a good investment on their part for many reasons, some of which I have mentioned and others I have not."

As Alex finishes what he knows, but with both Jocy and Alex knowing the entire conversation is for The Stiletto's surveillance ears, Jocy asks for her directions.

"Alright Alex, so what instructions have you been given in regard to this lunch date with Powers and myself."

Alex pulls out a 3X5-index card from his jacket pocket as if reading some notes. "I am to accompany you into the city. We will leave to go to the heliport around 9:30 in the morning. We will arrive at The Stiletto headquarters by 10:30, landing atop their building in the city. There will be an escort waiting to take us into one of The Stiletto's office suites. It is there we will both be wired so that The Stiletto can monitor our visit and conversations with Powers."

"You're going to the lunch date as well?" Asks a surprised Jocy.

"Yes and no," answers Alex. "I will go with you up the point where I have simply been your escort, but I will be around. Powers people will find something to do with me, I am sure."

Jocy feeling some concern, "but won't they check for wires?"

Alex answering firmly, "The Stiletto is counting on them not checking for wires, since Powers has no reason to suspect you of anything."

Jocy still not convinced, "but Alex, I would think his security people would check for wires. It's their job to do that sort of thing."

The phone rings while Jocy and Alex are conversing about the wires. They stop and look at one another. It's The Stiletto line. Jocy picks it up.

"Alex, The Box wants to talk to you." She hands him the phone.

Alex listens, then hangs up the receiver.

"Jocy, it appears that your anxiety over the wires is well founded. The Stiletto appreciates your thorough thought in this. You are of course correct. Powers would have nothing to do with it. His security force is one of the best in the world, and it is their job to protect him. They certainly would check for anything of that nature."

"The Stiletto, although you have them in a somewhat compromising position, by Dagger telling you their identity, does appreciate your care in keeping the appearance that everything is running smoothly for all concerned. They therefore, have no choice but to let you have free reign while you are with Mr. Powers. They trust you to some extent, so to speak. I will still go along as your escort into the city, and I'll be seated in the restaurant area during your meeting."

"So Jocy, unless you have further questions, both of us have things to get done before we can leave for a good part of tomorrow. I'll leave you to that."

Jocy feels relieved and ready. "No Alex, I'm clear. I'll be ready by 9:15 in the morning for you to lead the way from here to the city."

"Good, I'll see you then Jocy, and of course as always, if something comes up that you need me, just call."

"Thanks Alex."

Closing the door behind him, Alex leaves, and Jocy sits down in her chair with a sigh of relief. Musing to herself, 'constricted veins do not become her at all!'

50

While Jocy is having fun unconstricting her veins and preparing to head to New York to have lunch with one of the wealthiest men in world, Hank has already arrived in the Big Apple.

The small private plane that The Stiletto provided took him to a landing field outside of the city where a car was waiting to take him directly to Powers One.

Hank recognizes the driver of the car as the same driver that took he and Lin Chow to the docks, reuniting Lin Chow with his family. The driver walks over to meet Hank as he approaches the car from the landed airplane. "Good afternoon Mr. Ramsan, my instructions are to take you back to Powers One."

Hank adds, "and that is all the instructions you were given, and neither of us are to speak further, correct?"

The driver confirms; "Yes, that is correct, Mr. Ramsan."

Hank settles in for the 30-minute ride into the city. As of this moment, he doesn't know exactly what is next. He's hoping that Alex was able to communicate with Powers and secure him a way to London quickly.

The last time Hank was in London was when he and Jocy were there together while on assignment. Jocy not only has a keen eye for horses and art, but also knows how to take photographs that tell a story. They not only shared good work during that trip, they also played hard and loved often. She was born for him, he always told her that as a fact. Even through their separation, of which at the time he had no clue of why it all had happened, he still knew that Jocy was made for him.

Just as Hank is drifting further and further away in his mind with pictures of he and Jocy in London, the driver interrupts his thoughts. "We're here Mr. Ramsan."

The car pulls right up to the curb, and Hank helps himself out and says to the driver. "I hope I don't need to see you again, but it's been swell!" The Stiletto driver nods and grins, "yes Mr. Ramsan."

Hank steps away from the curb as the car drives off, turns and looks up at the huge entrance to Powers One. He says to himself, 'home sweet home.' He was glad to be on familiar territory. This place was friendly to him. Walking into the large atrium, he sees David moving toward him.

Extending his hand David says, "Hank, made it back safe and sound!"

"Yes, David, and I'd like to keep that way!" Hank responds laughing, but David knew he was serious.

"Well Hank, if we have anything to do with it, you will most likely be around for a very long time. However, we have work to do. To answer your question, yes we have arranged everything for your arrival in London by morning New York time, late afternoon London time." David guides Hank over toward the elevators.

"In order for you to get some rest, you'll have to do it on the plane. But you may want to freshen up, your suite is still your home."

Hank feeling a little frustrated says to David; "Man, between all the freshening up that I've been doing and the car rides I've been in, it's a wonder I still know what I'm really supposed to be doing!"

Both men share a laugh about the frolicking that Hank seems to be doing keeping him in circles of car rides. Nevertheless, they both know that important events have taken place between the showers and the various modes of transportation. Yet, another one is about to take place, which will take Hank to London Town.

Approaching the elevator doors, David says, "Hank, Lance would like to see you a few moments if you have time, he has coffee!"

Hank is most willing to oblige. "Lance Powers *and* coffee? A date made in heaven, lead on David!"

Stepping onto the private elevator, and David asks, "so Hank, how good was it seeing Jocy?"

Hank looks at him . . . "David, I melt into a puddle when she's around. Does that explain it just a bit?"

David laughing, "yes, that pretty much gives me a full picture, Hank."

The elevator opens to Powers' office suite, and as always Powers is standing, while talking on the phone; he waves them into the room. He hangs up, comes out from behind the desk, and extends a warm greeting and handshake to Hank, while David excuses himself to make Hank's arrangements to London.

Powers points Hank to the coffee and sandwich tray which was on a small buffet table. The blonde boy is happy and smiling.

One thing about Hank Ramsan, that all who know him, and who get to know him, they find out quickly that he is expressive in nature. He's very happy and loves to have fun. It shows in his demeanor wherever he is and whatever he is doing. He celebrates all of life, even the simplest forms, right down to coffee and sandwiches. Hank Ramsan takes no other and no one for granted.

While Hank is pouring coffee into a Powers One mug, he thinks to himself, 'Wonder if I can have this mug?' However, Powers has something he wants to tell Hank and interrupts his mug loving moment.

"Hank, David can fill you in further on some information that will be helpful to you as you arrive in London, but I personally wanted the pleasure of giving you some, well shall I say, special news?"

Hank sets his coffee mug down, as he has been known to be expressive enough to spew is coffee. Spewing coffee on Lance Powers' beautiful hand laid carpeting would not be a 'good' thing.

"Ok, Lance I'm ready, tell me."

Powers begins, "Hank, I'll spare you how it all was put together, but Jocy will be meeting me for lunch here, in this very office tomorrow at 11:30. We very much intend, once she is here, to keep her under our protection, and she will not be going back to the ranch. She knows nothing of this, other than she is to meet me to try and keep me calm over the freightliner still being stalled.

It's the hope of The Stiletto that I will in turn keep the other investors assured that everything is fine and going as planned."

"We want you to know that while you are putting your piece of the puzzle into full action, by retrieving the coin, and then moving on with what you are really to be doing, Jocy will be safe with us. The Stiletto will no longer be able to use her as a pawn, and you need not be overly concerned of her safety while you are gone. This way your full attention can be on what you have to get done."

Hank locks eyes with Powers. They both understand, and no words need to be said, but as usual, Hank has to say something!

"Lance, thank you," was all that would come out. Hank was extremely grateful, but his speech was stifled by thankfulness for what Powers had told him.

"My pleasure, Hank. I do know what it means to you, and it will mean a lot to Jocy to be free. Although she won't be entirely free until we make some changes in The Stiletto's activities. That's where you come into the picture. We can keep her from The Stiletto, but her total freedom as well as the freedom you are bringing to others, is up to you."

Breaking the tension, Hank says, "Piece of cake, Lance!" They both smiled, as they know this is a huge undertaking that has to be done, in order to be seen all the way through.

Hank interrupts the moment and asks, "is Talal around anywhere?"

"Oh Hank, Talal Halalad is always around somewhere," Powers jests. "But no, he is currently not in the city. He has had some background work to do for part of the project you are involved with. Powers glances at his watch; "Hank I have a meeting in about 20 minutes with 30 hungry lawyers, so I need to be on my way. David will be in shortly to fill you in on times you need to know for catching your ride London."

No sooner had Powers mentioned David's name that he walks into the office. "Lance, your car is waiting."

"As usual David, your timing is impeccable. Hank and I were just saying our good-byes. I'll leave you two to discuss Hank's agenda." Powers with his hand on the door leaves closing it behind him.

51

David begins filling Hank in on the details for his trip to London. "Hank you've got about three hours before we drive out to Powers' private hanger. You'll be flying overnight, U.S. time and arrive late morning London time. We were able to punch up the flight timing just a bit. Can you meet me in the lobby at nine this evening?"

"Sure David, that'll give me time for a power nap, and to organize my thoughts. I'll see you downstairs at nine."

"Great, I've got some phone calls to make, so I'll let you find your way back to the elevators." Then as David begins to wave Hank on, the phone rings.

Taking his time strolling to the elevator, Hank takes in the sights of the office and staff, which surround Powers. It's a peaceful feeling office and all of the staff people are friendly and accommodating.

In reflection of his surroundings, Hank knows when you are the best at your game, you get to choose the best players for your team. Lance Powers had certainly done that.

A gleam in his eye and a smile on his face, Hank is happy that he has done well. He's glad to be in the position he's in, having friends at the top of the world. Nonetheless, sometimes being in positions of this nature requires large deeds that need to be done. This was one of Hank's deeds coming up.

There were two goals he had to accomplish. The first one had to be successful in order to accomplish the second. On the surface, it looked seemingly simple, but part of the thread of the complexity was The Stiletto.

This thread was not to be taken for granted, and Hank would have to be completely on his toes and paying attention every minute.

As far as Hank knew, The Stiletto didn't know he was flying to London, but for sure, they would be watching him closely. The world's financial system as it is known to operate today, would change drastically if Hank succeeds. This would then topple and expose The Stiletto and the noose they had used to strangle the hearts and dreams of many. Money energy was something that belonged to everyone, only they didn't know it 'yet.' Hank was about to change that.

Arriving at the door to his suite at Powers One, Hank uses the new key card that David had arranged for him. This was a security precaution.

The Stiletto had returned all of Hank's items belonging to him. One of those items was his room key card, which he carried in his jeans. There was a possibility The Stiletto would have made a key copy.

"Home sweet home," Hank said to himself. It was the closest thing to familiar since he left Charlottesville, embarking on wherever 'next' would take him. Little did he know at the time, that part of his next would lead him to Jocy.

Hank kicks his boots off, throws himself on the bed, pulls two pillows out, and clasps his hands behind his head. Choosing to unwind a bit, his mind goes back to Charlottesville, both a writers and a horse town.

'Wouldn't it be great if he and Jocy could build a life there?' He starts building the home and horse barn in his mind. Of course, there is the usual bantering between he and Jocy, 'over who's in charge of dinner and going to the grocery store?' It would be great; it's what he wants.

Shaking himself from his dreamworld, realizing that for anything close to that happening, he first had some big events to solve. Pulling his ever trusty clipboard and pen from the desk Hank begins writing.

1. Find Sir Max
2. Get the coin back
3. Live through it

Thinking outloud, 'once I have the coin then what?' He writes more: *Blend the use of the coin with The Magic Wall.*

More words flow from his pen to the paper: *Where am I to go with the coin and the Magic Wall?*

Since this was such a huge undertaking, where would he first go for the most impact? He didn't know for sure.

Setting the pen and the clipboard on his chest, closing his eyes, he says to himself, 'Where am I to go, once I have the coin and the magic wall? To what group do I first make this introduction?' 'India' flew into his mind.

This was not the first time 'India' had played in his thoughts. Still Hank wanted more clarity. He opened his eyes, picks up the pen and writes: *Why India first?*

Immediately, these words popped into his thoughts and again he writes: *Due to the eastern religions, India is the most spiritually advanced country of the world. The people of India most likely would be more open to what I am bringing forth.*

Then thinking in his own logic, Hank realizes that in direct contrast, to other parts of the world, India is one of the largest poverty populated areas on the earth. He then went on to reason that this would be the perfect place to begin, and he would trust the momentum to take on a life of its own.

Hank writes, *India* in large letters then quickly lifts the phone receiver to call David, but changes his mind, hanging up quickly. Despite the fact that Powers had top security measures in order, this project of Hank's has been of a different nature than anything anyone had approached before. He was not taking any chances that his phone conversation would be overheard. What he does choose to do, is to call David, only to ask if they can meet now, leaving no further information as to the topic or reason.

"Sure Hank, why don't you meet me in the coffee shop. I'm on my way there now. See you in five minutes," was David's response.

Hank pulls on his boots, and leaves to meet David. Arriving about the same time, Hank stops David before going inside the coffeeshop.

"David this will be short, I don't want to take the chance of anyone overhearing us. Long story short, my next destination after I secure the coin, is India. Do you know of any good contacts there that would be willing to assist me as things develop?"

David smiling, "why of course Hank, does the name Talal Halalad ring a bell?"

"You mean, Tal is there?" Hank expressing much surprise and the questions begin.

"Wait." Hank stops. "I don't need the details, I am getting the jest that there are some things playing here, that I don't quite understand. I don't need to know right now." Hank continues, "but I will ask this David, once I arrive in India, is it safe to assume that Talal will find me? I don't need to go looking for him?"

"Precisely Hank." David grins back.

"Ok good, that's all I need to know David, see you at nine."

Hank turns to go back to his room. Leaving the elevator and almost to his room, he notices his door is jarred slightly open. Cautiously walking up to the door he pushes it. No one is there, and he knows he locked it behind him when he left to meet David.

Then almost in shock he looks over on the bed, and there is his pen and clipboard, but the piece of paper with his notes was gone! Hank's immediate thought, 'this could not be good!'

Hoping to catch David still in the coffeeshop, Hank rushes down the hall to the elevator. Still not using the phones, he laughs to himself at the exercise he seems to be getting. Regardless of what appears to be happening, Hank is still attempting to keep as lighthearted as he can under the circumstances.

Rushing to the coffee shop, he sees David at the cashier paying for a drink.

David looks up, sees Hank, and knows something is not 'right.' In almost a whisper, he asks Hank, "what?"

Hank guides David over to a quiet booth, and begins telling him of the missing note and the importance of it.

Sitting back in the booth, David takes a moment to take in what Hank has just told him.

They both knew the implications of The Stiletto having this information; they didn't need to discuss it.

Breaking the silence, David calmly says; "This one is for Maddy. Most likely, she knows about this already, but this one needs her expertise. I'll contact her as soon as I get back upstairs. In the meantime, you stay on course, even with the notes you took. If there is a change in direction or plans from your original notes, then you will be shown in some way."

Leaning forward to talk in a low voice David tells Hank, "You do know how this works Hank, so just use the same mechanics you are bringing to the world. The details will show up. I do need to get with Maddy on this now. I'll see you at nine, and if I have news of something to tell you at that point then I will."

"Ok, thanks David." Hank exits the booth, and grabs the elevator back to his room. Home, sweet, home isn't feeling so sweet in this moment. Still knowing he needs to get some sleep before the trip to London, Hank is determined to have that power nap.

The Power Nap. This was funny to Hank as he again threw his boots off. The idea of his power nap actually came from reading something about Lance Powers. He had read that Powers didn't sleep a lot, and took a 15-min nap at some point during the day. These so-called *power naps* would completely recharge him.

Hank took that recharge idea for himself, however his power naps last only ten minutes. He was about to have one of them now.

Dosing off after setting his cell phone alarm to wake up in an hour, in the event he would over sleep his 10 minutes, he hears it ring.

Sure enough, Hank's nap lasted longer than 10 minutes, but his cell phone ringing with a call from David 50 minutes later, woke him before the full hour was finished.

"Hank," David tells him, "we found out how your room was entered. It had to do with whom actually made your new room key card. I'll spare you the details, but suffice to say The Stiletto is very efficient. However, we will be more so, after this incident.

Can you meet me at 8:30 instead of nine, so that I can brief you on a few things before you leave?"

"Sure David, where?"

"Just meet me in my office, and we'll go from there."

Hank could tell that David was being cautious with what he said over the phone. He was not about to take any chances.

Changing his clothes seemed to be in order, as Hank sat on the edge of the bed trying to decide if he should take his duffel bag. He chooses to go ahead and pack as though he would be away for a weekend trip. Just the essentials would be taken.

'A fresh new pair of jeans,' Hank muses to himself, 'that fit me perfectly, and gee lets see, how about this denim shirt?'

When he and Jocy were together, she sometimes helped him with different shirts. She told him that he needed to change the styles of his shirts sometimes, just so she wouldn't get bored looking at him.

But he knew she always loved looking at him, no matter what he wore, or didn't wear. He gets lost in her sense of humor as he drifts off for moment.

Hank notices the room clock as he's tucking in his shirt and sees it's time to meet David. Grabbing his cell phone, duffel bag, clipboard, he heads for the door. Next stop, David's office.

52

Standing in his office foyer talking with one of Powers' employees, David notices Hank exiting the elevators. These elevators have private access as well, but are not the same as the ones leading directly to Powers' office.

David waves him into his office, and hands him a note. The note reads, *Follow me, do not talk until I tell you to. I'll explain later.*

Hank nods his head in understanding the hand written directive. Following David's directions, it becomes apparent they are going to Powers' private office.

Carrying his duffel bag, along the way, Hank asks with his eyes and hand gestures if he should bring the duffel bag with him. David answers 'yes,' with a nod.

Now inside Powers' office, David closes the door and locks it. Motioning Hank to follow him, David walks over to a wall, which displays photographs of Powers with the various elite of the world, from finance to politics.

David places his hands on one of the photographs and a large drawer, slides out from the wall. He motions to Hank to place his duffel bag in the drawer; Hank complies. David again touches the photo and the drawer goes back into the wall now containing Hank's duffel bag.

A huge portion of the entire wall opens up as David places his hand on another photograph. Gesturing again for Hank to step in with him, he follows. Both men are now standing in a room sealed off, about the size of a large dressing room. David snaps his finger and the wall closes.

Still not a word is spoken.

Opening a door within this small room, appearing as a small closet, David reaches in, and pulls out two hermetically sealed packages. Hank watches David open one of them. Taking what appears as a piece of clothing out of the bag, Hank sees that it is a long dark green robe. Without uttering anything other than simple body and sign language, Hank understands David to be telling him to strip himself of all of his clothes so that he may wear the robe. He, David will do the same.

David begins removing his first, so that he can show Hank where to put his clothes. They are to be put in a second closet room, and hung on pegs.

Now totally free of all of their clothing except for the long dark green robes adorning them, David turns away from Hank, and toward one of the walls.

Placeing both hands palm down on one of the walls, another wall opens at David's touch. He motions Hank to hurry behind him, and just as Hank passes the wall, he hears a swift swishing sound. The wall has closed, and the human eye can detect no opening.

Hank looks around to see what he can see in this 12 x 12 room. All he does see are four white walls. Except these white walls glisten and glimmer. Hank is dismissing it as fancy paint.

Finally, David breaks the silence. "Hank thanks for your patience while we have gone through this exercise. I'll explain now."

"Due to the episode with someone getting into your room, we needed to escalate things a bit in regard to the security levels of information as it relates especially to you. The fact that Powers' security was breached in this building is being addressed on many levels now, from the general aspect of Lance's life and business. But this moment with you is of a different nature."

"Lance has a special sound proof security room imbedded in his walls. He and I are the only ones that know of this room. Security does not even know of it."

"This room and the drawers and closets containing your clothes are highly sensitive. We need to know if your clothes had been set up for any kind of surveillance. The testing, shall we say, of which your clothes are now under, will detect anything man made that would cause security issues for us."

"This room we are standing in, is also highly sensitive. If either of us has anything not appropriate in or on us, it will be detected here."

Just as David is finishing his sentence, they are distracted by a swishing sound. A window or screen about 24 inches has opened in the wall.

"Ah, here we go Hank, the results of your clothes and your body makeup."

David reads from the screen; "Just as we thought. There was a tiny microchip embedded in each piece of your clothing, except the ones you had on. Which means this had to be done quickly while you were with me in the coffee shop and they were lifting the information from your clipboard. An instrument that can shoot microchips into various fabrics, is most likely that's what was used."

Hank interrupts with a question. "David, I don't get it. If The Stiletto is so efficient and smart, it seems to me, that they would not have taken the paper from the clipboard, but simply made notes as to what was on it. The fact that they took the paper immediately told us they were in the room, and knew our next step. If they had not taken my notes, then we wouldn't know they had broken into the room. Plus David, they left the door open, what's with all of that?"

"Good question, Hank," answers David, "there is an apparent reason for the ineptness as well as a hidden one."

"First, you've met some of the big guys employed by The Stiletto, they are not paid to think, but to follow exact instructions. The Stiletto hires big guys with demeanors to physically push, but have no real capability for leadership on their own. This usually brings a personality with lack of skill in other areas of expertise. The big guys most likely were instructed to search your room, and to shoot the microchips into your clothing. They did that."

"The rest would have required a personality that would think somewhat for themselves. The Stiletto's upper echelon does not want field people running around thinking for themselves.

Therefore, it does not give them any information that may be cajoled out of them."

"Only guys like Dagger have inside information, and still not a great personality choice to have in the higher rankings of one's organization."

"And the hidden part?" asks Hank.

"Well no matter how you look at it," David explains, "and no matter how efficient The Stiletto is, their motives are not constructive for mankind. Therefore, from an energy vibration perspective, that same energy of nonconstructive events boomerangs back on them in some way. It appears to them to show up in small ways. The Stiletto is willing to take those types of risks, and they know these risks exist."

"But what they don't know, is that it is in the small ways, that their success will be thwarted. Here's an example, and the reason we are now going into the next room."

David turns to another of the side walls, walks over to it and places both hands, palms down on the wall. It opens up. He motions to Hank to quickly follow him as the wall closes fast behind them both.

Hank stands in awe looking around this massive room. Equipment and monitors that Hank has never seen before are placed throughout this spacious place. One wall contains a huge screen with only a light blue and white mist flowing through it.

There are no other people in the room, except one female that Hank can see, but he has not yet seen her face. She turns around and starts across the room to greet them. "It's Jenny!" Hank exclaims.

"Hello again Hank, I understand you're in need of some more jeans!"

All three laugh, and Hank replies that, "Yes, apparently it seems so."

Jenny taps him on his arm saying, "Hank you will have new clothing and a new duffel bag waiting on board the plane. It's being taken care of as we speak."

"Well I certainly hope you picked the right colors Jenny." Hank chiding his female friend.

"Oh, you mean, a blue, blue denim shirt, and blue, blue jeans?" Is Jenny's quick-witted response.

The smirk and laughs were relieving the tension for Hank, and it was good to see Jenny.

"Ok, you two, it's time to get back to saving humanity now that Hank's clothes are in order!" David bringing things back to set point.

Hank interrupts with a question. "David, I know we've been here at least 30 minutes, what about our timing for nine p.m. and leaving for London?"

"Hank we set that time to give The Stiletto a time frame reference, in the event they were getting information somehow. Your arrival will be early afternoon, instead of late morning. So this will throw them off just a bit."

David continues, "Oh, here is a big piece of news Hank. This one will surprise you and make you happy at the same time."

"First, yes you have to get the coin back from Sir Max. By now, The Stiletto has informed him that you know he has it. Most likely, they are making arrangements for sure, of some kind. But you are still on course to get to London and to find him."

"Secondly, you will introduce your Magic Wall, along with the coin to The United States first, and not India. Without giving you all the details, simply by the U.S. having the information first, it will travel widely and with momentum to other areas of the world. If you were to begin with India, we would have to contend with The Stiletto knowing about it and have to deal with all the problems that would bring."

"On top of that, even if you were to influence many poverty stricken people from that country, the momentum would be slow in reaching other areas of the world. The lack of knowledge, and equipment available to those same people to help spread the word simply does not exist in the nature of what we need."

"By introducing it to America first, then both of those situations are remedied from the beginning. This will be a very exciting time for the world despite what the media reports of adverse feelings are of America from other countries. The United States is still a very much loved and honored country and looked to for innovations and ideas. This is a huge new one, and Hank Ramsan is its Administrator!"

"That makes sense to me David, especially due to the history behind the banking systems." Hank interrupts himself in mid-thought. "By the way, David, what's the big screen for? It seems almost three dimensional."

"Well you're not far from right Hank. That screen is a very high frequency screen. We have to go, so there isn't time to explain the vastness of the screen's capability. But for now, it is able to track you based on the radiance that you absorbed through that belt that Jenny gave you when you first got new clothes."

"It's time Hank, to go back into the closet and get dressed. You can put the same clothes on that you wore in here. They were not contaminated. Then we'll drive to meet the plane."

53

David and Hank hurriedly change back into their clothes while David's car is brought around in perfect timing just as they arrive at the lobby entrance. First to get to the waiting car, David opens the passenger side of the front seat door for Hank to get in, closes it, and walks around to slide into the driver's side.

A puzzled Hank says to David, "I didn't think you'd be driving me to the airport David."

David looks left to pull from the curb while answering. "Under the circumstances, I want to make sure you get to the plane safe and sound. But once you are airborne, everything else is up you."

The car moves forward to blend in with the New York City traffic.

Meanwhile, as Hank and David drive to the airport, The Stiletto has not been idle in attempting to thwart Hank's overall plan. They do not intend to let him get the coin back and continue with his Magic Wall Project.

The Stiletto still has the same obstacle involving Jocy. Jocy knows their identity and any attempt to kill or harm Hank would trigger release of that information. The same would apply, if they were to choose to harm her.

Not a group to roll over easily, The Stiletto had begun to put in place a highly sophisticated plan, which would get them what they wanted. And what they wanted was Hank dead, Jocy dead, and the power of the coin known to them. They wanted the power of the coin, as well as no longer having the threat of their identity being exposed, hanging over their heads.

It was an intricate plan. One that was so closely guarded that Alex would not be privy to it.

The Stiletto is aware that if Hank succeeds in his plans then there would be no need for the various stock exchanges around the world. Currently buying and selling stocks dictates corporate and individual financial futures. It's an income stream that has both a trickle up and trickle down effect.

Hank has a more simplified way of looking at things. If everyone could make their money, resources, and manifest what they wanted for their lives, as long as it was constructive, then the current protections and financial instruments around the world would no longer be needed.

Supply and demand would be an economic theory of the past. If there is something, a business or individual desires to have to expand their lives or lifestyles, all they need to do is to understand and apply the mechanics of The Magic Wall, and it would be done. Each person's wish would be the command of the dream come true.

This is not what The Stiletto wants. The Stiletto wants power to control the world and its resources. The Magic Wall would nullify that control.

While Jocy was preparing to go into the city to meet Lance Powers and Hank flying his way to London, The Stiletto had been busy.

The Stiletto power reaches far and wide. They knew that Jocy would go to the international newspapers and bureaus first, with what she knew. Therefore, The Stiletto would cut off that avenue as a threat to their exposure.

Between print and visual media, there are less than 10 CEO's that needed to be brought under control by The Stiletto. The Stiletto put its agenda into effect fast. Heads of corporations and their families were threatened if they did not comply with a certain directive.

The signed directive that was sent from The Stiletto to all media outlets upper echelon contained these words and language:

There is an individual threatening to bring down the financial markets, as we know them today. They intend on doing this by revealing the names and faces of those who make up the organization referred to as The Stiletto.

Furthermore, it has never been proven that this organization was anything but business like in its dealings. However, adverse publicity could bring great financial harm and undoing.

Therefore, any agency that attempts to publicize such untruth, let it be known, that the lives and families of those releasing this falsehood, will meet with untimely hazards.

All media outlets are being watched closely by The Stiletto. Also to assure that this directive is followed, let it be known that The Stiletto will not go down without causing worldwide destruction first. Therefore, if any among you feels brave and courageous, you may want to rethink your motives, as your actions will be resultant of killing hundreds of thousands worldwide. Signed: The Stiletto.

As this threat went out to all media outlets, including company chairmen, many with chills of fright running up their spine, they began calling other each other to compare notes. They all knew the power of The Stiletto.

They all also knew that The Stiletto on the surface always appeared to be operating above board, but if they ever were to be pushed into a corner, then you wouldn't want to be around to watch what happened. This was apparent as newspaper and TV heads talked to one another, all realizing this was one of those times.

People of power often use their influence as a vehicle to manipulate the media, but this was different. This was not a dog and pony show for expansion of some idea or business. This was the most powerful underground organization in the world backed into a big corner. Its back was up against the wall and there would be no prisoners taken. The Stiletto would not go down without creating worldwide havoc, including death and destruction.

With this agenda fully in place, The Stiletto could again use Jocy as a pawn to get Hank to give them the instructions to activate the coin. Their next step was to abduct Jocy. The perfect time would be when she thought she would be going into the city to meet Lance Powers.

Again, The Stiletto would have to be clever in protecting its accounts with Powers. They would do this by sending Alex instead of Jocy to the meeting with Lance. Alex would tell Powers that Jocy had a family emergency that came up just as they were starting into the city.

Score two for The Stiletto. Only they didn't know that Alex was a good guy. Nevertheless, there was nothing he could do about them seizing Jocy. Alex knew he had to maintain his cover so that Hank could do what he had set out to do.

The next day began early with Alex and Jocy boarding The Stiletto helicopter promptly at 9:30. While they are airborne, on their way to meet a car taking them to Powers One, Alex gets a call on the helicopters two-way system and not his cell phone. This told he and Jocy that something was up.

These words came through as Alex listened: "When the helicopter lands, the two of you walk to the waiting car. Just as you get to the car, Jocy will be detained, and you are to get into the car and drive to meet Powers. You are to tell Powers that Jocy had a last-minute family emergency and could not come, but sent you in her stead. You know about the shipment and some things about the customers involved. You should have no problem covering yourself with Powers. Make it work Alex."

Alex started to ask questions of what was happening with Jocy, but then he knew better. The Stiletto would not tell him anyway. Alex was given his instructions, that is all he was to know. "Do you understand what you are to do Alex?"

"Yes I understand," replied Alex.

"We will be in touch." Then click and silence. The Box hung up.

Alex made his way back to the seat beside Jocy. They had a code that when something was about to really go wrong, one of them would ask a question and the other would answer. This let them both know that something was about to happen and that some type of threat was eminent. They knew their conversations were being monitored, so they had to be careful.

Alex asked the question: "Hey, Jocy, what's your favorite song?" It was with that question that Jocy knew something was up. She needed to answer without appearing as though she had just swallowed a fish. "Well, lets see Alex, I have a lot of favorite songs."

Jocy catches herself about to blubber on and on due to her fear taking over. Then as would happen in natural conversation, Jocy asked Alex what his favorite song was. As he was about to answer, the pilot came over the intercom letting them know they were landing.

Alex was fiddling with a rubber band. He handed it to Jocy as some way to let her know, that things would be all right, although he had no idea how at this time. He didn't know what The Stiletto was up to.

54

Alex climbs out of the helicopter first, helping Jocy step down. They run hand in hand to the waiting car, with their heads down in order to protect them from the fierce wind of the helicopter propellers. Reaching the waiting car Alex opens the door for Jocy.

The moment the door opens, two men get out which surprises Alex. One of the big guys proceeds to tell Jocy that their instructions are to accompany her to another destination, and she'll need to get back on board the helicopter. She understood that to mean she would not be riding with Alex and certainly not meeting with Lance Powers.

Jocy began asking questions and per the usual method of operation of The Stiletto big guys, their only answer was; "Those are our only instructions, Ms. Preston."

Jocy and Alex stood and looked at one another. Jocy was gently nudged by one of the big guys, turned, and walked with them back to the helicopter as Alex got into the back seat of car.

Alex began processing thoughts rapidly. He would be meeting with Powers and for appearance sake, due to the surveillance, would have to use the family emergency story with Lance as to why Jocy didn't show. But Lance Powers would read into all of it and know that something was wrong, terribly wrong.

Jocy on the other hand, as the helicopter lifted off, had not a clue of what was next, or where she was going. She was beginning to feel afraid, and little did she know she had good reason.

While things were being set up for The Stiletto to have the upper hand, Hank was by now in the air thinking everything was under control, and feeling very good. His last understanding was that soon Jocy would be under the protection of Lance Powers. It would be a while before he would know anything different.

Hank began getting comfortable for the plane ride as a female attendant started his way. As she got closer, he recognized it was Jenny!

"Jenny, you pop up in the darndest places! Are you the attendant on this flight?"

"Well Hank, no I'm not the attendant, I'm one of your pilots!"

Hank laughing, "that's only a good thing, right?"

Jenny assures him that yes, it's a good thing, and that for the moment she needs to fill him in, so she 'thanks him to keep his pretty blonde face shut!'

Hank smiles and says, "ok, shoot."

Jenny begins; "Hank, we have a pretty close knit of people around you and what you are doing. David wanted to make sure there were no glitches on the plane, and that's why I'm here. I also have for your reading pleasure, instructions for when you land, of which may provide you some guidance in locating Sir Max."

Handing him a large manila envelope, Jenny in a sarcastic tone, tells Hank she will leave him to go and help 'drive' the plane.

Hank opens the envelope and pulls out a large color photograph of Sir Max. A Caucasian looking man, possibly in his 60's. Not a physical threat to Hank, so this made him feel good. This made him feel good until he continued looking through the envelope.

Sir Max has been for a long time, a powerful underground influence in the financial markets of the world. Further reading shows Hank that he also has deep associations to the Swiss Banking Systems, as well as the World Bank. He is The Stiletto Branch of the United Kingdom and a blood brother so to speak, of The Box.

Assuming Sir Max would be flanked by big guys and certainly would not be easy to get an audience with, he reads further hoping to make his search easier. It would help if Hank knew where he lived and didn't have to use precious time locating him.

'Lucky me,' Hank thinks to himself, as he pulls out some pages clipped together. The front page title: 'Sir Max's London Home: Underground Manse.'

This home is not a home in the normal sense, and Hank isn't surprised at what he is reading. Sir Max has lupus. This explains why he lives underground. Hank knew that people with Lupus exasperate the disease by being in sunlight. Many with this condition have to block the windows of their homes and wear clothing that covers them from head to toe before going outside during daylight.

Hank finds through the information packet, that someone with the status of Sir Max, has not only built a massive home underneath the ground but also constructed almost what appears to be a massive underground city. This underground city is similar to Crystal City Underground and one like the Atlanta Underground, both of which Hank was familiar.

However, this particular underground city was built catering to the likes of Sir Max. Although this city is open to the public, the selections are somewhat limited.

The residence of Sir Max is off limits to everyone, and is hidden from public view. Everyone would know it by 'The City of Sir Max.' That is how Hank was to find it.

That was all that the contents of the envelope contained, but it was enough to get him started in the right direction. Aside from this packet of information, Hank felt as though he might need a little more help.

He remembered that Jenny had told him his new duffel bag would be on board with fresh clothes, and he wondered . . .

Just as he was wondering, he rose out of his seat and began looking for the duffel bag, and there it was, above his seat. Pulling it down, and as he's looking, he sees it and says, "ah, good ole Jenny, a clipboard with notebook paper on it!"

55

Pulling out the clipboard, and tossing the duffel bag on the next seat, Hank prepares to write with the pen that Jenny had enclosed. Then just as he pulls his eyes to the paper, he notices some words written in script already present on the page.

Hank, this pen is a magic pen to go with your magic clipboard. The note goes on to say; *In addition to writing, when you say, 'Hank One,' it becomes a phone connection to me. When you say 'Hank Two,' it puts out a laser beam stun ray of sorts. Non-crippling, but gives you time if you need it. If you lose it, or it is taken from you, it serves as a beacon for us to find where it's located. Only your voice can activate it. Love Jenny.*

Reading those words reminded Hank of how serious things were, but he was comforted in the attributes of the pen. A fresh piece of paper was now in order and he began writing.

These words scrolled forth from Hank's hand: *I find Sir Max in ease, peace, and fun. I am easily led to the exact location of the Gold Coin with The Epigram.*

Stopping to look at the statement he just wrote, Hank begins asking himself some questions: 'Is this clear enough? What is my end result desire to have completed? What next?'

He decides to add one more statement. *I bring the gold coin back to the United States with me for its intended use, and I do so in ease, peace, love, and affection.*

Glancing again at the words, Hank felt his statement was complete. Reading the statement out loud three times took care of it for Hank. He folds the paper and stuffs it in the left back pocket of his jeans, his lucky pocket.

Hank has used a playfulness of sorts in designing his life on purpose. Once he found a way that worked for him, he began expanding the physics of it all. His life got easier and his dreams and goals manifested with momentum.

Early on though, Hank made a deal of sorts with whatever he was calling Spirit or God at the time. He would do 'this,' whatever he was to be doing, but along the way, he wanted it to be fun, and he wanted to celebrate this life. As it was turning out, that is exactly what had been happening for him. This all began, after he lost Jocy.

Now, things were different. Hank was embarking on concepts of which he didn't have full understanding of how they worked. He kept it simple in knowing that all he needed to do was to follow what was in front of him, as it would always lead him to the next thing. The trick was to have whatever was next to come to him in easy ways instead of hard ones. That was one of the larger more important strategies he had taught himself, and one of the major themes he was choosing to assist others in along the way.

Hank felt strongly about helping people make large amounts of money in easy and fun ways. He knew the constructive power and its application, and intended on showing others. This was exactly why he had entered the dangerous territory of *The Stiletto.*

Those who chose destructive power to control the world would soon lose that power. It would happen because millions more would discover a stronger, softer power that would bring them anything they chose, including wealth. This would trickle up and down the chart of humanity from the rich to the poor and from the diseased to the healthy.

It always filled Hank with enthusiasm just to think about the possibilities. When anyone would ask about it, he'd lose himself in the excitement of telling stories of how things would change. This was his mission. It's what he came to do, and he knew it.

Hank fell into a daze musing over things and one of those famous power naps seemed to show up just at the right time. He rested for 10 minutes and is awakened as he hears Jenny on the intercom. "Landing gear is down, please fasten your seat belt Hank."

Hank is a bit surprised as his 10-minute power nap appears was more like three hours! He figured he needed his rest!

"Hank, if you'll check in your duffel bag's side pocket, you will see your accommodations for your stay in London," came from Jenny over the planes intercom.

The Vista International on the Chelsea Harbor, is what is neatly written on his itinerary along with a notation; *The financial arrangements for your stay, including food and beverage, have been provided.* Hank assumes it's Lance Powers taking care of his accommodations.

Just as he considers his accommodations, and begins putting his notes back in the duffel bag Jenny walks back to brief him. Wanting to know for sure, Hank asks Jenny, "Hey Jenny, is Powers taking care of the Vista? I'd like to know who is being so generous with me."

"No, it's not Powers this time, and this individual prefers anonymity." Jenny continues, "just know that you are well-taken care of Hank. Also your room overlooks the marina, so you should be quite happy, for as long as you are in that room!"

They look at each other, with no words needing exchanged. Hank's duration of home away from home is unknown at this time, but it would be home for as ever long as he was there.

Jenny interrupts the silence. "Hank, we're landing in a private airstrip just outside of London. From there, the same benefactor of your current accommodations has a car waiting to take you to The Vista. Once you are there, you're on your own to find Sir Max."

"Ok, got it, Jenny. Mind if I ask what you'll be doing, while I'm chasing Sir Max?" Hank trying to keep things light, but also wanting information that may be helpful to him.

"What I end up doing Hank will depend on you. I am to monitor you through the radiation from the initial belt that you had on, as well as through the pen. We will always know where you are. But you have the bulk of the job on your big shoulders."

Both smiling, as the light goes on over the cabin, Jenny turns to go back to the cockpit while telling Hank, "seat belt on blonde boy."

56

From the plane window, Hank notices a small airfield below. He was hoping to see some markings or other planes that would give him a clue of who was payrolling his stay in London. Reflecting upon how he's been living since he left Virginia with all of his needs taken care of, Hank is aware of his own Magic Wall at work. This time his wall was taking him to London.

There were no identifiable markings on any of the other planes from what Hank could see from the air. As they approached landing, Hank notices all the planes are generic looking including the small jets. There was nothing helpful in identifying any certain person or company to give him a clue of his benefactor.

The plane gently sits down and taxi's along the runway cruising toward a small hanger with a side building attached. Still looking out his small window, Hank notices near the building a white limo and assumes this is his ride into London. No one seems to be around, only the white car, a hanger, and a building.

The seat belt sign is turned off and Jenny begins opening the cabin door, pushing the collapsible stairs forward. She turns to Hank just as he's making his way toward the front of the plane.

"Your chariot awaits, Mr. Ramsan!" as Jenny motions him on to the now open doorway.

"So this is it, Jenny?"

"This is it for this moment, Hank." They both hug goodbye, and the underlying affection is felt by both. Jenny makes light of the moment, saying, "enough of this Mr. Ramsan, the world awaits your work!"

Hank reaches down and picks up his duffel bag, while Jenny watches him walk down the stairs and then over toward the car.

Wondering whether he was to get in the car or not, Hank sees the driver's side door begin to open. To Hank's surprise it was Talal.

"Talal!" Hank blurts out, as Tal makes his way over toward Hank.

"Well Hank, you didn't think we'd leave you to your own wits to work this out did you?" They laughed with Hank half-agreeing. "Hop up front, Hank and well catch-up a bit on our ride into London."

Hank is full of questions, and Talal just smiles. "Oh, Mr. Ramsan, I had soon, but not soon enough forgotten your curious nature! Slow down and I'll catch you up on some things you need to know."

Talal puts the car into drive and begins giving Hank some details.

As Talal is talking, it occurs to Hank how the ease and fun in finding this Sir Max has already begun, just as he had written it down. Here is his now very good friend Tal, meeting him in London, being his chauffeur, and giving him some details that will help him along his way. He smiles for a moment to himself, while paying attention to what Talal is telling him.

"The packet of information on Sir Max is up to date except for one thing. He is aware you will be trying to find him and he's going to make it easy for you. He will be looking for you as well."

Tal continues briefing Hank. "Since Sir Max has the gold coin, or access to it, it's a natural assumption that you would be traveling to find him. This will put you and the coin in proximity of one another, and Sir Max likes those odds. He knows you can activate its power. He will make it easy for you two to meet, but don't count on him handing over the coin. He won't make it that easy when you do finally meet. You'll have to be creative for that to happen."

"Hank, things could get dangerous for you in London. Sir Max is a well-loved man here due to his generosity in many areas. He and his reclusive lifestyle are a fun mystery for the people of London.

Talal's cell phone rings interrupting his update mid-sentence. Hank notices Talal is listening, he's not having a conversation. He's not smiling, nor is he expressing anything. Hanging up, Tal takes a deep breath, slows down, and pulls off to the side of the road.

"The Stiletto has Jocy," came from Talal's now serene demeanor.

This changed the intensity for Hank, as he learns how Jocy never made it to the lunch with Powers. Instead, she was taken to The Stiletto's headquarters, while Alex met with Powers.

Talal didn't know the background of the events. He didn't know that Powers was of course angry, but he had to be on his toes and play the game.

When Alex showed up for the lunch meeting, it was assumed by The Stiletto, that the lunch plans would have meant that Lance Powers would meet Alex and Jocy in the restaurant of the hotel.

Powers had other plans. Plans made dependent on Jocy showing up. However, before Lance knew the change in those plans, he had sent David to meet his lunch guests. David's instructions were to bring only Jocy to Powers' office suite.

When David walked into the lobby and saw Alex standing there alone, he knew something was up, but still had to also play his role. David knew The Stiletto would have surveillance equipment on Alex, and would be monitoring the encounter.

Alex politely introduced himself to David, and offered his apologies for Ms. Preston not being able to attend. Explaining at the last minute, she had a family emergency, but that he, Alex understood the nature of the meeting between Jocy and Mr. Powers, and he would like to continue the appointment, if appropriate.'

Alex feeling some stress was overly polite in his request of David.

"Yes, I understand," was David's first response, then pausing, "if you'll pardon me one moment Alex, I'll have to inform Mr. Powers of this development and see if he wishes to meet with you under all the new circumstances presented."

David already knew Lance would meet with Alex, but it would be a controlled atmosphere; one that The Stiletto hadn't counted on.

57

David walked over to the lobby's registration desk to call Powers from his cell phone, his back turned to Alex. While on the phone he turns and looks at Alex, closes his cell phone and sticks it in side blazer pocket. David walks back over to where Alex had seated himself and reports the result of the phone call.

"Alex, Mr. Powers of course is very disappointed that he will not be lunching with Ms. Preston. However, under the circumstances and due to wanting to keep his friends happy in trusting his investment advice, he has agreed to meet with you. Please follow me."

It's as this point that Alex and David move toward the elevator making small talk as they step in for the ride upstairs. The light chat would help keep The Stiletto under the assumption that things were being controlled by them and not Powers.

Arriving on the main floor of Powers' office suite, the elevator door opens to four men standing waiting. David turns to Alex explaining, "due to security," of which he assumed Alex would accept, "these gentlemen would be checking him as a pre-cautionary measure. Lance Powers' stature simply required this action."

All Alex could say was, "yes, I understand."

Then in Alex's earphones he hears 'The Box.' "Alex, we may lose contact. We trust you to do all in accordance with The Stiletto."

No sooner, than the statement had been made, one of the security officers asked if Alex would remove his earphones and hand them to him. Alex did so, and under his breath, gladly.

Having finished a non-evasive search of Alex, David thanks him for his cooperation and again asks that he follow along. David was taking him to Lance Powers' main office suite.

When they enter the room, Powers is not there. David takes Alex over to the same wall of pictures that he had shown Hank earlier. He puts one hand on a particular picture, the side of the wall opens up, and he asks Alex to quickly come in behind him.

Alex responds to David's request to remove his clothes and hang them on the peg within the closet, which was opening up as he was talking.

David begins unwrapping one of the hermetically sealed green robes which he pulled from the closet drawer and instructs Alex to put it on. Alex complies with it all, and no conversation takes place, other than instructing Alex to remove his clothes.

David did not want to take a chance that an embedded microphone was somewhere on Alex, so he kept his comments brief. Intending to get Alex into the white room where they could talk freely, was the plan.

Alex removed his clothes and puts on the robe as David had given him. The wall opens up with David's touch and both men walk into the white room.

David kept his street clothes on, feeling no need to be the example for Alex as he was for Hank. Hank was new to higher level security measures.

Saying nothing, David puts his index finger over his lips letting Alex know he is not to say anything as he is waiting for the screen to appear.

Seemingly out of nowhere pops the screen. The message shown was, 'nothing detected in Alex's clothing or flesh.' Therefore, they are now free to talk.

David begins with a short explanation to Alex. "Alex, you and Hank are the newest ones to be given entry into this room. Only a select few are aware it exists. However, under the circumstances we had to bring you in, so that we could talk freely and fully protected. So now Alex, tell me what is going on."

"Yes, Alex tell us," came from a voice that entered the white room, it was Lance Powers. Lance had just entered through the same wall that David and Alex had appeared.

"Hello again Alex, it's been awhile!" Powers greeting Alex with a firm handshake, and telling him; "I had to naturally wait until you were fully cleared before I could meet with you Alex, and now that has occurred, so tell us what has happened."

"I don't know a lot of details," Alex begins, "but it's pretty apparent that The Stiletto is going to hold Jocy hostage in order for Hank to show them how to implement the coin. I received a call from The Box, as we were on board the helicopter to meet our ride into the city. All I was told is that I was to meet you alone and to say that Jocy had a family emergency. Then as we landed and walked to the car, two of The Stiletto's big guys got out of the car and told Jocy that she was to accompany them back to the helicopter. Those were the only bits of instructions they were given."

David finishing his story, "I assume they have taken her to The Stiletto's headquarters."

With that comment, Powers begins to feel his blood boil just a bit, but calms himself quickly so that he can think clearly. His thoughts no longer kept to himself, he tells Alex and David; "Well this must mean that they have an ace up their sleeve or they wouldn't have taken this chance. They know that Jocy could expose them and that she has a plan in place in the event they would do harm to her or Hank. They are up to something, and we have to find out what that is and now!"

All three men stand in silence.

Suddenly the small screen appears on the wall, and David reads the words outloud: *Please, all three go into the Big Picture room.*

Both Powers and David knew what the Big Picture room was and now Alex would be introduced to it. David placed both hands on one of the walls, it opened up like a mist, and all three men walked through.

Alex just stood in amazement in what he saw in this room, much of what he saw he had not a clue of what it was. David interrupts his thoughts.

"Alex, I know you would like to know more about this room, but now is not the time." And with that, there was a swishing sound and in addition, from Powers, Alex hears, "Maddy!"

Lance points to the screen graciously, "Alex, this is Maddy."

Alex is speechless. His thoughts are running in confusion not sure of what he is seeing. His eyes open wide while this huge screen in front of him seems to take up an entire wall. It's lifted somehow from ground level. His stare at the screen brings him this vision of the most beautiful blonde female. She seems to glimmer, but how could a person glimmer? Realizing it's not just a vision, she is somehow real, and he's too amazed to ask questions.

Alex has never seen anyone, or any painting as beautiful as this person Maddy that he was now locked onto. Then from that very screen and it's beautiful face come these words; "Hello, My Good Lance, David and Alex, it's good to finally meet you in person, although Alex, I have been aware of your assistance."

Alex still can't speak, and Lance and David just grin at one another.

David chides Alex a bit, bringing him back to earth. "Alex, take a deep breath, Maddy doesn't show up just to socialize."

Alex comes out of his daze. "Yes, right, I'm with you!"

Powers acknowledges the moment; "Maddy, please begin."

"This is where things are gentlemen. The Stiletto is holding Jocy as a hostage. She is comfortable, they are not being unkind to her other than she is their prisoner, which she has been for some time. She is now confined within their private barracks in the city."

Maddy continues. "You of course are correct Lance, they do have an ace up their sleeve, and they have played it. The Stiletto has used world wide power and influence to inform, threaten is the better word, all of the media outlets at the CEO level. They have put out a directive that if any media enterprise, from print to electronic or otherwise, is sent any information regarding the supposed identity of The Stiletto then the families of those, as well as the CEOs themselves would be in hazards way, as in eradicated."

"This was made clear in a hand-delivered memo to all of the top media management around the world. What this of course means, is that even if Jocy had set a plan in motion due to her being harmed, she would be killed without anyone ever disclosing her secret. Business and finance as the world knows it would continue as it has been, under the control of a few."

"Therefore, once again, it comes down to The Stiletto using Jocy as a pawn to get Hank to give them what they want. They allowed the two of them to spend just enough time together that Hank has an emotional investment. This will weigh heavily upon him now."

"However, The Stiletto does not know the power that Hank has at his disposal, and *that* is our Ace."

Maddy finishes and it appears to Alex that twinkles came from her eyes. He had to blink twice to be sure his eyes were okay!

Maddy goes on to explain that currently 'they,' meaning Lance Powers and his organization, could pretend they were holding Alex captive. However, in doing that, The Stiletto would know that Powers was involved in more than mere investment interest with Jocy. She further suggests that Alex is to return to his work with The Stiletto, as that is helpful to both Hank and Jocy in many ways.

Maddy then asks Alex to report back to The Stiletto that Lance has agreed to keep his investors calm over the delay, but that he would only do so for nine days."

"At the end of nine days," Maddy further explains, "Lance would have returned from some overseas interest. This issue with the paintings and the horses needed to be well cleared by that time, in order for Powers to continue in good standing with his friends and business associates."

Alex understood clearly and agreed this was the best route knowing also, what he knew of The Stiletto's method of operating. He would report to The Stiletto as Maddy had suggested.

58

David suggested that Alex get back into his clothes as it had been now an hour and a half and The Stiletto will expect him to report in soon.

All agreed and David escorted Alex back to the changing closet while Powers remained behind for further briefing from Maddy.

David stops Alex just short of going into the changing closet.

"Alex, once we get back into the closet our conversations go back to being aware that The Stiletto is listening. We all know you will do what you can in every moment." They shook hands, and David opened the wall leading to the closet.

Neither one spoke another word until they both were outside of Powers main office door. Then Alex back in his street clothes and with his earphone in his pocket said to David, "thank you for arranging this meeting with Mr. Powers, David, especially under the circumstances."

David shakes his hand and acknowledges the comment by saying, "yes, thank you, take care Mr. Saber." Alex is then escorted to the elevator by one of Powers' plain clothed security guards.

As soon as Alex was back down in the main lobby of Powers One, he put his earphones on and quickly contacted The Stiletto. He knew they would be waiting impatiently to hear from him.

Hearing the connection in his ear, Alex immediately proceeds to tell Mr. Box that he is now leaving the front doors of the building. He goes on to explain that Powers security guards frisked and checked him over for surveillance equipment, and that the lunch was not in the restaurant but in Powers office suite. Alex wanted The Stiletto to know how it was set up for Jocy in the first place, so that they would not think anything odd, since plans had changed.

Telling The Stiletto that Powers committed to 'us' and will keep his investors calm for nine days more due to his travel agenda, helped Mr. Box remain calm.

However, upon Powers' return, Alex emphasized full expectations from the entire Powers organization for full, immediate satisfaction. Powers insisted that his investors were to be happy with him and with us in the investment provided, despite the holdup up with the freightliner.

The Box seemed satisfied with Alex's answer and was glad for the nine days.

"What do you want me to do next?" was Alex's question to The Box, as he knew not to ask anything more specific than that.

The Box always wanted anything and everything to be his own idea and Alex did not want to put on airs that he had a tendency to have his own ideas as well. The Stiletto does not appreciate creative thinking by its employees. Not even someone like Alex, whom they trusted in part of their hidden circle.

The Box instructed Alex to do whatever was necessary without calling attention to The Stiletto. He was further instructed to get the freightliner situation cleared up within three days. This would give them enough time to move the artwork and the horses to the ranch.

Alex knew someone would have to be at the ranch to help organize the shipment. He knew it wouldn't be Jocy and he knew not to ask. Just as he was thinking those words, The Box told him they had sent someone new to the ranch to oversee things. The introduction would be made upon Alex's arrival later in the day.

In the meantime, The Stiletto driver who was by now waiting out front of Powers One while Alex had been on the phone with The Box, gets out of the car and makes his way toward Alex. The driver says to him, "my instructions are to get you back to a waiting helicopter that will then take you to where the freightliner is docked."

Everyone with instructions in tow, Alex gets into the back seat of the black stretch limo as the driver opens the door.

While things are beginning to feel tense around Alex due to his playing both sides, things have gotten fiery tense on the other side of the ocean. Hank now knows Jocy's situation to an extent and his job has gotten more complicated than it already was.

Talal and Hank are sitting in the parking lot of the Vista International and know for the moment, their conversation is somewhat protected inside the car.

Hank knows he needs to calm down and control his emotions in order to be of any use, whether it's one single person as Jocy, or anyone else for that matter.

Hank asks Talal; "Talal, why can't Maddy do something?"

In his understanding manner, Talal offers; "Hank, Maddy is doing many things behind the scenes. Some events have to be handled by what would be perceived by others, as the human perspective. That human perspective is you."

"You Hank, have to do this, and yes it appears it has gotten more complicated. However, you have to be the one to do this Hank. Just use what you know and keep doing as you have been doing."

"Where will you be Talal?" Hank asks, wondering if his friend and confidant will be in London with him.

"Well Hank, I'm not sure yet. Some of my activity is based on yours. It's best that you not know I am around. You have to depend on your own wits in this, or it won't work."

Talal sensing it's time to get Hank on his way says; "Go on into the hotel and find Sir Max unless of course he finds you first. In that case, take very good care of yourself."

Hank smirks, gets out of the car, waving Talal on his way.

Walking into the lobby, Hank notices it carries all of the style of a fine five star European Hotel. Due to the time of evening he has arrived, the front desk isn't busy and he's able to walk right up to check in.

The clerk checks him in and mentions, "oh, by the way Mr. Ramsan, you have a message waiting for you," as she hands him a brown sealed envelope. The envelope contains no identifiable markings. Hank opens it while standing at the desk and silently reads these words; 'It would be my pleasure to have your company for dinner. Please meet me in the hotel's main restaurant at nine this evening. They know me here, just ask for Sir Max.'

Chills ran up Hank's back. "Here we go!" flew into his mind.

Hank knew there was no sense in running from this meeting. Sir Max was at least making it in a public place. This meeting would appear to be of a non-threatening gesture to Hank. This is precisely what Sir Max wanted at this time.

Already hungry and knowing that Europeans prefer to eat later than the rest of the world, Hank decides there has to be some kind of food bar in his room. He goes on up to take a look at his suite which is on the ninth floor. The hallway is quiet and has as lavender aroma, giving him a feeling of calm. "Room 936, ah here it is!" Hank says to himself as his hunt for his new home away from home was over for the moment.

The sweet soft essence of flowers, roses came to mind, flowed to Hank as he opened the door inward. The room is light, airy, and expansive. More room than he needs, but feeling great to be in it just the same.

He sets his duffel bag on one of the two beds, and walks over to the large window. Sure enough and to his liking, he had a great view of the marina and the beautiful yachts of the rich and famous going in and out of the harbor.

Quickly he remembered he had walked right by a fresh tray of bagel sandwiches and a fresh pot of coffee as he went to the window. This added to the aroma of the room. Hank had noticed it as he went to put his duffel bag on the bed.

The blonde boy was smiling. Someone had done their homework and he was so hungry he didn't care in this moment if it was a good guy or bad girl. While thanking the stars and heavens as he lifted a turkey sandwich to his face and blessed coffee and not tea, Hank was feeling at home.

Holding the bagel in his mouth, he opens the note that was with the tray of sandwiches. It's signed in gold letters, *Enjoy! Love Maddy.* Then as all of Maddy's writing had the habit of doing, the gold letters disappeared from the note.

This made him feel better already. He especially knew that this food was safe for him to eat, which the opposite notion had crossed his mind.

Hank had about an hour before he was to meet Sir Max, which wasn't much time to really do anything that otherwise, might jeopardize him being late. Opening his duffel bag, he pulls out his clipboard, fills his coffee cup, walks over, and plops on the bed, while keeping his boots on.

Sitting his mug down after taking a big swig of coffee, he begins writing: *This meeting with Sir Max leads me to the gold coin in ease and peace.*

Then he writes a question: *What do I need to know about this meeting that maybe I don't think I know?* Hank closes his eyes for a moment and just as abruptly, he opens them. This phrase softly planted itself in his mind. *Turn the Tables.*

Now talking outloud to himself he says; "Great, one of those statements I have no clue what it means!" Hank's thoughts kept moving to this; 'Does it have something to do with the dinner table when he meets Sir Max? Should he look under the tables in his room?' Which by now he was looking under the desk in his suite and finding nothing. He decides he will know what the phrase means at the right time.

It's 8:45 in the evening London time as Hank washes his hands and decides to change his shirt for dinner. He looks in his duffel bag and lifts out a clean shirt. "Oh, I think I'll wear this blue denim shirt!" And he laughs to himself, he quite often thinks he's very funny!

Checking himself out in the mirror, Hank looks back in the room to see if he needs to bring anything with him. Noticing the pen that Jenny gave him lying on the clipboard, he knows he'd better take it along.

59

The headwaiter looks at him funny as he walks into the main foyer of the hotel dining room. Hank thinks to himself, 'must be the jeans!' He asks for Sir Max, and the waiter motions for Hank to follow.

Sitting back in a dark corner booth, with dark clothes on, awaits the famous Sir Max. Hank recognizes him from his picture. Surprisingly to Hank, Sir Max gets up from the booth to introduce himself while motioning him to please have a seat.

Sir Max wastes no time in getting to the point. "Mr. Ramsan, I have something you are looking for and you have something I want. I also have a proposition for you."

Hank listens as Sir Max promises him the moon and safety forever with 'Ms. Preston,' if he will show him how to implement the coin.

Hank respectfully listens to the offer while asking; "And if I say no?"

"Well Mr. Ramsan," Sir Max leans forward, "then we will have to do away both with you and Ms. Preston. We will be no further along in our use of the coin, but also we will have no further nuisance with the damage that Ms. Preston attempts to do."

"Also, Mr. Ramsan, this would remove the nuisance of you always being around like a pest trying to get the coin from us. It would just clean things up a little for us if you were dead and not around. You are better off to us shall I say, dead than alive?"

"Well, I don't cater to the dead part much, Sir Max, so lets play a bit." Hank now punting of sorts and with no clear direction.

"What guarantee do I have that you won't kill me after I tell you about the coin? Speaking of which, Sir Max, are you aware that I am the only one who can ever implement the coin? If I tell you how, I still must be the one to provide the application."

Sir Max sits back in his seat. "No, Mr. Ramsan, I was not made aware of that fact. How do I know you are telling me the truth?"

Hank continues: "Well Sir Max, if you will notice, I'm the only one trying to get the coin back. If it were of value without me, then others would be trying to get it from you and not need my services. I am the only one with the power to bring the coin alive. That's why I am here, and not an army of others."

"Very well, Mr. Ramsan. What would it take to make you happy and to help me in using the coin for my own benefit?"

Just as Sir Max said those words, Hank heard again these words in his own mind, *Turn the Tables*, and he knew just what to do.

Hank sits back in his seat and begins to present a deal for Sir Max to consider.

"Here is what I want, Sir Max; I want to live happily ever after with Jocy. I no longer want her or myself ever threatened by The Stiletto again. I want peace of mind, wealth and the girl of my dreams. I want all of that."

"Continue Mr. Ramsan." says Sir Max, as he is amused at what he is hearing.

"This is what you don't know Sir Max. It is The Stiletto's agenda, and by that I mean Mr. Box; do you know of whom I speak when I say Mr. Box?"

Sir Max replies, "yes, of course go on."

"Mr. Box has no intentions of sharing the power of the coin with you, Sir Max. In fact he plans on using it to destroy you so that he has full share of the world's financial instruments, holdings and resources."

"Surely you bluff Mr. Ramsan," Sir Max questioning the moment, "otherwise why would he send the coin to me for safekeeping?"

With a ready answer, Hank replies; "Are you aware Sir Max, that there are actually two coins with the same power? The Stiletto knows where the other coin is located. Has The Stiletto mentioned that to you, Sir Max?"

Sir Max is silent, then speaks.

"Mr. Ramsan, what is it that are you proposing, as I feel one coming. My difficulty is that I tend to wear black and you wear white. How can we meet that both are satisfied?"

By now, Hank is flying by the seat of his pants. He needs one piece of convincing information for Sir Max to agree to regarding the plan he's about to propose. But he is fumbling and it's not coming. Then like lightning, it shot into his mind.

"Sir Max, why do you want the power of the coin?"

With a ready reply, Sir Max explains his position. "Well up until this point, I have been acting under the auspices of The Stiletto. I was actually getting the coin in order for them to use the power, and I was told I would have a larger place in the world market. Now that you tell me there are two coins and I have not been privy to that information, when I should have been, it makes me question some things."

"Ok, but Sir Max," Hank again pressing his question, "if you had the power of the coin, what would you want it for? Power, correct?"

"Well yes, of course." answers Sir Max.

Hank continuing, "does it matter to you if the power is for bad or good as long as you were a recognized player of power?"

Sir Max pauses to ponder a moment. "Well now that you put it that way. No, I would be willing to use it for good, if I had the power to pull some strings and was recognized for my Power. I am quite the ego maniac you know," Sir Max half-smiling.

"Yes, I understand. The ego quite often gets a bum rap. However, if you are willing to tilt more toward the power of the good guys, then I think we can make a deal." Hank feels he has now successfully turned the tables but adds a little more information to ensure his position before asking for Sir Max's final answer.

Hank proceeded to tell Sir Max of his plan regarding The Magic Wall. He could implement his plan without the gold coin, but it would work faster if he had it to use. As he is expanding his story it appears that Sir Max is still unclear as to his role as Hank is being 'Mr. Change The World.'

Sir Max wanted to know specifically what his role would be, and how it would give him power. He wanted to know what was in all of this for him. So he came out and asked Hank to explain it to him, 'exactly.'

Hank begins to spell it out clearly. "Sir Max, The Magic Wall is going to create wealth all around the world in all sectors and cultures. People will know how to create their own wealth and resources in ease. They won't need to stay in jobs they hate or eat out of trashcans, or rob Peter to pay Paul. They won't need to risk losing their home by borrowing money from a bank with escalating interest rates, in order to stay afloat."

"Most of all, the creative flow of people will be expressed and new ideas and inventions will spring forth because the stuck money band has been finally broken."

Sir Max interrupts Hank's speech. "Yes Mr. Ramsan, quite noble and all, but where do I fit in a way that keeps me happy?" Sir Max is now insistent.

"Sir Max," Hank begins explaining, "all of this new wealth will need to be organized. The role of banks and financial instruments will change drastically. Someone has to put it together. And whomever does that, will be looked upon with trust and admiration. This position will carry much power around the world."

"Right now, The Stiletto is not known to the world because they misuse money and resources for power that does not belong to them. Along the way innocent people get hurt."

"You would take on a role of hero of sorts, while at the same time be in charge of the new system of wealth that presents itself."

"I can hand you all of that on a silver platter. Can you guess what your role in this transaction would be, should you accept it, Sir Max?"

"Kill The Stiletto," is Sir Max's blunt reply.

"Well, I don't know if killing The Stiletto is necessary, but I assume you know who The Box is?"

"Yes of course I know," replies Sir Max with assurance.

"Well it stands to reason," Hank continues, "that The Stiletto is not being open with you. It also stands to reason, you were going to lose out big time. But if you and I work together to get what we both want, then you have to diminish the power and the long reach of The Stiletto. Can you do that?"

Sir Max, again in a confidant manner, "Yes, I can do that."

"Ok I have one last question, Sir Max." Hank hoping this will bring him the answer he both needs and wants from Sir Max.

"Ultimately what you will be doing are things that will bring you power and hero status. It is actually a good thing. Do you have any problem being a good guy, Sir Max?"

Eager to answer, Sir Max responds quickly. "Oh no, Mr. Ramsan. In fact I was always a good guy until The Stiletto got something over me and I couldn't free myself from them. Similar to your Ms. Preston, only a much larger arena."

Hank going in for the close, "Ok then, Sir Max, do we have a deal?"

"Yes, Mr. Ramsan we have a very good deal!" An enthusiastic Sir Max actually feels some sense of relief in this transaction.

Shaking hands, they laughed at the play on words, and then decided to celebrate their transaction by enjoying a meal together.

60

Things are beginning to come together on Hank's end of the world. Having solicited the help of Sir Max was a brilliant stroke of genius. Hank knew that he created this stroke of genius, this lightening bolt of thought, to turn the tables with Sir Max, with the same magic wall concept he was taking to the world.

However, there was still the situation regarding Jocy. If The Stiletto gets any idea of what's going on between Sir Max and Hank then Jocy's life would be over just for the pure sake of getting back at Hank. This as well, would seal the fate of Sir Max.

The Stiletto would be anxiously awaiting word from Sir Max on any progress regarding the coin. However, what The Stiletto didn't know is that plans had begun to be in place a good while before Hank and Talal had met for the first time. Their meeting on board the plane was planned from another place.

Unknowing to them, The Stiletto was being surrounded on all fronts. Hank's mission would take place and it would meet with success. The turn of events with Sir Max, all but insured it. Or did it?

There was still getting Jocy out from possible peril, which had to be addressed with finesse. The Stiletto did not attain its vast power without being smart and resourceful. Hank would have to be careful as to what took place now, and how it would be handled with Sir Max. There was no room for error.

Hank decides to bring this up during the dinner conversation so that Sir Max understood clearly about Jocy needing to be somehow free. He went on to point out, that if the arrangement between he and Sir Max was found out, then Jocy would be killed, with Sir Max, and Hank right along with her. Extreme care had to be taken to ensure that The Stiletto had no idea, no sniff of anything backfiring on them.

Sir Max understood clearly the implications. The next step would be for Sir Max to come up with some story to give to The Stiletto. He and Hank discussed some options.

While Sir Max and Hank are fine tuning the next step, Alex has arrived by helicopter aboard the freightliner. Since the freightliner was under the supervision of The Stiletto's men in Holland, the arrangements for Alex to board the ship were easily carried out.

When Alex arrived on board the ship, he was immediately taken to the Captain's Quarters. Captain Helvik greeted him and asked him to be seated across to the right of his desk.

Alex was seated in a high leather captain's chair that faced the large porthole looking out to sea. The chair swiveled around so that he could easily see the captain and the door.

The first question came from Alex. "Captain, do you know what the real hold up is with the freightliner? Apparently there is something going on that neither I, nor my company knows anything about."

As Alex asks this question, he is consciously aware of The Stiletto monitoring his conversation.

"Yes, I do know what the hold up is, answers the Captain. There is a shipment on board destined for a U.S. investor that someone does not want to be released. Apparently this partial item was stolen, which as you know Alex is the nature of many pieces of artwork that we ship. But something or someone has found out about this piece and is trying to get the authorities to seize the entire cargo."

Alex asks the next natural question. "Do you know Captain Helvik, who the person is attempting to stop the shipment?"

"No, I do not," returns the Captain, "and the only reason I know what I have told you is that I bribed one of the coast guard officers, who is of high ranking. Now I owe him a favor, which does not put me in a good position, especially since all that I do is ship the goods. I have no real control or interest over buyers and sellers."

Wanting to make the Captain feel secure Alex says, "well, Captain, I'm sure The Stiletto will make it worth your effort, for finding out this much for us."

More questioning from Alex; "Do you happen to know what exactly the piece is, that we are playing a tug of war over?"

"Yes, it's actually three pieces, and they come together and must not be separated. It is called *The Sword of Three's.*" answers the Captain, as he continues the story of the cargo.

"Apparently there is some type of legendary power in this artifact, and it would not do to be in the wrong hands."

Alex sits back in the chair waiting for a comment in his earphones, he knew one would be coming. Sure enough, in his ears he hears The Box.

"Alex, The Sword of Three's must be delivered to the ranch. We have already paid a huge some of money for our own private shipment. Plus we have granted many favors for its possession. The fact that someone has changed their mind, or another party has gotten involved, is of no consequence to us. Alex, get the ship with the full cargo including The Sword of Three's docked so that we can unload it and have everything at the ranch within three days."

"Just get it done Alex," The Box insisted. "Alex, this has to be a smooth transition, all of it, especially The Sword of Three's. And if it is not a smooth transition, then make it appear so! You have your instructions."

61

Life at The Stiletto headquarters is getting tense. The Stiletto is thirsty for more wealth and power. It knows what it plans on doing with both the *Power of the Gold Coin* and *The Sword of Three's*. However, right now both elements of The Stiletto plan are stuck.

'The Box,' is not willing to come out of the box to be known. Therefore, he has to depend on others to due his bidding. He must depend on Sir Max to get the power of the coin from Hank and he needs Alex to get The Sword of Three's delivered. The Stiletto's focus for over a long time had been set up for this moment.

As far as The Stiletto is concerned, both goals would be attained no matter how much money or whose lives had to be taken as an end to their means.

Jocy for the moment was safe from harm. The Stiletto put her up in one of their lavish apartments, securely located in The Stiletto's main building headquarters. She has all the food and electronic equipment one could want. Still she is a prisoner. She cannot call or go out and is to communicate only with The Stiletto.

Not being one to just sit around, Jocy's mind goes to many ways that she could try and escape, but she knows it will do little good. She decides to count on Hank and Alex, her two men, to somehow have everything turn out all right. But then again, what would 'all right' look like to Jocy?

A magazine cover stacked on the patio table near Jocy catches her attention. She had been gazing out into the New York skyline when she happened to look down at the stack of magazines.

On the cover was a perfect picture of Malibu Beach in California. Both she and Hank were celebrity geeks. They loved the fascination of celebrity and studying the profiles behind them. Some of their best times together had been in the Los Angeles area. The first time they fell in love was there. They knew in the same moment.

Jocy's mind began to wander back to those special times. She and Hank were assigned to cover some art galleries and were attending a special opening of a new artist. This was also where Jocy began developing her natural flair for art and made some new friends. Later these new friends became part of her art brokering business.

One particular artist, Doretta Bendalin, drew Jocy's attention. As she looked further into the painting of this artist, it seemed to draw her more. It was as if this artist painted from some special place.

Doretta Bendalin, was one of Jocy's first artist friends. Little did Jocy and Hank know at the time that Doretta's artwork would become world renown and that Jocy would be brokering stolen pieces of Doretta's work.

Soon after that gallery opening, Jocy would have to abruptly leave Hank with no explanation, in order to save his life.

What Jocy didn't know at the time, was that her leaving Hank would have such a devastating blow to his heart and mind, that he would go on a search for 'something.' Something he was not sure he was looking for, but found that it was actually looking for him.

It was this search that eventually led him to his life's work. It was in this life's work that Hank would need all of his wits about him in order to eventually save his life. Not only his life, but Jocy's as well as many others around the world. This was all of course assuming he could pull it off successfully.

As Jocy is falling deeper into thoughts of fun and affectionate days with Hank, the phone rings. It was Alex.

She knew he couldn't be open with her, but it was great just to hear his voice.

"Jocy, The Stiletto has asked me to check in with you from time to time. Plus, I've found out what is holding up the shipment and will be trying to undo that. I may be checking in with you when I return to the ranch. There is someone temporarily in your place and I'm sure I'll need to help her along, but will do so with your help if you will give it."

After listening intently, Jocy responds to Alex. "Sure Alex, it appears I'm not going anywhere!"

"Yes Jocy, I understand, and thank you for your help as I need it." And with that Alex hung up.

It was good to hear Alex's voice, Jocy thought to herself, and at least she knew he was okay.

emotional, mental and physical planes. If we write it three times, it then goes into the etheric record. It was from that point of the Swords that we became aware of all things running through life that was made up of three's. We find it the beginning of various religions through what is called The Holy Trinity. Actually, a religious zealot buried the original Swords of Three's and the parchment behind the wall. He did not want the general population of that day to know of the power of three's, much less the power of the swords themselves."

"Ok," Alex queries the Lieutenant further, "assuming this is an ancient truth, then it works anyway for anyone who would apply it. What did the swords have to do with anything? Why are they important enough to keep this freightliner stranded and why does someone not want them realized to the current buyer?"

The Lieutenant continues; "The story passed down is this. The Swords carry a specific energy given in radiation from one of the Ascended Masters."

The Lieutenant pauses and offers, "Alex before you ask, I do not know what an Ascended Master is, I am simply repeating the legend."

"Yes, I understand, please go on Lieutenant." Alex responds in kind.

"The Radiation within the sword cannot be removed except by an Ascended Master. Anyone having possession of all three swords, placing them on a platform of a natural element, and then placing them in the form of a triangle has set the stage. Then with either writing a statement and putting it in the middle of the triangle, or saying something three times while standing within the triangle of the swords, this will bring instant manifestation of the thing decreed."

"So Alex, as you see, anyone having this knowledge along with the actual swords would then have much power at their disposal."

Sitting back in his chair, the only words that would come from Alex's mouth were; "Yes, now I see. It's all very clear to me."

With Alex drifting off into a daze, he comes out of it as all of the men laughed at his rhyme. This broke him from his concentration of what he had just heard and the implications of the information.

63

While Alex was drinking from his coffee cup and musing over the new information, he receives a call from The Box in his earphones. The Box is going to arrive at the ranch the next day, and Alex needed to have the Swords at the ranch by then.

Alex is both dumfounded and bewildered that The Box is actually going to show himself at three in the afternoon the following day. As this is being set up in his mind, he begins to wonder how things are going on Hank's end. Was he able to find Sir Max, and could he get the coin without getting himself killed in the process?

Unknown of course to Alex, Hank has done very well. Sir Max has agreed to work with him under the condition that he, Sir Max, would come out looking like a hero and having power as well. The side benefit to Sir Max, which he never thought would happen, is that he would also realize his freedom from The Stiletto.

The next step in Hank's mind was to have the gold coin containing The Epigram in his position as soon as possible.

Before Hank and Sir Max ended their dinner evening together, Hank asked him straight out; "Sir Max, when may I have the coin in my possession?"

"We can get it now, if you'd like Mr. Ramsan." Both men burst into a laugh. They both knew of course that Hank wanted it now!

Hank felt no hesitation in going with Sir Max to his residence, which is where he had indicated the coin was located. On the other hand, Sir Max made sure to remind Hank that while in the company's car and at his home, their conversations and actions were being closely monitored.

Hank's response to the surveillance; "Sir Max, while we are in your car and home, please simply follow my lead, no matter what it looks like. I will assume you will react to me in your being a Stiletto employee. Are you ok with this?"

"Yes, Hank," responds Sir Max, "I think we shall proceed as we both have agreed. We have intentions to be met that will only be produced if The Stiletto is rendered powerless in some way. I will yield to you and your actions, however please understand that I will represent myself with you as having control over the circumstances."

Enthusiastically Hank replies, "yes, I understand, so lets get to it!"

Both men shook hands across the table in agreement. Sir Max signaled for one of his entourage to escort Hank to Sir Max's waiting car.

The working plan was now in motion with Sir Max representing The Stiletto and Hank representing all that he held dear to him, including his projected mission.

As both men climb into the back of the dark windowed limousine, Sir Max starts to play the game quickly.

"Mr. Ramsan, now that you have agreed to cooperate with the power of the coin, I must ask why you are now so willing to do so?"

Hank follows Sir Max's lead; "Well Sir Max, there are some things I can control and some I cannot. One of the things I want for my life is for Jocy to be free and for us to spend the rest of our lives together. This is of course assuming she wants that as well. I don't want to keep fighting with The Stiletto over this coin, when it may end my life in the process."

"Yes, but Mr. Ramsan," Sir Max now questioning Hank's reasoning, "my understanding is that you had some larger motivation in addition to the gold coin. What happens to that mission?"

Hank responding, "I can still do in part what I want to do without the coin, and without upsetting the apple cart of The Stiletto. It will just take me longer. But that's a good exchange for me considering the other options, which would be Jocy and me dead."

"Yes, I see your logic Mr. Ramsan. A smart choice on your part." Sir Max plays his role in agreement.

From the front seat, the driver asks over the intercom which entrance Sir Max would like to drive through. Sir Max answers, "just use the main underground entrance."

After parking, the driver walks around and opens the back door for Hank to first slide out as Sir Max follows. Hank is noticing the dismal atmosphere from no allowance of natural light.

Sir Max, his bodyguard, and Hank step onto an elevator that travels sideways instead of up. Hank has many questions about this under-ground manse he is approaching. Only, he knows it cannot appear that there is camaraderie going on between the two, so he keeps his silence.

The elevator door opens to a large dark foyer. Dark colored slate is the covering for both the floor and the walls of the foyer.

The bodyguard opens the large double doors to Sir Max's office, and they both walk inside. Hank looks around noticing all of the genuine artwork by the Masters. He wonders if they are stolen.

Sir Max interrupts his thoughts. "I guess you are wondering if these are originals and if so, are they stolen?"

"Well yes the thought did cross my mind." Hank shakes his head while responding.

Sir Max begins to tell Hank the history of the art on his walls.

"Well Mr. Ramsan, I have a deep appreciation for fine art and continue to study the history. I gladly pay for the privilege to give these pieces a home. The Stiletto pays me very well and it affords me to live among the finer things despite the environment of living underground."

"Excuse me Mr. Ramasn, but I need to check in with The Stiletto to see the procedure since you have agreed to cooperate in showing us how to implement the power of the coin."

Just as Sir Max, said the words, the phone on his desk rings.

"Excuse me Mr. Ramsan that is the private line from The Stiletto."

Sir Max walks over, answers, and simply listens. Showing no facial expression so that Hank can't pick up anything, Sir Max hangs up the phone.

"Mr. Ramsan, there has been a development in the United States with The Stiletto. I do not know the details, I only have my instructions."

"I am to give you the coin, and you are to leave immediately under safe guard by my men who will accompany you on my private plane. You are to arrive at the ranch in Massachusetts by two in the afternoon tomorrow, U.S. time; no later than two o'clock."

"And if I don't?" typical Hank Ramsan response in times like these.

"Then Jocy is dead," just as surely comes back Sir Max with the response.

Hank fully understanding the message replies, "I guess I have no choice then."

"It appears not Mr. Ramsan," continues Sir Max based on his newest instructions. "If you are ready, then let me get the coin from my safe and you can be on your way."

64

Sir Max leaves the room, and the body guard stays with Hank as The Stiletto would expect. The artwork and sculptures in the office alone Hank surmised were worth millions, many times over.

Sir Max re-enters the room. "Enjoying my collection Mr. Ramsan?"

"Well yes Sir Max, it is all quite amazing the worth you have on your walls alone."

"Living beneath the ground," Sir Max goes on to explain, "tends to make me want to spruce up the place a lot with the finer art world. Speaking of which your gold coin certainly represents itself as a Master Piece of sorts."

Sir Max walks over to where Hank is standing and lifts the small box, which is covered in jewels, toward him. He opens it so that it is facing Hank.

It's the coin looking back at him. "There is something about that coin, Sir Max," as Hank reaches into the box to pick it up.

"Do you not want to carry it in this fine box, Mr. Ramsan?" asks Sir Max.

As only Hank would respond even with a coin such as this, "Well no Sir Max, I like to travel light, so I'll just stick the coin in my pocket."

"Fine then Mr. Ramsan, let's get you on the plane back to the States. John here, will take you to my private hanger at Heathrow."

Extending his hand to shake with Sir Max, they both locked eyes with an understanding of their agreement, something that The Stiletto would not pick up on its surveillance equipment.

Hank assumed he would be back in the United States late morning New York time. He would need the time on the plane to get himself organized, but first he was looking forward to being in Heathrow for a few moments. He hadn't been in this magnificent airport since the last time he and Jocy were there.

It was nice for Hank to be alone in the limo except for John, the driver. He needed to catch his breath without feeling he had to be 'on.' His thought then wandered to the Christmas he and Jocy had spent in London, which was the last time he was in Heathrow. This would be a nice trip down memory lane for Hank before his trip back to the U.S.

The driver pulls up to the main terminal and tells Hank to walk to the private hanger area. He explains that Hank would see signs for it as he entered the terminal. If he got lost, the driver instructed him to just to ask for the hanger of Sir Max. According to the driver, everyone in London was aware of all of Sir Max's facilities.

"What? You don't have instructions to come with me to make sure I show up?" quips Hank back to John.

"No Mr. Ramsan. My instructions were to drop you off. It is assumed the nature of this meeting is enough to make sure you show up without you having to be guarded."

"Yes, I guess that's true," referring to Jocy, but John was referring to The Stiletto. Hank slides out of the car, steps up onto the side walk and enters the giant doors of Heathrow. He stands and looks around at the portals of the world this airport provides. Shaking himself loose from amazement he begins walking through the maze of people as he looks for the private hanger area of Sir Max.

Then over the intercom he hears: "Message for Mr. Hank Ramsan. Please check the main information booth on Concourse A."

Hank sees 'Concourse A' ahead about 100 feet, walks up to it and says he was paged for a message. The information officer says, "yes Mr. Ramsan, an envelope was just placed here for your arrival." The officer hands him the message.

Wanting a bit of privacy as he opens the note, Hank walks over to a side wall near a bank of phones. He opens the envelope and pulls out a white piece of paper and written in gold letters are these words:

Upon your meeting with The Stiletto, the coin will be charged with its full Radiance. Use it according to your wisdom as events arise. The note was signed *Maddy.*

No sooner had he read the words, they disappeared from the paper.

Trying to keep from the seriousness of what was ahead of him, Hank thought to himself, 'Ok, got it.' Turning to get his bearings he looks up and sees the signs to the private hangers. Hank begins his way toward them, as if almost in a daze. He walks briskly on, paying no attention to his surroundings. Despite his earlier desire to enjoy a few moments in Heathrow reflecting back on he and Jocy, the time was not for that now. All parts of him knew it.

Then he sees it, the sign: 'Sir Max.' One thing for sure he thought, Sir Max did enjoy the recognition! Hank smiled knowing that Sir Max was truly soon to be known as a great one.

Moving at a brisk pace toward the hanger, a man in a light-colored casual suit walks toward Hank as if he were going to greet him. "Mr. Ramsan, I am here to escort you for approximately the next eight hours," says the man.

At first, the phrase that this escort used didn't register with Hank, then all of a sudden he realized the words, *I Am,* and *eight*, were used by this new escort in a sentence. Hank still didn't understand it all, but at least he knew he was in good company.

The attendant shows Hank on board the plane and settles him in his seat. Hank loved these smaller jets. They were comfortable to fly in and he had lots of room. Speaking of room, it then occurred to him that his duffel bag was back at the Vista International.

Just as Hank remembered about his luggage, the attendant walks back to his seat and is carrying what looks like Hanks duffel bag!

The attendant politely tells Hank, "Mr. Ramsan, this was just delivered by The Vista. Someone there felt you might like to have it." Hank bewildered, just shakes his head and thanks the attendant, then puts the duffel bag on the seat next to him.

The fasten seat belt lights go on, and Hank chooses to take advantage of his duffel bag being there and reaches in and pulls out his clipboard.

"Ah, magic clipboard, speak to me," Hank said in a whisper.

Hank concludes that now is the time for him to get very clear on the power of the coin and his particular association with it. He begins to outline the power of the coin.

65

Beginning at the top of the page, Hank writes:

The Power of the Gold Coin: The Epigram.

Continuing with pen and paper these words flow to Hank and onto the page in the form of an outline:

I. What does the gold coin do?

The gold coin cannot do anything unless The Epigram is invoked with it.

II. What is The Epigram?

The Epigram is a statement made, beginning with a fiat. The fiat for use with the epigram is: I AM.

The words 'I AM' are written symbolically on one side of the coin in raised gold letters. The phrase, 'The Epigram' is written along the edge and a symbol of a sideways figure eight intertwines the symbol.

The understanding and combination of these words and symbols brings power and momentum to anyone holding the coin as they repeat the Epigram three times.

The Epigram statement is a desire or intention to be manifested. This combination works, period. It therefore can be used for both constructive and non-constructive elements, giving the intended end result perfectly.

The outline that Hank had just written would be what he gives to The Stiletto. However, there was a piece missing from what Hank had written. The Stiletto wouldn't know this piece was missing. The most powerful use of the coin and its stated epigram would only come to perfect fruition by someone who fully understood and applied the mechanics behind the words, *I Am.* The Stiletto would have no idea of this information.

In addition, the power would only be able to be applied by someone who had begun to build a bridge of higher vibrational frequencies between the human and divine self.

Hank had reached this level of bridge building. Therefore, he had more power in using the coin than The Stiletto, or anyone associated with them would have. The very Masters who precipitated the coin into existence set a safety mechanism in place. It could not be used against humanity. The mechanism simply would not allow for it.

Giving a surface definition of the figure eight would be done if The Stiletto pushed Hank to do so. Otherwise, Hank understood the figure eight symbol would be withheld from The Stiletto thereby affecting its use of the power. The safety mechanism was built into the *Figure 8.*

Hank knew those were two aces up his sleeve. If The Stiletto had him killed, and they retain the coin, they would still be missing the primary power of activation. They would not know the full use and understanding and the application of the power of the, *I Am.*

The current level of information on the paper outline would at some point backfire due to the destructive intent by The Stiletto, versus constructive intent by someone such as Hank Ramsan.

Drifting into the early morning hours, the flight continued over the ocean. Hank folded the outline, put it in his back lucky left pocket, and put the clipboard back into his duffel bag. Settling back and getting some sleep was next on Hank's agenda and he dozed off into a restful nap.

While Hank was outlining the epigram and napping, Alex had made his way back to the ranch. The helicopter was setting down on the same helio pad that he, Jocy, and Hank had all landed days earlier. Looking down Alex saw a female figure standing near the landing. It was getting dark so he couldn't recognize who it was. He knew someone was to take Jocy's place but he didn't know who exactly.

The helicopter runners set down, and Alex jumps out. A female hand helps him as he gets steady from the wind. Alex is guided away from the swirling air as the chopper lifts off the pad.

In a welcoming voice Alex hears, "Hello Alex, I am sure you know of me, I am Jenny and I arrived here about eight hours ago." This was a quick signal to Alex that Jenny was sent to help see things through to a favorable outcome.

"Hi, Jenny, yes, I've heard your name mentioned briefly in the company of Talal Halalad. We only have a short way before our conversations are picked up by the surveillance equipment."

Jenny responds her awareness of the circumstances. "Yes, I know, so I have to talk quickly."

Jenny begins filling Alex in on her understanding from events based on what The Stiletto has told her.

"Alex, I'll tell you what I've been told by The Stiletto and then I'll tell you what I know in addition to that." Jenny continues talking very fast.

"The Stiletto will arrive here around one o'clock this afternoon. Then following at two, Hank is to show, then at three p.m. the person who has been holding up the shipment, will arrive."

Alex interrupts Jenny. "What do you know about the Swords showing up, Jenny? When I left the ship, I was in the middle of finding out about them and received a message from The Box to get back to the ranch. Those of course were my instructions, with no explanation."

"Alex, some kind of a deal was made is all that I know. Something about the swords would show up only if The Box came in person to collect them. Apparently, that is exactly what is going to happen."

"Alex, things will be happening very fast," continues Jenny. "Hank is bringing the coin, the Swords will be here, and The Stiletto, in his person will be here. The Stiletto is thinking this moment is his, we have to make sure that it is not."

"I am sure The Stiletto will not be showing up without taking some harsh precautionary measures. Therefore, we must be on our toes every single moment. As far as The Stiletto are concerned, they think you and I are loyal to them, so we have that in our favor."

Just as Jenny finishes that sentence, they reach the full surveillance area and they both know their conversation and demeanor must change instantly and does.

Jenny switches to Stiletto employee by saying: "Alex, I have instructions to clear two separate wings of the ranch. One for the two p.m. meeting and one for the three p.m. meeting. We are to have a minimum of five guards in each wing, fully armed. Can you take care of what's called the West Wing, and I'll take care of the East Wing?"

Shaking his head in agreement, Alex responds, "yes, of course, Jenny; do you know what other precautions are being taken?"

"No Alex," answers Jenny. "I was only given instructions to secure all of the horses away from the stables, so that is going on now, as well as securing the ranch house. I don't even know if The Stiletto is arriving by land or air. I guess we'll find out when he gets here."

"Alex, there's one more thing. Due to the nature of who The Stiletto actually is, you and I are to make an announcement to all arriving, that under no circumstance is the real name of The Box, The Stiletto to be spoken. If anyone even breathes his name, The Stiletto has ordered the guards to shoot and kill the individual instantly. Please be sure all in your wing are aware of this instruction."

"Ok, that's one I'll not forget, even for myself." Alex muses under his breath.

Glancing at his watch, Alex sees that it is it's almost four a.m.. He tells Jenny he's going to get some sleep in his office barracks and will meet her at nine the next morning to coordinate further. Jenny agrees she'll do the same, as everyone needs to be well rested for the events of the coming hours.

66

Events are being put into place that neither Jenny, Alex nor Hank are aware of, to ensure the success of the meetings. However, it is both sides that are playing things close to the vest and not letting many in on what is coming up next.

Maddy, Talal and Powers have been working earnestly on their end, as well as The Stiletto has been active in their world. This moment is do or die for The Stiletto. The Box doesn't care who has to die in order for him to have what he's wanted for such a long time. He won't miss this opportunity for world power. The Stiletto has world power in the financial markets and anticipates more with supernatural tools. It is with this belief of power that comes with the coin and the swords that The Stiletto will rule the world and all of its activity.

While Hank is in the air and Alex and Jenny are sleeping, the wide-awake Stiletto are making plans to ensure that they won't be taken by surprise. Their plan is to have the coin in their possession after taking it from Hank at the two p.m. meeting, and then using it to secure *The Sword of Three's* in the three p.m. meeting. This would assure them a smooth transition of ownership.

Leaving no rocks unturned and ensuring that they get the coin from Hank with no problems, The Stiletto is bringing Jocy along for the ride with them. They will threaten her in front of Hank to guarantee he do their bidding. The Stiletto has covered all bases for success with backup plans upon back up plans.

Jocy doesn't have a clue as to what's going on or going to transpire. She's been a prisoner in the secure apartment of The

Stiletto's main headquarters, only being told to be ready to leave for the ranch at noon.

The Box left instructions for 20 of his best big guys to meet in the large dining room of the main Stiletto headquarters at eight a.m. sharp. This meeting of big guy instructions was taking place as Hank's plane began circling the airport to land outside of New York City.

During this meeting, The Stiletto's men were instructed to carry to the ranch, rapid-fire pistols and were to wear chest protectors. One of the big guys was an explosives expert. He was instructed, once they landed at the ranch, to make a stick of dynamite out of Jocy. The Box would be holding the detonator to Jocy during the meeting with Hank. This was to be ready and set with Jocy by 1:30 that afternoon.

The Box went on to tell the big guys that if this project failed to do what The Stiletto intended, then not only would he torture and kill these 20 big guys, but he would also see that all of their immediate families were tormented and killed as well. The Box wanted this done, and no lives would be spared to see that it happened his way. Instructions clearly given, The Stiletto dismissed his men to get ready for departure on four armed helicopters.

Not far away, Hank's plane was landing. The seat belt sign had just flashed above the cabin as the attendant walked back to inform Hank that they would be landing in about 10 minutes.

Hank wanted to know, "where are we landing exactly?"

"Mr. Ramsan, as an employee of The Stiletto," answers the attendant, "I am not at liberty to tell you anything about the next eight hours."

All Hank could get from that answer and its coded message, is that this attendant was around just in case something went wrong. This helped Hank feel a bit more secure as he understood the attendant had to protect his role.

Hank simply said, "well I guess I can wait 10 minutes to find out."

"Yes, thank you Mr. Ramsan," responded the polite attendant, "and now if you will buckle your safety belt for our landing, we are soon making our approach. Also, Mr. Ramsan, there will be a car waiting to take you to your next destination."

Hank didn't know for sure what that meant, since he didn't know where he was landing. Was this car going to take him to the ranch or was there another stop or helicopter ride? He would have to wait and find out. It was his only option under the circumstances.

Finally the plane gently sets down and taxi's swiftly toward a hanger, seemingly in the middle of nowhere. The wheels stop, and the attendant opens the door and pushes the stairway outward. Hank has already started up the aisle with his duffle bag in hand. He and the attendant exchange only a nod of goodbye to one another. Down the steps Hank goes, not knowing what or who is next.

Making his way to the open door of the hanger, Hank notices a dark blue limousine and the driver's side door begins to open.

Someone steps out, apparently a man who then signals Hank to come to the car. Suddenly Hank recognizes the man, it's Talal! He almost blurts out his name, until he sees Talal put his index finger over his lips telling him not to speak.

Talal signals Hank to follow him behind the building and then tells him; "Hank listen carefully. The driver of the limo is a Stiletto, but he is napping thanks to a quick trick on my part, but he will wake soon, thinking he just dozed off. He will wake up when you tap on the window asking if he is your ride to the ranch. You are about an hour away by car. Your meeting is set for two p.m. but you will arrive about noon, before The Stiletto gets there. Alex and Jenny are already there."

Talal continues briefing Hank. "You will have to act as you understand Alex and Jenny are Stiletto employees. Much of what is to take place after you arrive at the ranch will be up to you and your instinct. It will come down to what you have learned along the way including your use of the coin. You will have to pay very close attention to every thing going on around you in order to save and change many lives. Further supernatural gifts can only be used under certain conditions, and we hope that those conditions do not present themselves or else it will upset a balance that I haven't the time to explain."

"What I am trying to tell you Hank, is that this is up to you to do. You are ready, do you understand?"

"Yes, I understand Talal," was all Hank could say.

Hank wasn't quite sure what it was he understood he just knew he would do what was needed at the right time. He knew it as well as he knew his name was Hank Ramsan.

It was time for things to move forward and Talal put Hank in motion by suggesting he get on the road to the ranch. "Ok, Hank, it's time for you to wake your driver friend up and be on your way."

The two friends shook hands and Hank turned toward the car. He stopped and turned back to say something to Talal, but he had vanished.

Hank walks up to the driver's side of the car and knocks on the tinted glass. The window slowly comes down as the driver pulls himself up from laying down position. Hank says, "I'm Hank Ramsan, are you my ride?"

The driver, still a bit groggy responds, "yes, Mr. Ramsan, I must have dozed off waiting. Please help yourself to the back seat and we'll be on our way."

Hank walks around and gets in the passenger's side of the back seat. He prefers not to set directly behind the driver in case he could have a conversation, but as usual, as they start and Hank asked the driver a question, he got the usual response from The Stiletto's driver; "My only instructions are to drive you to the ranch. It's about an hour away, Mr. Ramsan."

67

Midmorning New York time has arrived. The Stiletto's big fellows are packing up the helicopters while The Box is on the telephone with his partner in Japan. Japan is an important financial market to The Stiletto. So important is Japan, that The Box has been keeping this part of the world, which is also under his control, informed as to what has been happening all along.

The end of this day would be of extreme benefit to The Stiletto and its organization throughout the world. The Box has made many deep and far reaching promises to assure the continued cooperation from those with their fingers on the pulse of wealth.

The partner in Japan, was not of Japanese origin but was placed there many years ago by the visionary organizer of The Stiletto. Only The Box knew the identity of the counterpart. No one else within The Stiletto organization knew of this partner or even that one existed.

Once The Box held what he perceived that the *power of the coin* and *The Swords of Three's* would give him, his next goal for total power, would be to control all of the world's governments. With this control, he would have full run of worldwide resources, as well as governing jurisdiction over all peoples. He would own the world, which was his plan from the beginning. The Box distinctly wanted not only to rule the world, but also to *own* it.

With so much at stake nothing would be compromised. He was gloating over this next step in discussion with his Japanese partner. To own the world, no one had ever really owned the

world. Not literally. However, The Box using the organization o
The Stiletto was about to do just that.

In a matter of a few hours, The Box would own the world. Within those same hours, things were being put in place to assure that means to The Stiletto's end.

The Box checked in with helicopter pilots on their readiness. "We are ready to leave now," was the response. He makes another phone call to the big guy in charge of getting Jocy to one of the helicopters. "We are moving her now," came the answer. Then the check in with the expert dynamite builder, "all is aboard and ready to make a stick of dynamite out of the young lady." Everything smooth as clockwork, and The Box was satisfied.

Feeling all was in readiness, The Box makes the last call to Alex at the ranch. "Alex, are the wings set up for our arrival?"

"Yes," replies Alex, "and the horses have also been moved."

"Fine Alex, we are leaving within the next 30 minutes." The Box sensing the readiness of all systems. "We will be there shortly before one this afternoon. The Box hangs up.

Alex was in Jenny's office when he took the call from The Stiletto. After hanging up, he turns to Jenny to let her know they will all be arriving a bit prior to one o'clock. They both look at one another knowing they cannot comment.

Hank will arrive at the ranch about the same time as The Stiletto. The ride is very quiet for Hank, and he doesn't feel like talking.

of the ranch." Hank folds his portable magic wall and sticks it in his right front pocket.

68

Arriving 30 minutes before The Stiletto is due to show, the car in which Hank is being delivered makes its way up the driveway to the ranch house. Alex walks out from the house to the spacious drive, knowing that Hank is the passenger. Opening the back seat door for Hank to slide out, he wanted to give Hank some sense of comfort, despite the circumstances.

"Mr. Ramsan, I've been instructed to take you to the west wing, and secure you in the conference room. The Stiletto will conduct his meeting with you in the conference room.

Alex and Hank look at one another other as friends and brothers, but cannot exchange any words as to not bring any attention to their true affiliation.

Accompanying Alex into the main lobby of the house, Hank notices a female figure and then recognizes Jenny. He starts to blurt out her name, until Alex pretends to accidentally step on Hank's foot, bringing him back to understanding that shouting Jenny's name would not be a good thing to do! He's glad to see her, for more than one reason. The fact that she is there gives Hank further comfort in having his own troops to help in some way, if needed.

The three of them stand in the hallway in silence. Alex quickly introduced Hank to Jenny in the event any of the conversation is picked up, as he didn't want the silence to appear conspicuous. They hear the four helicopters loudly over head and Alex nudged Hank; "We need to move you to the west wing, Mr. Ramsan."

Alex guides Hank down the west wing hall to the conference room, while Jenny moves over to the large picture window and looks for the helicopters. It appears like an invasion. All four helicopters are dark and menacing looking with some kind of gun barrels fastened to their sides. Jenny watches as they land near the horse stables, and all of the occupants appear to be going into the one of the stables. Jenny notices a female also being walked in with two big guys at her sides, she assumes this is Jocy.

The office phone rings as Jenny is peering out the window. It's the exclusive Stiletto line. Jenny answers, it's The Box. "Is Mr. Ramsan secured in the west wing conference room?"

"Yes," was Jenny's reply. Then click, The Box hung up.

The same moment that Jenny had laid down the receiver, Alex walks into her office. "That was The Box checking to see if Hank was in the conference room."

"Ok," Alex uttered under his breath. He was very nervous.

The two of them stand there not knowing what to do or say in this important and dangerous moment. Again, The Stiletto line rings. "Have Alex open the end doors to the west wing, we are coming in now."

Jenny hangs up. "Alex, they are coming in now for the meeting with Hank. You are to go and open the wide doors at the end of the west wing."

Alex turns to go without saying a word. He is nervous and doesn't have a clue as to what's next. He passes the large mahogany closed office doors where Hank is located, and walks the 20 feet toward the end of the wing doors. Alex opens both doors inward, as he does he looks up and fright fills his mind.

The first three people he sees are Jocy flanked by two big guys. The fright was Jocy was covered in sticks of dynamite. Jocy is escorted closer to him and begins to pass him. They both look at one another and Alex is choking back tears. This is his sister and his friend. This was a human stick of dynamite. All of Alex's thoughts went to the human side of the moment. He is a praying man; he began a silent huge prayer.

Following behind Jocy about 10 feet was a small stature of a man, with a heavy brimmed hat and a large scarf around his face. This was to disguise The Box until the last minute, is what Alex was assuming. Four very large big guys flanked the disguised Box with chest protectors and pistols already out and in their hands in ready position.

Alex quickly moved to the side and out of the way. He could feel the tenseness of the moment. It was very heavy and thick.

Everyone was in the hall. The doors had not yet been opened to the conference room where Hank was waiting. Jocy was placed at the front of the door. It was apparent to Alex that Jocy would be the first one in, and the first thing that Hank would see.

This for sure would throw Hank for a loop and send him off balance, which is what The Box would want for that moment. The Box still in his disguise was standing about 5 feet behind Jocy. All of a sudden the signal in the form of a nod was given, and two of the big guys opened the doors inward.

Alex couldn't see. In that moment there was deafening silence.

No one was moving or speaking. Alex as quiet as he could moved over about 4 feet holding his breath that he would not be heard. He wanted to see what was happening.

As he lifted his eyes from his position, his heart stopped beating at what he saw.

The tallest most beautiful blonde creature of a woman he had ever laid his eyes upon was standing next to Hank. It was Maddy. She had a large, long barreled handgun pointed right at Hank's head. The barrel was dug into his head and her finger on the trigger. Dressed in white and blue, an iridescent white and blue, this tall blonde seemingly dangerous woman was more beautiful in Alex's mind than a princess. She was glistening beautiful and in this moment, she was also deadly.

No one spoke.

69

The silence was finally broken with these words from the blonde gun bearer still pointing at Hank's head: "I Am Maddy. I am your three p.m. appointment. I have chosen to arrive early so that I would not be surprised in a fashion that would be detrimental to me, or my investors."

"There is much at stake here Mr. Box, I'll thank you to have your men drop their weapons from where they stand. If they do not or any shot is fired, Mr. Ramsan dies first. If you look around, my associates surround you all. Please have your men step away from you."

As they step away, Maddy and Hank both see that Mr. Box is holding the detonator to the dynamite connected to Jocy.

"Now it's my turn to play as you say, 'Maddy.'" The Box voicing his control. "My finger is holding the pressure point on this detonator to Jocy. If I fall, or take my finger from this button, Jocy blows up and all within this room, and the largest part of this ranch, goes with her."

Maddy responds, "It seems we may have a stand-off Mr. Box. However, it also seems you would not want all of your plans and work to go to waste. I am only here to protect my investment regarding *The Sword of Three's* and where they go."

"My understanding from Mr. Ramsan is that he has something you want, but he is the only one with the instructions on how to activate the coin. If he is dead, you miss that. If I am dead, then you don't get the swords, and you would be dead anyway from the same dynamite. It seems there would be a more workable solution."

Hank has an idea. "If I may speak, I may have a solution that just might make everyone calm at least."

The Box speaks first. "Go ahead Mr. Ramsan."

"My understanding is this," continues Hank. "Maddy won't release the swords until she sees and knows who you are, Mr. Box. That was part of your deal, which I assume Maddy will honor. And you Mr. Box want the instructions for activating the coin, of which I agreed to, if you would free Jocy. I'm not interested in either Jocy or myself dead. It defeats my purpose for making the deal with you."

"Since our meeting was set up first, I will honor my end of the deal. You release Jocy, and I will give you the instructions of the coin. At the same time, you honor your end of the transaction with Maddy by uncovering your face, so that she knows who you really are. Otherwise, you could leave here with the instructions to the power of the coin, but not have *The Sword of Three's*. You would lose all of your investors of which Maddy has strong connections all over the world. Both your art and horse businesses which are lucrative to you in money and contacts, would be lost forever."

The Box speaks; "Mr. Ramsan that sounds good on the surface, but how do I know you will give me the instructions to the coin, after I remove the dynamite from Jocy and uncover who I am?"

Quickly Hank answers, "Because I lost Jocy once before due to you and your organization. In this moment, she is all I care about. It's how you set it up to happen, Mr. Box. You wanted the issue of the coin to come down to my care for her. Here is the moment as you designed it. The instructions to the coin, for Jocy's life."

"Yes, you are correct Mr. Ramsan, it has happened exactly as I have planned it." The Box speaks in agreement.

The Box signals the big guys who covered Jocy in dynamite to untie her and release the wire to the detonator button that The Box was holding. Everyone holding their breath as one wire was unhooked and The Box releases his finger from the button. There was no explosion, and everyone in the room was grateful at the same time and on the same side. That however, changed quickly back to the triangle of The Box, Hank, and Maddy.

The room stood in silence as the next thing to happen was for The Box to reveal his face. Alex was still out in the hall not believing all that he had just experienced and the moment was bringing more, as The Box would uncover his face.

Hank stands relieved that Jocy is no longer a human bomb but also is waiting to see who The Stiletto really is. The one who had controlled all of the world's financial markets, the one who until this moment, no one knew the identity of the person behind The Stiletto.

The Box lifts the hat and the scarf at the same moment. You could have heard a pin drop. It was a woman!

While everyone except Maddy is standing in awe of the moment, The Box next reaches behind 'her' collar and removes something from around her neck. As she speaks, she has a normal female voice. Apparently a man-made voice box placed around her neck distorted her voice to make it sound like a man, or simply it was not easily deciphered as a woman, therefore it was always assumed it was a man.

This woman was no one that anyone would know. The Box spoke. "I'll give you a brief explanation, and then I'll ask that we move onto you holding up your end of the transaction."

"Never mind my personal reasons behind this," The Box begins, "I chose to control the world money systems, and I had to find a way to get close to the men that pulled the strings. As I did that, I got my way, so to speak. All of these men were well known and had much to lose if others would find out about our liaisons."

"I used that power to seize more and more control in high places, and of course, along the way my own life was threatened. With each whisper of a threat to me, I immediately brought harm to that one's life. It then quickly became known not to mess with or threaten or stand in my way."

"And now we are here, and this is the moment I take it all. I have kept my end of the bargain in regard to both of you. Now may we proceed to your handing over the instructions for the coin?" The Box had completed her overview.

70

Hank answers The Box. "Well, if this Maddy person will take the gun from my head, I can hand it to you. The coin is in my left front pocket, and the instructions are written in my back left pocket."

Maddy slowly lifts the gun away from Hank's head. Hank first reaches into his left front pocket and pulls out the gold coin. He shifts to puts the gold coin in his right hand. Reaching into his back left pocket he pulls out the folded piece of paper with the instructions written on it.

With the coin, now in Hank's left hand along with the piece of paper, he extends his palm forward to hand both pieces to The Box.

The Box takes it from Hank and looks at both the front and back of the coin. All in the room are standing still and watching as The Box opens up the paper and begins reading the instructions.

The Box reads the instructions silently to herself. Her next step, which was also planned, was to use the coin to take control of the room and all within it, now including Maddy.

Feeling she has the instructions understood in order to be able to use its power, The Box lifts the coin clasping it tightly. Out of her mouth and with a grin full of venom, she repeats loudly, three times: "I Am the ruler of this room! I am the ruler of this room! I Am the ruler this room!"

Suddenly, The Box collapsed, dropping like lead weight to the floor.

No one moved.

Alex saw what happened, and still acting as a faithful Stiletto employee rushed into the room, and bent down to check her pulse. "She's dead."

None of The Stiletto's big guys knew what to do. Most of them always did only what they were told to do, and nothing else. Since The Box was dead, they didn't know how to act.

Alex took charge, acting still as The Stiletto employee. "Gentleman," he said, "due to this untimely death of The Box, we all are without an employer. I suggest you go back to The Stiletto headquarters and find out where you stand with accounting and payroll. I will contact the accounting department about a healthy severance for each of you for your honorable service to The Stiletto. Please leave your guns here as you go."

After Alex's remarks, no questions were asked as all 20 of the big guys filed out of the room to get back to the helicopters. Some of them thanked Alex for taking care of things.

As the last big guy left the room, Alex closes the large conference room doors, and falls back on them with a sigh; "Boy that was a close one!" They all laugh, as they were all glad to still be alive.

Then there is a light knock on the door, Alex opens it slowly, and it's Jenny. In a perky quip she says, "so, seems the guys in white won?" This again broke the tension.

Jocy turns to Hank. "Hank, who is Maddy?"

Hank steps aside to make a proper introduction, but there is no Maddy. She had vanished.

Just as Hank tries to find the words for answering Jocy, Jenny walks over and introduces herself.

"Hello Jocy, I'm Jenny, and I was sent to replace you by The Stiletto, but in all actually, it was Maddy who arranged it all."

Jenny, almost as if to assist in making everyone comfortable begins to explain how she and Hank met in New York City. She tells the story that he tried to pick her up in a bar. Everyone agrees that yes, Hank would try to do that!

Jenny reaches down and takes the paper and coin that were being clinched tightly in the now dead hand of The Box.

Jocy wants to know what happened and asked for anyone knowing to answer. "Why did the use of the coin and instructions kill The Box, instantly?"

Offering an explanation Hank begins; "Jocy, the power of the coin can only be used for constructive purposes. The Box with her very powerful epigram statements did carry power with her use of what she was invoking. However, I left out two very important pieces of information. Anyone holding the coin, and invoking a decree of harm to others, then the power instantly boomerangs back on the one invoking."

Jocy full of questions says, "yes but I thought the power of the coin could be used for positive and negative forces."

"Yes, that's true," Hank goes on to say, "but the very reason for Maddy being here with me, had to do with that one moment. We knew that The Box would attempt to use the coin against us."

"Both Maddy and I have built a bridge of sorts between our human and divine natures. Maddy of course has built her bridge and mine is still under construction."

"But the point is, The Box had none of that vibration bridge building action going on. And when she tried to influence our vibratory rate coming from such a dense lower place within her self, the power in front of her, between Maddy and me simply shot back and canceled her out, so to speak. It's like a 3-legged stool. It needs all three legs of the same strength to hold the seat up to do what it wants. The box didn't have another leg to stand on, so it fell."

"Ok, I think I understand part of this, and I am so glad to be alive, and free!" Jocy responds and then another question. "But I have to ask. What is next? I mean here is this great ranch and horses, and all of that art work?" Alex interrupts, "yes, and the freightliner is still held up."

Jenny offers an answer; "Well, if Alex can make arrangements to take care of this body in a discrete way, then I'll have the cook fix us an early dinner. I may have some information on the 'next' that you would be interested in, and we can discuss it then."

They all agree to meet in an hour, and in the mean time, Hank wants a few moments alone with Jocy.

71

Jenny and Alex walk out the door together, and Hank grabs Jocy's hand and whispers, "come on, lets go." Hank is pulling her by the hand, and she's most willing to be pulled by this man, she knows what he is doing. He has pulled her by her hand many times in their past days together.

Hank peeks in various rooms, not finding one to his satisfaction. Then he finds one, and he pulls Jocy in with him and closes the door. He turns to her, picks her up, and cradles her in his arms as if he were carrying her over a threshold. He gently lays her down on the bed.

Leaning on his elbow, he just stares at her. He can't take his eyes off of this girl. Looking back at him, Jocy's says, "after all of that blonde boy, aren't you at least going to kiss me?"

There it is, that big blonde smile, that happy boy smile that melts Jocy in a moment. She closes her eyes, and she feels his soft lips on her upper lip. He always went for that upper lip of hers. Then he moved his mouth down over her lower lip. This only made her want him in her mouth more. She loved the way he kissed her.

Moving his warm tongue up under her upper lip sent her over, and Jocy was a 'goner.' Then with his full mouth over hers, they stayed spell bound within each other and nothing else on heaven or earth existed in those moments. Nothing except the two of them and the love and sweet adoration they had for each other.

They didn't talk about the future or the present. They just wanted to feel one another from the depths of themselves. That's all and only what they both wanted. But with a knock on the door from Alex, they realized others seemed to want them as well.

Through the door they heard Alex, "Ok you two, soups on! We've got things to get to, hurry up, come on!" Hank is laughing because he knows Alex won't shut-up 'til he answers. "Ok Alex, five minutes and we are there!"

Hank turns to Jocy and says, "don't ever leave me again, deal?" Jocy returns, "deal." Hank pulls her up and they begin their way to the kitchen area.

Jenny and Alex are already seated and look up at two beautiful smiling faces entering the room. Jenny and Alex look over at one another and roll their eyes.

Pulling her chair out, Jocy begins to set down, looking over at Jenny saying, "now what was this about Hank picking you up in a bar?"

Jenny amusingly answers, "well you know Jocy that blonde smile of his can turn a girl's head!" Jocy agrees and they all chide Hank about his affection for women.

Trying to save himself Hank says, "ok you people, don't we have something a little more to discuss than my weakness for women?"

Hank notices there's a fifth place setting on the table and asks, "hey Jenny, can I guess who's coming to dinner?"

"And your guess would be me?" comes from a voice entering the room and it's Talal. Hank gets up and hugs his good friend, and he is very glad to see him.

Hank introduces him to Jocy, and Talal in is his usual polite gentlemanly self takes Jocy's hand.

Talal pulls his chair up to the table as the cook brings in layers of freshly oven-roasted turkey and a huge jar of Hank's favorite mayonnaise. Hank knew the coffee and iced tea couldn't be far behind. "It's really great you all cater to my needs so well!"

"Yes, or you wouldn't cease about what you needed!" jokes Alex, as he grabs the breadbasket first before Hank can get to it.

"Ok people," Talal begins, "here's the new plan, now that The Stiletto is out of the way. The markets will appear confused because no one is pulling the strings. However, the men overseeing the various financial instruments around the world will reorganize events and the confusion will subside. The good news is the banking system and the way the world sees money, including dissolving the money band around the earth, will only be remedied as Hank introduces his Magic Wall. The momentum to spreading *The Magic Wall* and its power will be given as Hank uses the power of the coin."

"Here it is in the larger picture of things." Talal continues the next stage. "Hank will begin introducing his Magic Wall in his home base city of Charlottesville, Virginia. Jocy will begin to move the horse farm and art work business to Charlottesville. This will meet with Hank's intention set of he and Jocy living and working together from Charlottesville. Does that work for you two?" Tal glances over at Hank and Jocy.

They both just smile.

"Alex, the freightliner has been released, so you have to oversee the horses and paintings from this shipment. *The Sword of Three's* are back with Maddy."

"Jenny goes back to New York City and her work with Lance Powers, but she will also be a liaison for the two of you." Tal nods to Hank and Jocy. "You both have some big operations expanding, and Jenny can coordinate much of it, with Lance and David."

Hank interrupts with one of a million questions swirling his mind. "Great Talal, where will you and Alex be operating from?"

Tal continues his organized answer. "Alex will help Jocy move the ranch operations to Charlottesville, then he is free to work and live from there as well, if that is his desire." Talal looks at him, knowing that yes, Alex would very much enjoy Charlottesville with Jocy and Hank.

"And you Talal, where will you be?" Hank asks.

"Hank, you know I always show up, but for now, let's just say, I'll be between Powers One and Charlottesville. Just give me my own room to come home to! Deal?"

"Deal!" Hank agrees enthusiastically.

Continuing to keep the conversation on course, Talal looks directly at Hank. "Hank, I know you've been through a lot, but we have to get you back on track with your overall mission of *The Magic Wall*. Are you ready to begin showing how it works to others?"

"Sure, I am!" replies Hank, "and just to show you, take a look at this!" Hank pulls out *The Magic Wall* he drew when he was being driven to the ranch this last time. This of course was his portable Magic Wall depicting how things would turn out during the ranch meeting. Sure enough, The Stiletto no longer existed.

"Ok good Hank," as Tal studies his crumpled Magic Wall, "because your first opportunity will be coming up in about two weeks in Charlottesville."

"How is that going to happen Talal?" queries Hank.

"Well," Tal begins, "one of your books has begun taking on a life of its own. Within that book, as in many of your writings you mention *The Magic Wall,* and people quite simply are starting to talk about it more and more as they see the success of it in their own lives as well as that of others."

"Your first public appearance will come from a local celebrity that will set up the opportunity. The celebrity name will draw the people to the function, but you are to be the main attraction with your Magic Wall. Then from there it just steam rolls around the world, from person to person, and email to email."

"This then changes the need for the financial systems as they are now functioning. They will have to change to serve better. And they will serve, and not dictate, which is what it has now become."

Hank never without the next question, "Talal, how was all of this set up?"

Tal looks at Hank and says one word, "Maddy."

Alex beaming at all that is transpiring, reaches over to pour everyone a glass of champagne, and offers a toast to the future!

72

Everyone seemed satisfied from the early dinner and Tal begins getting people moving again. He asks Jocy if she would travel with Alex to the freightliner to help supervise the unloading of the goods. Since things had changed hands a bit, Tal thought it might be a good idea. Jocy agreed.

Turning to Hank, Tal says, "Hank, I know you and Jocy want to be reunited but there are some things we have to do before you begin your Magic Wall activities. One of them is to move you from your loft. You have an appointment at 11 in the morning, with an agent to show you some farms in Virginia. In order for you to get some rest and gather some things we have a plane ready for you to leave at seven this evening, putting you in Charlottesville around 10 tonight."

"That's fine Tal," Hank being flexible, "Jocy and I have the rest of our lives together and this must be done. I'll be ready on time."

Jocy interjects, "Just don't buy any horse farm without me taking a looky see Mr. Ramsan. You don't know squat about horses!"

Hank comes back with, "Jocy you know that's not it, you want to make sure the kitchen is the right color, since you like spending so much time in it! Or should I say need to spend more time in it?"

With that comment, Jocy and Jenny just look at one another, and Hank looks over to Alex and asks him if 'he won that one or not?'

Alex tells him straight out. "Hank you already won big time with Jocy, don't push your luck! Take the defeat in stride." Hank concedes that yes, Alex is right.

Tal needing to make sure Hank makes the flight says, "Hank you might want to gather your things soon. We will be taking the helicopter I flew in on to the airport. It's scheduled to leave here in about 30 minutes."

Jocy turning to Alex. "Alex, if I remember correctly there were four Friesian Stallions being shipped in this shipment. They've been held in tight quarters for days on that ship. We need to get them here as soon as possible and getting them feeling their oats again before we give them up for the investors."

"You're right Jocy," agrees Alex, "but I do know that Capt. Halvik is a horse lover himself, and he will have done his best to care for them under the constricting conditions. I'll have two of the grooms drive the large trailer and we'll get them all in one trip."

Jenny pipes in; "Ok, then Jocy unless you object, while you're gone, I'll see that the other horses that were kept away from the stables find their way back home. Then I'll head back to New York when you and Alex return."

"That will be great Jenny, thanks." replies Jocy in kind.

"Good then. It sounds like everyone knows what they have to do. Hank 30 minutes?" Tal looks over at Hank.

"Yes Talal, I'll be ready. Will you be going with me on this trip to Charlottesville?"

"No Hank, we will part company after the helicopter drops us off at the hanger area. I have to get back to New York for a few days, but I'll be in touch. And you have my cell number, right?"

"Yes. I do," Hank smiling, "426."

Hank leans over kissing Jocy on the cheek to say goodbye, and that he would call her. The two women who now were becoming fast friends, just smiled at the familiar, "I'll call you."

Hank says, "What?"

They all get up to go along their way as Jenny says loud enough for all to hear; "Jocy per usual I guess we are stuck with the dishes!"

Alex offers quickly, "no girls, I who am Alex, shall provide my own stud services for help in the kitchen!"

"Great Alex, thanks, because since all of the kitchen help except one was a Stiletto employee, I'd just feel better if we started from scratch on new personnel." Jocy already was planning the new staff with her comment.

Both Jenny and Jocy agreed on that note and the three of them moved onto the kitchen with hands full of dishes.

Hank needs his duffel bag, which is in the conference room, the room where everything crested in one moment. He excuses himself to retrieve it. Alex follows and enters the room soon behind him.

"Thank you for doing your part in this Hank, so that it turned out the way it did."

Aware that it wasn't only he who played a role, Hank tells Alex, "Alex, you know it was a team effort, I couldn't have gotten any of my part done without you and Talal all along the way."

"Yes I know, Talal is a special breed of individual." They both looked at each other knowing that what Alex said in reference to Tal, really meant more under the surface, but both knew the time was too short to get into it.

Hank looks around the room while asking, "by the way Alex, what did you do with The Box's body?"

"I had a well-connected friend in the Mafia take care of it for me," responds Alex as he was readjusting the windows for light.

"My Alex, you certainly have an array of friends, and very useful I might add."

"Yes Hank, I'm one very resourceful guy. But I'm also a very thankful brother of Jocy's, so thank you, man."

They shook hands, Hank grabbed his bag, and Talal was calling for him all in the same moment. They all converge at the patio door at the same time.

Jocy is standing at the door with Hank, as Tal looks back and says, "Hank two minutes!"

Hank shouting back, "great, I can kiss this pretty girl for two whole minutes!" Hank sits his bag down, takes Jocy's face in his hands, and kisses her while holding her close.

Just as he pulls his mouth away from hers, they both say 'I love you,' in the same breath. On that note, Hank picks up his bag and rushes to the helicopter, where Talal has already boarded. Hank is on his way back to Charlottesville, where this all began with a saber in his door, and an Alex Saber in his life.

73

Hank had been back in Charlottesville for almost two full weeks. He'd been looking at horse farms, which led him to horse people. Some of the horse people were also celebrity writers, producers, and actors. Some of them were all three wrapped up in one person.

What Talal had told Hank about one of his books getting a lot of attention, was happening. Almost everywhere he went in town, someone recognized him. He never went in for that part of things, but figured it came along with the ride he had chosen.

The time came when one of the local commercially successful writers offered a suggestion to one of the large art community sponsors, who also happened to be a book publisher. The yearly nationally known art festival was to take place and they needed a substitute speaker. It was suggested that Hank Ramsan be contacted.

When the local writer was asked, "why Mr. Ramsan?" His reply was, "I've used his Magic Wall, and that's the reason, I am as successful as I am. It would be a great thing for the festival to be known for bringing this out into the public eye on a national level."

All of the board members agreed that Hank Ramsan would be a good replacement, and should be contacted as soon as possible.

Hank received the call that evening from the arts festival board chairperson, asking if he would consider being a replacement for one of their scheduled speakers.

Hank agreed and asked what topic they would like him to present. The chairman suggested he discuss a bit of the theme of his books, *User Friendly Physics,* and "oh yes, there seems to be some interest in your Magic Wall," recounted the chairman.

This was it. This was the real beginning of Hank's desire that the entire world would have a Magic Wall. Hank knew the implications on an individual level as well as in commerce.

There was nothing in the way now. All of his dreams were flowing to him, just as he had placed on the Magic Wall of his loft. Jocy is back in his life. They would live together in Charlottesville and build a horse farm. Providing a place that art investors could trust their choices to, along with the horse business, would keep them both happy and stimulated.

It was all perfect.

The night of the presentation came and Hank was dressed in his usual jeans, boots, and blue denim shirt. He did add a suede blazer to appear a little dressed up.

Hank is standing in front of 300 very enthusiastic people, because most of them had heard of his Magic Wall. The local press gave it wide coverage. He was feeling very good this night as he looked out among the faces in the crowd.

He may not have felt quite as good if he and known about one particular face in the crowd. The one no one knew about, sitting smack dab in the front row, the Japanese partner of The Stiletto.

The End of The Beginning of 'The Millionaire Maverick'
(sj)

Appendix

Special Acknowledgments

In some way, these individuals have contributed to *The Millionaire Maverick* through my own expansion.

Madonna
...For her willingness, no matter what, to step over herself, irrespective of public opinion, in welcoming her full potential.
...For the raising of the spirit of millions of humanity, in ways of which many are unaware.
Thank you for honoring your gifts, Madonna.

Donald Trump
...For his love of architecture and the art he made of his buildings.
...For his writing of it in books, so that we may get some insight into his success in love for what he does well.
Thank you for honoring your gifts, Mr. Trump.

Richard Branson
...For showing us through your writing, your process of building your companies.
...For showing us that your notebooks were a primary catalyst for your days and the love you had for what you do.
...For your willingness, to do it just for the fun of it, and making fun a primary criteria for your business life, which built your life and lifestyle. Thank you for honoring your gifts, Mr.Branson.

As I studied what was there for me to see, I was able to see the physics behind how your lives evolved to the level they have. Thank you all, for the opportunity to 'see and apply' it to my own life. **(sj)**

References/Resources/Acknowledgments

Tales from The Arabian Nights (Aladdin and the Enchanted Lamp) (Ali Baba and the Forty Thieves) Retold from the Original Arabic by N.J.Dawood Illst Ed Young (1978 Doubleday)

Unveiled Mysteries (St. Germain Foundation/St. Germain Press)

The Magic Presence (St.Germain Foundation/St. Germain Press)

Webster's Dictionary (Merriam-Webster)

Building A Company / Roy O. Disney and the Creation of an Entertainment Empire by Bob Thomas (Hyperion)

Richard Branson: Losing My Virginity:
(Time Books/Random House/Virgin Publishing Ltd)

Walt Disney Company / Burbank, CA

Flash Dance / Paramount Pictures
Producer: Jerry Bruckheimer Written by: Joe Eszterhas

The Stepford Wives (1975)/Anchor Bay Entertainment
Producer: Edgar J. Scherick Written by: William Goldman

Levi's / Levi Strauss and Co.Worldwide

The Magic Wall / The Sword of Three's/ User Friendly Physics

About the Author

Susan James writes and speaks of the mechanics behind energy and spirit. She self coins these concepts the basics of *User Friendly Physics* to the higher level of understanding in *Genius to Brilliance*.

James' underlying theme in all of her publications revolve around raising our individual illumination, and the effect we have on all of humanity, as well as our individual lives, as we do so.

The application of the mechanics of energy and spirit to our lives, lifestyles and businesses continues to be a quest for Susan as she offers it to all who are interested in following their potential path. She does this through her many forms of writing, including books, newsletters, courses, consulting, and speaking engagements.

User Friendly Physics assists us in having what we desire in our lives "without goofin' it up first." **The Millionaire Maverick** is Ms. James second fiction among several non-fiction titles, which surround this theme.

Other Titles by Susan James

Manifesting 101 & Beyond: Essays & Tools for Creating
Manifesting 102 & Beyond: The Design Continues
Manifesting Methods for Would Be Millionaires
The Millionaire Maverick
Harley & Jelly Bean
17 Seconds to Weight Loss: The Guide
(More on the Way!)

Contact and 'The Magic Wall' Information

Susan James
Vast Five Productions
Suite 218
644 Greenville Ave.
Staunton, VA 24401

email: susanjames@rica.net
website: http://www.susanjames.org

Want a free copy of 'The Magic Wall?'

If you'd like a copy of ***The Magic Wall*** and or the writing exercise ***The Sword of Three's***, email Susan James at susanjames@rica.net request them! They will come to you in your email.
Hank says 'Thanks for asking! **(sj)**

Printed in the United States
963400001B